"You okay? You went white as a sheet. I thought you were going to pass out,"

Max said gruffly, bending his mouth to Maggie's ear as he gathered her closer.

Tiny balloons burst in her brain, letting all her common sense escape and float away. She could definitely get used to this, a man who'd be there when she needed him. Maggie let herself lean back into his strength. Gave temptation its head for a second and luxuriated in the male scent of him, the solid bulk of his chest that could almost make her believe she could rely on him.

If only for a second...

Dear Reader,

It's the beginning of a new year, and Intimate Moments is ready to kick things off with six more fabulously exciting novels. Readers have been clamoring for Linda Turner to create each new installment of her wonderful miniseries THOSE MARRYING McBRIDES! In *Never Been Kissed* she honors those wishes with the deeply satisfying tale of virginal nurse Janey McBride and Dr. Reilly Jones, who's just the man to teach her how wonderful love can be when you share it with the right man.

A YEAR OF LOVING DANGEROUSLY continues to keep readers on the edge of their seats with *The Spy Who Loved Him*, bestselling author Merline Lovelace's foray into the dangerous jungles of Central America, where the loving is as steamy as the air. And you won't want to miss *My Secret Valentine*, the enthralling conclusion to our in-line 36 HOURS spin-off. As always, Marilyn Pappano delivers a page-turner you won't be able to resist. Ruth Langan begins a new trilogy, THE SULLIVAN SISTERS, with *Awakening Alex*, sure to be another bestseller. Lyn Stone's second book for the line, *Live-In Lover*, is sure to make you her fan. Finally, welcome brand-new New Zealand sensation Frances Housden. In *The Man for Maggie* she makes a memorable debut, one that will have you crossing your fingers that her next book will be out soon.

Enjoy! And come back next month, when the excitement continues here in Silhouette Intimate Moments.

Yours,

Leslie J. Wainger
Executive Senior Editor

Please address questions and book requests to:
Silhouette Reader Service
U.S.: 3010 Walden Ave., P.O. Box 1325, Buffalo, NY 14269
Canadian: P.O. Box 609, Fort Erie, Ont. L2A 5X3

The Man for Maggie
FRANCES HOUSDEN

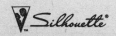

INTIMATE MOMENTS™
Published by Silhouette Books
America's Publisher of Contemporary Romance

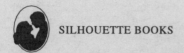 SILHOUETTE BOOKS

ISBN 0-373-27126-3

THE MAN FOR MAGGIE

Copyright © 2001 by Frances Housden

All rights reserved. Except for use in any review, the reproduction
or utilization of this work in whole or in part in any form by any
electronic, mechanical or other means, now known or hereafter
invented, including xerography, photocopying and recording, or in
any information storage or retrieval system, is forbidden without
the written permission of the editorial office, Silhouette Books,
300 East 42nd Street, New York, NY 10017 U.S.A.

All characters in this book have no existence outside the imagination of
the author and have no relation whatsoever to anyone bearing the same
name or names. They are not even distantly inspired by any individual
known or unknown to the author, and all incidents are pure invention.

This edition published by arrangement with Harlequin Books S.A.

® and TM are trademarks of Harlequin Books S.A., used under license.
Trademarks indicated with ® are registered in the United States Patent
and Trademark Office, the Canadian Trade Marks Office and in other
countries.

Visit Silhouette at www.eHarlequin.com

Printed in U.S.A.

FRANCES HOUSDEN

has always been a voracious reader but never thought of being a writer until a teacher gave her the encouragement she needed to put pen to paper. As a result, Frances was a finalist for the 1998 Clendon Award and won the award in 1999, which led to the sale of her first book for Silhouette, *The Man for Maggie*. Frances also teaches a continuing education course of her own in romance writing at the University of Auckland.

Frances's marriage to a navy man took her from her birthplace in Scotland to New Zealand. Now he's a land-lubber and most of the traveling they do is together. They live on a ten-acre bush block in the heart of Auckland's Wine District. She has two large sons, two tiny grandsons and a wheaten terrier named Siobhan. Thanks to one teacher's dedication, Frances now gets to write about the kind of men a woman would travel to the ends of the earth for.

For my mentor, Enisa Hasic, my critique partners, Jean, Judy, Judith and Rowena, and for Joanne Graves, who never minds me bending her ear over the phone for hours, while I listen to myself talk out my plots.

And in memory of Margie Rameka, who always believed I'd succeed one day.

Chapter 1

"I won't tell him! You can't make me."

Maggie Kovacs heard the quaver in her voice above the soft rumble of conversation flowing around them. She heard feeble. She heard fear. And it annoyed the hell out of her, when what she really wanted was to bang the wineglass in her fist on the table. She would have too, if she hadn't known every last person in the bar, ninety percent of them male, would turn around to see who was losing it.

Jo looked at her over the rim of her beer glass, took another swallow and put it down. "The choice is yours, Maggie. No one's forcing your hand."

Choice! She had none.

All she had were delaying tactics, as she hoped against hope the police would do their job and her problem would go away. No such luck. Life became intolerable when you regarded all your friends with a jaundiced eye, wondering who...? She'd never thought the day would come when she thanked God for having no family to call her own, but thank Him she did.

Maggie let her gaze drift past Jo between the crowded tables to where the fire crackled. The old fireplace was widemouthed and loaded with logs, someone's attempt at cozying up the old pub. Anyone could see the bar was a relic from New Zealand's early closing era. There weren't many left in the inner city, and this pub, like most of the modernized ones, sported more paint than a K Road whore looking for business. But the bar owed its popularity to convenience. It was practically next door to Auckland Central, the city's main police station.

Wood smoke sputtered from the logs every time the door opened, joining tainted air already tangy from damp wool steaming in the heat. With each breath the scents filled her mouth.

She tasted winter. The dead season.

Quickly, she gulped down some wine to rid herself of a taste turned bitter, and glanced at the clock over the fireplace. Hard to believe she'd been here less than half an hour. There was a clock ticking in the back of her mind, not unlike that one, and it had been getting louder and louder in the last week until she'd panicked this morning and rung Jo.

The evening hadn't gone the way Maggie had planned, and her friend had caught the brunt of her failure. Hopes of Jo easing the stress jangling her nerves had died the moment her friend turned the tables and put the onus back on Maggie. And who could blame her? Not many people cared for spooky stuff. Not even Maggie, and she was its source.

It was her own fault for not realizing Jo might have changed. In three years, her dark eyes had grown wary and a tight, repressed line had replaced her smile. Her face and chin, once soft and youthful had grown finer, as if someone had drawn them with a harder pencil.

From across the bar Maggie had watched Jo arrive, taken in the forever irrepressible mass of dark brown curls hanging over the collar of Jo's leather jacket, and been fooled. But cops had always been able to fool Maggie—she should have remembered. There were some who could cozen you into telling all your secrets, then laugh behind your back and blab them to the world.

Was Jo, too, calculating the changes and taking a guess at their meaning? How had they turned out such opposites, when as girls they'd been so alike? Had all their years in identical school uniforms hidden their true selves? Leaving time to solve the mystery.

Jo drained the last half-inch in her glass, then set it down with an exasperated click. "If you didn't want my advice, why'd you bother to look me up?"

"Come off it, Jo. You know why. I've never been able to talk to anyone but you about it. Where else would I go?"

"You managed it once—"

"Yeah." Maggie placed her arms on the table, her elbow accidentally hitting her wineglass. She heard it skitter across the laminated top, but if a crash came she blanked it out as unimportant. "And only just lived to tell the tale. Look what happened!" *Look what they did to me!* "I won't let it happen again!" *I can't.*

"Is this a private argument or can anyone join in?"

Maggie looked up, startled by the deep resonant voice. Immediately, she went into denial. "We weren't arguing." Out of the corner of her eye she saw Jo smile at the new arrival. Someone special?

"Max, I didn't think you'd be here this evening." Delight rang in Jo's voice. "I thought you were pulling an all-nighter. Come and join us."

So this was Max. Detective Sergeant Max Strachan, to be precise. Jo's boss. The man she'd been pressing Maggie to speak to.

"Never spilled a drop. Neat trick. You'll have to show me how to do it." A large hand, slim fingered with blunt tips, set the glass it had caught back on the table. All she could see was his hand with its sprinkling of dark hair as the lights behind him captured all but his silhouette, making his features invisible.

"It's not something you can learn overnight. I've had years of practice," Maggie said, watching him hook the leg of a chair from the table next to theirs with a large, black-shod foot.

She flinched as the chair scraped across the tiled floor and he pulled it up to their table. His gabardine-covered thigh, cold from the night air, brushed against her nylon-clad knees as he sat down between her and Jo. At the same time a searing heat from the hard-muscled flesh molding the soft cloth made her ache to pull away. But that would be too obvious.

Wide shoulders blocked the rest of the bar from view as he settled into his chair, giving Maggie the uneasy feeling of being trapped. He could easily be six-five. Built like a brick outhouse. A man who would make male offenders shake in their shoes and female ones want to get down and slobber over his size twelves. A man to avoid. And as soon as she could, Maggie aimed to do just that.

"This is my friend Maggie Kovacs. Maggie, Max Strachan."

Max held out his hand. Automatically she placed hers in it and felt her own swallowed up by a mass of contained strength. Since he was impossible to ignore, she let her reluctant gaze travel over him. A scar ran from his left eyebrow to his hairline, and a streak of silver made his dark hair, as dark as hers, look jet-black. Was there irony in the way the silver striation turned his already handsome face, with its black winged brows and aesthetically high cheekbones, into a prototypical pirate? In the midst of all that perfection, the slight bend in the bridge of his nose should have been a reminder that the man was a cop who had more than likely done battle before. It wasn't. Cops were supposed to be good guys, but Maggie usually took them as she found them; her last experience had colored most of them charcoal-gray. But in Max's case she'd rather remain in ignorance.

His eyes paid Maggie the compliment she'd given him—a detailed inspection. She swallowed at his intense look as their gazes collided. His eyes were truly blue. The truest blue she'd ever seen, ringed by long sooty lashes any woman would envy. True blue eyes that searched and sought out her deep hidden secrets. Maggie blinked in self-defense. He was the last man she wanted to share secrets with. Especially the one she'd just added to the list—the mind-blowing attraction he stirred, like a sleeping volcano wakening. Max smiled, just a slight curve of his chiseled lips, but enough to make her insides quake.

"Margaret Kovacs." Her name rolled off his tongue one syllable at a time, as though he savored each nuance with teeth and tongue before letting it go.

Someone had let loose a whole load of geese in the grave-yard. How else could she account for the shivers running down her spine?

Maggie gauged his thoughts. Was he trying to place her name, flicking through the filing system in his brain for where he'd heard it before? "Maggie," she corrected. "I prefer Maggie." By repeating her name, she hoped to nudge him off the track his mind had started down.

"Maggie it is. And what brings you to this neck of the woods, Maggie? We don't usually see ladies like you in here."

"I wanted to catch up with Jo. It's been a while," she said and flashed him a scathing look. He'd had to state the obvious. It hadn't taken a detective to recognize her as the most over-dressed person in the bar. Or did she mean underdressed? The only person in a miniskirt in this place where jeans and casual gear were the uniform of the day.

Even her hairstyle set her apart, with its precision cut. She'd let her stylist crop it ruthlessly to the shape of her head, leaving a shiny black length of hair to swirl across the tops of her ears and eyebrows. "It's a crime to hide that bone structure, my dear. Your cheekbones are to die for," was Stefan's cri de coeur.

Maggie took a deep breath. At twenty-eight she should be past the age of letting people like Max get to her. But at least she hadn't let it show how much his comments had bothered her.

"Almost three years," confirmed Jo. "I couldn't even make it back to Maggie's father's funeral, and that must have been a year ago, when I was in Gisborne."

"Fifteen months."

"A year this past March. That would have been Frank Kovacs?"

Maggie caught the gleam of recognition in his eyes, the slight tensing of his hand around his glass, and knew the seed of speculation had been sown. This was exactly the situation she'd wanted to avoid. "Yes. Did you know him?"

"I've heard of him."

I'll just bet you have.

Suddenly she just wanted out of there, wanted to run away from eyes that saw too much. Too easily.

She'd come to talk to Jo on a wave of courage, and the longer she stayed the more it ebbed. She'd already had her fifteen minutes of fame, and taking a chance on thirty might just push her over the top.

Max drained his glass. "Can I buy you both a drink?" He looked at their glasses, Jo's empty one and the half glass of red wine of Maggie's that he'd caught and replaced. "Not your usual vintage, I imagine? Maybe I can do better?"

That was all the confirmation Maggie needed. Max remembered her story and wasn't too subtle about letting her know. "I doubt it." She took another sip as if to prove him wrong.

Jo pushed her glass toward Max. "Thanks, I'll have my usual," she said, giving him another of the smiles she'd been rationing, as if the undercurrents in the conversation were passing her by. Maggie knew Jo wasn't that dumb. Jo was sending a few signals of her own, and Maggie got the impression they were all for her benefit. Showing her the lay of the land. One minute Jo was practically pushing her to meet the guy, the next Maggie could see a sign in bold writing: Hands Off.

Maggie took another look at the clock with its small brass pendulum swinging back and forth. No chance of time slowing for her.

"Would you look at the time? I have to go." She stood up and slid her arms into the camel-colored, cashmere coat she'd left hanging over the back of her chair. She turned her collar up till it framed her face, ready for the biting wind that had sprung up as the sun set. "Jo, give me a call when you've got the time. You've got my numbers. Nice to meet you, Sergeant Strachan."

Max stood up and Jo followed his example. "Do you have to?" she asked.

Maggie slung the strap of her bag over her shoulder. "Yeah, I have to. Bye now." She left them with an inane wiggle of her fingers, which showed the panic in her mind. Unable to get away quickly enough, she aimed for the door with the distinct feeling that Max's eyes were boring into her back. With every step she took the door seemed farther and farther away.

A finely turned ankle.

Now, where the hell had that come from? It was one of those long-forgotten expressions lurking in the recesses of Max's mind, but it fitted the pair of sheer, black-nylon covered ankles to a tee. The ones playing hide and seek with his libido through the long slit in the back of Maggie's coat. Each glimpse made his breath catch softly, miniature versions of the drawn-out hitch in his breathing when he'd first spied her across the room beside Jo. He'd never been an ankle man, until now, but he'd always been a quick study.

Max watched her walk away, head high, shoulders straight, as if she didn't give a damn. Each movement, from the tilt of her head and the slippery sheen of her black hair sliding over her upturned collar, to the firm click of her slender-heeled shoes on the tiles, were lies. A demonstration of body language lying through its teeth.

He knew it.

She knew it.

It wasn't what had been said earlier. It was the denial that they'd had anything to say. The subtext had been deafening from the moment he'd seen her slender body surge across the table toward Jo. Passion and energy etched every line. Sparks bursting from that energy had lit a fuse inside him, and he'd known straight off it was too late to douse it. Max prayed the fuse was a long one, and a slow burner. He'd need all the time he could get to garner his defenses. From the moment he'd heard her name—maybe even before, when lust had driven him across the room, and Jo's presence had eased the inevitability of their meeting—he'd known this was one situation that could blow up in his face.

The double glass doors, with their dull, fingerprint-yellow brass handles, swung on their hinges after her exit. But relief didn't come as quickly as the doors shuddered to a halt. Max turned back to Jo and picked up her empty glass from the table. ''Same again, you said?'' He didn't wait for her nod or the question shaping her eyebrows. He needed a moment to himself and his thoughts, and he'd get them at the bar while he ordered Jo a beer and himself a whiskey. A double.

Maggie Kovacs. Her father had been the one whose plane had crashed, but she'd been the one who'd hit the headlines.

He remembered the sergeant on the case, if you could call it a case—more like a retrieval job for the police divers, with a mop-up by the air-accident inspector.

Until Maggie had reached the scene.

To hear Sergeant Gorman tell it, she'd been out of her tree. Gorman was a bluff, red-faced character who looked as if he'd be more at home on top of a tractor than riding in a cop car. Still, it took all types. The man was retired now, and Max reasoned he'd only been handed the Kovacs case to get him out from behind his desk. The rest had been a bonus. The guy was probably still raising a few laughs at Maggie's expense.

Maggie.

Sometimes prejudice got in the way of reality. Where were the hoop earrings and spangled head scarf? The "cross my palm with silver, mister?" Maggie didn't look anything like the advertisements with their 0900 numbers littering the tabloids and women's magazines. Madam Zelda and the likes, who'd read your fortune from cards, or your future from the vibes singing down the phone line, and charge you $3.95 a minute for the privilege. For a while there he'd almost let them get away with annihilating his future. They'd certainly robbed him of a fortune—and his marriage. It was something he'd never forgive or forget. Like the day he'd opened the final demand from the phone company, and felt the bottom drop out of his world.

He downed his first whiskey while they poured Jo's beer, and was into his second before he reached the table. The heat entered his stomach and had spread to his veins by the time he sat down. He caught Jo's glance and knew she'd be speculating about the second drink. Usually he nursed one glassful till the ice melted and the whiskey was as hot inside the glass as when it hit his tonsils.

"So…" he sighed. "Good-looking woman, Maggie. Catching up on old times, were you?" He tossed back another mouthful of the desperate man's anesthetic and waited for Jo's reply. The bombshell wasn't unexpected; he just wasn't ready for it to go off this soon.

"She came to see me about a murder. Three of them, to be precise."

"Cut the crap, Jo. Next you're going to tell me she dreamed them!"

"She's psychic."

"Then you're going to tell me you believe in all this mumbo jumbo." Max took another swallow. The effects of the anesthetic were wearing off quickly. He'd known Jo for five years now. Worked with her on and off for three of them. She was a good cop, with a quick, keen mind. She never flinched, even when things were at their hairiest. But believing in this psychic twaddle had to be a female thing.

"For heaven's sake! This is a new age, Max. Sooner or later you'll have to give in and open your mind to the possibilities. Hell, I like my job too much to put it on the block, but I've known Maggie all my life. You I've only known long enough to learn how hard you can dig in your heels."

"I'm not interested in a rundown on her dreams. I'm not a shrink. Tell her to try the yellow pages." He'd had enough on his plate with three unsolved murders in as many months. Not even a fool could deny they were connected, and he was no fool. Which was a good reason for staying away from anything that smacked of paranormal. Now if only he could convince his libido of the same thing where Maggie was concerned, he might be a damn sight nearer to suppressing the urge to get up and follow her out the door.

"Well, don't get your Jockeys in a twist. It just so happens she doesn't want to speak to you, either." An edge of satisfaction colored Jo's voice as she tossed the ball back at him.

"So what was this tonight? A social call, or is she after a little more publicity to keep the punters rolling in?" At the base of his skull a pain throbbed, and he wondered who he was really trying to hurt—Jo, Maggie or himself? "You thinking of flagging the police and taking up marketing, Jo?" The steel in his voice would have made a wiser woman back off. Not Jo.

"Okay, Max. Let it all hang out, spill your guts," she retorted.

Jo's breasts heaved under her blue chambray shirt and spread the zipper edging of her leather jacket farther apart. Boy, she was angry with him! Max had never seen her this mad before. How much would it take to make her blow her stack? There was a calm, calculating part of his brain that thought maybe this was a good thing. Cruel, but good. Good for him.

He'd been thinking for a while now that maybe Jo was

getting too fond of him. And he wasn't the only one to notice, judging by a few of the comments written on the men's room walls. The only thing to cut that out would be to make the place unisex.

At one stage he'd toyed with the idea of getting her a sideways promotion out of Central. A word in the right ear was all it would take. But was it fair to nix a good cop's career, just because she thought the sun shone on his sorry behind?

"I knew who she was the moment you said her name," Max growled. "Maggie's reputation precedes her. If you'd been here fifteen months ago you'd know to keep away from her, unless you actually *want* your credibility as a cop to go down the drain." He swallowed the last mouthful in his glass. Who was he trying to remind, Jo or himself? His divorce was six months old, and the only relationships he'd had in the last two and a half years had been the types that pass in the night. A quick tumble in the sheets and a few more weeks relief were all he got out of them. One look at Maggie and he could tell that wouldn't be enough.

"Just because I haven't seen her in three years doesn't mean we haven't been in touch. I can read, and not just the rubbish Gorman let slip and the media blew all out of proportion Maggie wrote me about it, about the crank calls and the lies. I was trying to persuade her to tell you about the dreams when you arrived."

"Good one! You'd send her to me when you know my opinion of these fakers."

"I thought if you saw her face-to-face—"

"It takes more than a pretty face to bowl me over."

"Tell me about it. I know it never worked for me."

"Don't let's get into that, Jo. You're a friend. Friends last longer than lovers." He hoped Jo would take the words as they were meant and not as a put-down. It was the first time either of them had openly acknowledged her infatuation.

Jo shrugged and laughed ruefully. "Can't blame a girl for trying. But we're getting off the subject. I'm worried about

Maggie. She sounded desperate. Didn't you notice how edgy she was? Once you arrived she couldn't wait to get away.''

''I thought it was my lethal personality she couldn't stand.''

''Well... She doesn't like cops, but her manners are usually better than that.''

''You're a cop.''

''Yeah, but we were at boarding school together and we both come from the same background. It makes a difference.''

''I didn't know your family made wine.''

''I was talking about Dalmatia. Both our families came from there originally. In some ways Maggie's father hadn't changed much from the old folks who first settled there. He had a closed mind on some things.'' Jo tilted her head to one side, her expression serious as she looked him up and down. ''Remind you of anyone? Frank Kovacs forbade her to talk about her dreams. Not that he didn't love her—he adored her. It was the only thing he was ever strict over. Said he only did it to protect her. Seems he had to die to prove himself right.''

Max watched Jo swallow, lick her lips, then swallow another mouthful of beer. He could tell she wasn't finished, so he waited and said nothing.

''I know these dreams do come true. But I can't help her this time. I haven't enough clout, but you do. And I'm guessing from the way Maggie's acting, she's going to have to give in and pay you a visit.'' Jo leaned across the table and gripped his sleeved arm just above the wrist. By the strength of her fingers, he guessed her desperation was as strong as Maggie's. ''I need you to believe she got nothing from me. Nothing, yet she knows everything, down to the red scarves.''

Max felt his stomach clench and acid rise. Heartburn.

Could he believe Jo? The possibility posed too many questions he didn't want answered. He'd rather keep Maggie in a box marked This One Makes You Hard Just by Being in the Same Room. He'd rather plan strategies to get her into his bed. To start figuring out the way her mind worked would draw him in too deep, and no amount of paddling would keep him near the surface. Not unless it was the pale olive, satin skin covering Maggie's surface from head to toe.

There had to be another explanation. Damned if he could think what it might be, though. To give credence to what he'd just heard meant admitting he'd been wrong about a whole lot of other things, including his wife and his marriage, and he wasn't ready for that just yet…or ever.

"There must have been a leak. Check the newspapers—we might have missed something. If someone on the case has a loose mouth, your job is to find out who. And I need answers by this time tomorrow. Heaven help us if this gets out," Max muttered, knowing that, so far, heaven was the only place they hadn't gone for help. That sounded too much like the area he was trying to avoid.

"So, you believe there could be a leak? And you're satisfied it's not me?"

"No, I'm not. You'd better work your little butt off and find me someone, or there's only one conclusion I can make."

"Great! I give you a gift from the gods and now you're going to make me pay for it."

A blast of raucous laughter had them both turning toward the bar. Max recognized the bulk of their team, milling around the barman, singing out their orders. "C'mon, Jo. You might as well start right now."

"Why do I have to be the spy?" she complained, getting to her feet.

"You won't be alone. I'll stick around for a while. Check first for anyone who might have worked with Gorman. Maybe you're not the only cop Maggie knows. If it'll help, I'll shout the next round. The guys needed some downtime to relax and work some of the frustration out of their systems, so I gave them tonight off."

Max stood up and, as he did so, caught sight of a scarf under his feet. He reached down and picked up the scrap of silk, patterned like a leopard in black, tan and gold. "This yours?" he asked.

"No, it's Maggie's." Jo held out her hand. "I'll take it."

Max rolled the long strip of silk around his fingers and released Maggie's scent. It filled his head like a haunting refrain he couldn't shake. "Would she have gone back up north tonight?"

"No. She wouldn't drink and drive, and I know she walked here from the apartment Frank had in the Viaduct Quay tower. She'll probably stay the night there."

"In that case I'll hang on to it." Max pushed the ball of silk into his pocket. "From what you told me, chances are I'll see her before you do."

In fact, he would bet on it.

Chapter 2

Maggie's body glowed pink, blooming from the aftereffects of a hot shower and brisk rubdown with a thick towel. Her comb slid off the long, creamy slice of marble below the huge mirror and into her palm. Holding the comb firmly enough to mark her skin, she slicked her wet hair back without once looking at her reflection. Her father's dark green silk robe hung on the back of the door and she slipped into it, hiding her nakedness.

A hint of Frank's favorite cologne still lingered in the soft folds after all these months, the fragrance teasing at her memory as she wrapped the robe's generous width around her. Doubling it over at the front, she crossed her arms tightly against her breasts, trying to remember the last time her father had held her—and failing.

So long…so long ago since the dreams began and the hugs had stopped. Puberty at least. But then, maybe all fathers began distancing themselves from their daughters at that age, and everything else was in her imagination. The way the dreams were, according to Frank Kovacs. Her father had had a way of saying things, like an edict from on high, and Maggie had known not to argue when he used a certain tone of voice.

Stubborn, arrogant man.

If only he'd believed in her.

Maggie's lips quivered and she pushed the thoughts away before they undid all the good the shower had achieved. Just give her one dreamless night and she'd be okay. Thoughts of Max Strachan were banned as well. Thoughts like the ones that had made her stumble out of the shower, grab the towel and attempt to erase the graphic visions with rough friction.

The water had been hot, so hot—not as soft as the tank water at home, but with more pressure—and she'd luxuriated in the difference, letting the needle-sharp jets tingle against her skin, tilting her head back to let the water pour over the tightness in her throat, then split into three streams as it coursed around her breasts. She could put up with the smell of chlorine just for the way the spray sent her blood zinging through every particle of her skin till she felt as hot inside as out.

Then she'd glanced down while she'd soaped her breasts.

And seen Max's hands.

His broad palms cupped her breasts from the sides and his fingers created patterns of tanned and pale skin across the full mounds. Max used the contained strength she'd felt earlier to conjure the silkiest of caresses from pure, latent power. His touch, gentle yet hot as fire, seared through to her soul as the water careened over the growth of dark hair, plastering it to taut, lean sinew and bone until it spilled off his wrists. Here was a vision that could shatter her fragile control, and as her nipples tightened into sharp points and stabbed into his palms, she squeezed her eyes shut and still couldn't blank it out.

Damn, she was losing it.

Maggie hitched the belt of the robe around her waist and tightened it. Pulling hard on the ends until she could hardly breathe, she formed a bow with short jerky movements of her hands. Who was having the last laugh now? She could hear her father's voice echo in her mind.

"Too much imagination."

Thick carpet soaked up his footsteps, and heavily embossed, light blue wallpaper, hung with reproduction artwork, ate up all other sound, obliterating his presence. As he reached the terra-cotta door, which emphasized the similar-colored pattern on the dark blue carpet, a swift glance over his shoulder confirmed he was on his own. One more strike against the up-market apartment tower. If anyone was going to creep up on Max, he wanted to hear him coming. Sure, the tenants had probably paid a bundle to achieve this high-tech impression of peace and solitude, although if he lived ten stories up, his number one priority would be knowing no one had come along and kicked the rest of the building out from under him.

He reached out and rang the bell to the left of the solid wood door. A peephole had been set dead center in the thick plank bisecting the door. He eyed it for a moment, just a moment, and considered sticking his thumb over the aperture, then changed his mind. At thirty-four he was past playing those kinds of games.

Maggie would let him in—she had to. There was an awareness, an attraction. It had shimmered between them like a living, breathing thing no smelly, clamorous pub could pollute. He'd felt it, and he would swear she had, too—he wouldn't have risked calling on her otherwise.

From his first sight of her on the other side of the bar, tension had begun to claw at his gut. Even learning her name and knowing her history hadn't dulled the sharp edges of neediness he'd felt at the touch of her hand. And unless he mistook his instincts, it had driven her away. Among other things. But she would recognize what it had cost him to come here tonight. He was certain of that.

Max rang the bell again and stood close to the door, his hands braced on either side of the frame, waiting, wondering what he'd do if she wasn't inside. Although she should have been expecting him. He'd shown his ID to the security guard at the desk when he'd asked for her on the way through, and if the guy had been doing his job he would have told her the police were on the way up.

Max could feel her watching him. He sensed her presence on the other side of the door as surely as if she'd reached out and touched him. That was all it took. His groin tightened and all the blood in his brain rushed down to his crotch. Max closed his eyes and swallowed, fighting for control.

A few more minutes and Maggie would have been sound asleep. She'd curled up on one of the sofas with the robe wrapped around her knees and her feet tucked under it. While the fire flickered gaseous flames up the chimney, she'd dozed lightly, with the TV droning softly, turned to a program guaranteed to cure the worst of insomniacs. It had taken her ten seconds to come to. Longer till the second ring confirmed the noise wasn't coming from the TV.

A shiver splashed with excitement and muddied by apprehension flowed through her as she looked into the viewer's fish-eye lens.

She knew him.

It made no difference that he was standing so close to the door only the lower half of his face was visible. She recognized the dark green shirt and loosely knotted, matching tie under the jacket of small, muted-green checks he'd worn earlier. Recognized the movement in the strong throat as he swallowed, and most of all she recognized the hard, square-cut jaw. Nothing had changed in the last few hours except the deepening shadow of a relentless growth of beard.

Maggie's pulse quickened and the nerves on the surface of her skin vibrated the way a piano wire does when a fingernail scratches it from end to end.

It didn't stop her asking, ''Who's there?''

''The police.''

''How can I tell? Hold your ID up to the security viewer.''

"For Pete's sake, Maggie! Stop fooling around. You know it's me, Max. Sergeant Strachan. Your memory can't be that short." His exasperation showed in the explosive bursts of language, harsh at first, then softening, cajoling. "Please, Maggie, open the door and let me in. I need to speak to you."

She hesitated long enough to elicit another plea.

"Maggie, you know we have to talk."

She could only guess why he'd turned up at her door at ten o'clock at night, and neither conclusion brought any comfort. But it appeared to be business as usual, otherwise he would have said "Max here" instead of "the police," and the only way to discover if her suspicions were right was to let the man talk. "I don't know what you think we have to say to one another, but you can come in—just for a few minutes," she said, qualifying her previous statement as she undid the chain and clicked open the locks.

She stepped back, swinging the door so its full width separated them instead of mere inches. "Come in," she said, increasing the distance between them by another step.

Nothing had changed.

Whatever effect he had on her imagination, Max Strachan up close and personal sent it off the graph. He walked past her into the apartment and her heart lurched, starting a fast, syncopated beat as she watched his wide shoulders fill up the archway that separated the foyer from the main living area.

The soft brilliance of table lamps and wall sconces blinded Max after the muted lighting in the corridor. Here, cream and pale gold melded on squishy cushioned sofas, carpets and curtains. What wood there was in the room had been limed to fade unobtrusively against walls the color of thick, rich cream straight from the milking shed. In contrast, his and Maggie's reflections drifted over a night-dark sea and sky. And behind the sheen of glass, the scene shifted and changed as car headlights traveled the Harbour Bridge and merged with the carpet of small, unwinking stars on the North Shore.

It made his own small apartment seem dead. Like comparing poor-boy minimalist with rich-man lush. For the first time that night Max questioned the urge that had chased him all the way down Hobson Street and around Viaduct Quay.

"Well, Maggie. No one can say you haven't got style."

"My father had style, or rather his designer did, but it's not mine. On a sunny day it's like living in a white-out. I hardly use this place. In fact, this is the first time I've stayed here since my father…"

"Crashed his plane?"

"Yes, round about then." For a split second he thought her face would crumple, but she ducked her head, hiding her expression, before he could be sure. When she did return his gaze her shoulders had squared and a fraction of a smile shaped her full lips. "Would you care for a drink?"

Max nodded, marveling at her self-control. She'd got it down pat, compared to her behavior the day Frank Kovacs's plane had taken a nosedive into the sea.

"Good, I could use one myself, but I hate to drink alone."

So his visit wasn't to be limited to a few minutes, after all. Max took that as a sign of encouragement.

Maggie padded around him on bare feet. Swathed all in green, with her hair straight back and her face natural and free of makeup, she might be mistaken by some for a woodland sprite. Not by him. He liked the play of light on the silky robe, changing its color from light into dark over the curve of her lush little butt, as it swayed to a rhythm all its own.

Maggie didn't have a stitch on under that thing. Max tugged at his tie, loosening it some more. He needed something to kill the heat spreading from his loins. He needed Maggie, or at a pinch, air.

Opening one door of a long, hand-carved sideboard on the far wall, Maggie hunkered down to look into the wine rack. The robe pooled on the carpet and bloused around her middle. "What do you prefer, red or white wine?"

"Whichever you pick's fine by me. You're the expert," Max replied, following her, drawn by a need to be closer. He leaned one elbow on top of the sideboard as she pulled one bottle after another from the rack and examined the labels. Her clean, fresh scent wafting up to him was more intoxicating than anything she could find in the wine rack. Now if only they could bottle Maggie Kovacs...

Someone ought to shut him away for staring down the gaping neckline of her robe. He wouldn't mind for a minute as long as they locked Maggie up with him. She had the most perfect breasts he had seen in all his life. Mounds of smooth olive satin—not too big, not too small—hand-size and tipped with sweet, tight, treacle-brown nipples that had him craving for a taste. Man! If he caught anyone else trying this—

What had gotten into him? Possessiveness? Get a hold of yourself, Max!

"This is an excellent one, a six-year-old shiraz. I think you'll enjoy it."

"Looks good to me," he said, fastening his jacket as he straightened, to prevent Maggie from getting an eyeful of the bulge distorting his zipper. As she got to her knees, Max held out his hand, and she drifted up to him until he couldn't tell who needed steadying, her or him. Her night-dark gaze held his till her eyelids fluttered and severed visual contact, though her hand still seared his palm.

"There are glasses in the other cupboard. Can you get two out while I open this?" Did her voice sound as shaky as it felt? Having Max this close made her limbs feel like Jell-O. There was just so much of him, and all of it male. If she licked her lips she would probably taste testosterone.

Maggie lifted the gold wine steward's knife and wondered that it didn't melt in the heat of her hand. Her stomach clenched and her hips bucked slightly. If only she could rid herself of the picture she'd created in the shower, of Max's hands on her breasts. It seemed her brain and her hormones were at odds. So far she felt brainless and out for the count, with three rounds to go. No wonder she'd asked him to stay for a drink, when all she'd meant to do was have a little conversation and show him the door.

She gripped the bottle like a lifeline. With the knife open, she ran the razor-sharp edge around the cap. Two clicks in quick succession told her Max had placed the wineglasses near her elbow. She flicked the seal up, catching it between her thumb and the knife, and began to peel it back, revealing the cork. The buzzing in her ears started about two seconds before the stars came out in front of her eyes, and the bottle tilted, sliding on its edge across the tray. Somewhere on the edge of her peripheral vision lay a sight she wanted to deny.

"Whoa, there!" Max's arms came around her, catching the bottle with one hand and relieving her limp fingers of the knife with the other.

In the midst of all the heat radiating from Max's body, Maggie shivered. He'd returned the bottle and knife to the sideboard, and he supported her with his strong, tightly muscled arms, pulling her shoulders back against his hard chest.

"You okay?" he asked gruffly, bending his mouth to her ear as he gathered her closer. "You went white as a sheet. I thought you were going to pass out."

Tiny balloons burst in her brain, letting all her common sense escape and float away. Oh, she thought. She could get used to this, someone who'd be there when she needed him. Maggie let herself lean back into his strength. Gave temptation its head for a second and luxuriated in the male scents, the solid bulk of his chest that could almost make her believe she could rely on him. If just for a second.

The pressure of his steely hardness against her hip felt like a rod to her back the same moment the thought *No wonder Jo is keen on this guy,* crossed her mind.

Jo! Her best friend!

What was she doing?

Moving in on her best friend's man!

Maggie clutched the edge of the sideboard with both hands. An old Mae West joke raised its feeble head, but Maggie was absolutely certain he wasn't packing a gun. Which only went to show how jittery she was, a case of jangling nerves with a bit of mild hysteria thrown in for good measure. "I guess I stood up too quick, but I'm all right now," she said to excuse her behavior. Forgiving herself for being carried away by the nearness of Jo's man would take a bit longer. No matter how much Maggie was tempted, only hurt could result from ignoring the signals her friend had been putting out at the pub.

As for Max's part in the incident, he was a man. She'd heard it was a mechanical reaction.

A heavy sigh tore from his throat and he stepped away from her. "Yeah, you look better, more color in your cheeks. Though for both our sakes it'd be best if you got dressed and I took care of the wine. When I first arrived, I suspected you might be naked under that robe, but now…"

Maggie turned to face him, her hands crossed defensively on her chest. She felt a flash fire of color race from her cheeks to the roots of her hair. Max reached out and stroked her skin where the cuff slid back from her wrist, setting her heart pounding erratically.

"Now I'm positive," he said, trailing one finger—only one—against the shadowy blue veins where her pulse did bumps and grinds from this simplest of contacts.

"Maybe you should just go."

"No. I'm not done here. But don't worry. All I want for now is to talk. You go get some clothes on. We can sit over there with a sofa apiece and the table between us. What could be safer?"

By the time Maggie came back, Max wasn't so sure he'd put the right handle on the situation. Dressed in the black miniskirt and high-necked sweater she'd worn earlier, she sat down opposite him, and Max decided she'd proved the less-is-more theory in reverse. Covered in black from the toes of her tights to the turtleneck collar under her chin, Maggie settled against the deep cushions of the sofa with her knees glued primly together and swung to one side so her toes just touched the floor. The contrast of dark wool with honey-gold skin, and her protective position, made her look fragile. Compared with him, she was. Probably only five-ten to his six-five.

Yeah, getting Maggie to put some clothes on had only added to his problem. Her sweater clung to every curve, but more than her curves affected him, though he couldn't put a name to exactly what. Basically, in his eyes, Maggie Kovacs was sexy as hell.

The oversoft sofa cushions looked good as he sank down into them, but his overactive libido made getting comfortable a lost cause. He watched Maggie raise the glass of red wine to her lips, saw the dewy film it left behind, knowing if he kissed her she'd taste of wild blackberries and sunshine, and her lips would feel as soft, full and earthy as the wine they sipped.

Maggie took another mouthful then lifted her brows while she asked, "What was it you wanted to talk about?"

Max blinked and tried to bring his mind back to the present. Rescue came in the form of Maggie's silk scarf. He dug into his pocket and pulled it out, letting the opaque leopard-skin print coil sinuously onto the glass table separating them. "This for starters. You dropped it on the floor at the pub."

"You should have given it to Jo. She'd have taken care of it."

"Yeah, so she said, but I wanted to do it myself."

"So, what's so important it dragged you up here at this time of night?"

"Can't you guess?"

"I'm not a mind read—" Maggie stopped midsentence, and his eyes mocked her slip of the tongue. Her first guess had been correct. "Jo blabbed, didn't she? Well, I'm sorry, Max, you've had a wasted journey. No matter what Jo told you, I have no intention of discussing it with you. I've learned my lesson!" *Boy, had she learned it.* Gorman had left her wrung out and hung up to dry.

"That's not why I'm here. In fact, I refused to listen to Jo and I have no interest in any dreams you might have had, past, present or future. I don't believe in that garbage." The air between them parted like the Red Sea as he thrust his wine-glass onto the table. Bottle in one hand, glass in the other, he filled it with wine, then remembered his manners. "Would you like a refill?"

Strike one! It looked like she'd been second-guessing, after all. Saying nothing, she held out her glass and let him top it up. Looking him straight in the eye, she said, "I get it—you've come to warn me off."

"Wrong! You'll get no warning."

"Come off it, Max. You know, and now I know. You want me to keep away from Jo. Hell, it's not catching. I won't contaminate your lady friend."

"My lady friend?"

"You and Jo." Maggie held up her hand and crossed the first two fingers. "You're a couple. A blind man could see it. She lit up as soon as you came in to the bar. But don't worry, she wouldn't help me. Actually, she tried to palm me off onto you, but I told her no way." Maggie knew she shouldn't tease him, but she'd had just enough wine on an empty stomach to make the attempt. He looked so serious, so grim with his jaw clenched tight. "I knew you wouldn't want to hear about my dreams." She leaned forward, concealing her true intent with a lazy droop of her eyelids, and tilted her head to one side. "Maybe I really am a mind reader. Would you care to cross my palm with silver?"

Hearing his thoughts from the pub echo back at him knocked Max for six. He stared at the strong lines dissecting the hand challenging him, and garnered his wits. Coincidences did happen. They happened every day. He had no problem with that. No one could look into your mind and extract a thought. His gaze shifted from hand to eye, and he knew without a doubt Maggie was enjoying herself at his expense.

"I don't think I'll waste my money, because if you can't

see there's no more than a working relationship between Jo and me, you aren't much good. I'm her superior at work, and I can't help it if she likes me—a lot. But I don't mix business and pleasure. Which is another reason for not listening to tales of your nightlife.'' Max tilted half a glass of wine down in one swallow. Hell! He'd sounded like an egotistical jerk. ''I think she's mixing pity with attraction because of the way my marriage ended.''

''How long ago was that?''

''A bit over two years.''

''Then I think Jo's gone way past feeling sorry for you.''

Max sighed out loud. ''All right. She may care more for me than I do her. We've talked about it and hopefully sorted it out, because I don't want to lose her as a friend or a colleague. As for your friendship with her, if it doesn't impinge on police business, then it's none of mine. I believe you two go back a long way.''

''It feels like a lifetime. Maybe we don't see each other as much as we used to, but when we get back together it's as if nothing's changed. I would hate anything to hurt that.'' Maggie watched him through narrowed eyes, but even that couldn't diminish his size or his presence. Her friendship with Jo was precious to her. All the while they'd boarded at Saint Mary's Convent School, Jo had been her rock—strong, stubborn, immovable and on Maggie's team. And she had an uneasy feeling Max could be the catalyst that could blow their friendship apart. No way; it was unthinkable. Jo was all she had left.

''You can trust me, Maggie. I won't let that happen.''

There was nothing Maggie would like better than to be able to trust Max. But she couldn't. She'd long since decided cops were born with an instinct to catch people at their most vulnerable and use it against them. That's what had happened on the day she'd watched the divers search for the remains of her father's plane. A day when she'd been at her lowest ebb. Even now she couldn't remember which hurt most, her father's death and the fact that it could have been prevented or what came after. The memory of the way her father had scoffed at her warning made her shudder. Life had been good to Frank Kovacs, given him all he'd ever needed or wanted. Nothing could touch him. He'd thought himself invincible, and had died trying to prove it.

Max knew it was too much to expect Maggie to simply acquiesce, too much to expect her to trust a stranger—trust him. They were at the beginning of a journey that could be rough, full of twists and turns and occasional dead ends. But chances were, if Maggie was half as strong as he thought, they'd both go the distance. The silence stretched between them until Max could wait no longer and broke it by clearing his throat. "How about you? Are you in a relationship?"

Maggie's laugh had a fragile edginess that set it half a note off-key. "Who, me? You must be joking. I'm too busy for a relationship. I have a winery to run, and don't tell anyone, but I'm feeling my way here. I've hired a new wine maker, and if he doesn't come through for us we could lose a lot of our markets. Don't get me wrong. He's good. I just don't know if he's got the flair Dad had. We'll start releasing his first vintage in October and I'm organizing a wine fest for Labour Weekend. I just hope it's a success. This is a new concept for us. I always wanted Dad to run one, but he said our wines sold themselves. I can't count on that anymore, so I'm working on promoting it whenever I can." She cut off her words in midstream, pushed at her hair and rolled her eyes in embarrassment. "Oh, boy! Will you listen to me?" She excused herself with a shrug. "For the last year the winery has been my life."

"Join the club. This would be maybe the third night off I've had in three months."

"And you're wasting it on business?"

"No…pleasure."

"So, you're saying this isn't business?"

"It isn't business."

"Then why are you here?"

"For starters, your scarf. Secondly, I wanted to get to know you and I seized on the scarf as an excuse. But I'd have come without it. I couldn't keep away."

"I don't believe I'm hearing this."

"Well, hear this," he said bluntly, as he got to his feet and walked around to Maggie's side of the table. He took the glass from her hand and set it down, then pulled her to her feet so she wouldn't feel intimidated by his height. Her eyes had gone black and opaque as if she were dazed. He'd forgotten she had no shoes on, and he towered over her. So he slipped an arm around her and pulled her up onto her toes. He felt himself tremble and abandoned all reason. Maggie Kovaks was David to his Goliath and he would die if he couldn't taste her lips. "I want you, Maggie."

Her hands pushed against his chest and he heard her breath quicken. "Don't be frightened, Maggie. I don't mean here and now, but someday, you and I are going to get together. When the time is right, it will happen." He tilted her chin up and felt a tremor run through her, mimicking the ones weakening his body with desire. "Like this," he said, and feathered his lips over hers. "And this." Max slanted his mouth across Maggie's, tasting wild blackberries, tasting sunshine.

Her hand slipped around his collar as he caught a sigh from her lips and breathed it in. The kiss deepened as she opened for him and his tongue searched out the dark, sweet cave of her mouth, savoring every nuance and flavor. Knowing this might be all he had of her for quite a while, he memorized the subtle textures of satin and pearls to keep him going during the sexual drought ahead of him.

Maggie's hand fisted in his hair as he felt her tongue seek his out. When she stepped onto his shoes, pressing closer, his hand cupped her hips, plastering them together from knee to shoulder. Hunger, hot and dark, slashed through him as her breasts cushioned his chest and he ground his hard, aching need against the softness of her belly, giving passion its rein.

Max didn't want to stop. He had to stop. Now—before he

threw her on the floor and took her there and then, like an uncontrollable animal. A groan of pain ripped from him as he put his hands on her shoulders and pushed her away while he had the strength. The look in Maggie's eyes almost broke his resolution as he set her back a step, leaving his hands as their only link.

He brushed his thumb over the full redness of a bottom lip that looked thoroughly kissed. "Seems the feeling is mutual." Max heard her small gasp of shock as realization hit. "I ought to go while I'm still able."

"Oh, no, you don't!" Maggie felt like spitting tacks. So, he was right. The feeling *was* mutual. She'd been caught up every bit as much as Max, so much so that she hadn't wanted to break the contact, the kiss. And it riled her that he'd been able to…to push her aside. It rankled that it could never happen again. He was wrong for her, wrong in every way. She'd lived the first part of her life with a man who hadn't believed in her, and had no intention of getting caught up with another. One who called the part of her that should have been special "garbage!"

"This ends the moment you walk out that door," she declared.

"You mean you want me to stay?"

"No, dammit! I mean this is it. Over! Kaput! I won't hurt my best friend and I've no intention of having an affair with a man who reminds me of my father."

"Don't try to tell me you kissed your father like that. I won't believe you."

Maggie almost spat in disgust. " What I'm getting at is that my father never believed me, either. If he had, he'd be alive today and you wouldn't even be in the picture. You've got too many counts against you, Max. I've already suffered at the hands of the police and now I'm gun-shy. I need a man who isn't frightened of the unknown, one who can open his mind to the possibilities."

"I never said I didn't believe in fate."

A rueful note wove its way into Maggie's laughter. He was a beautiful man, and she bet he stripped off well. She'd already felt the lean strength of his arms and would like nothing better than to rest her head on the hard bulk of his chest at the end of a day when things had gotten too tough. She was tired of shouldering everything alone. Strength was good, but she wanted more, she wanted a man who would listen—listen and empathize—without cringing.

"I'll bet before you met me, when Sergeant Gorman was slinging his mouth off to the tabloids, you thought I was weird."

"Truth to tell, I probably thought a lot worse. I would have been separated about a year by then, and there was a lot of stuff I didn't like about women, and so-called psychics would have topped the list."

His words hit Maggie like a slap in the face, wiping out her last scrap of hope, a scrap she hadn't even realized she'd been saving.

"Humph, that sounded pretty harsh. It wasn't meant as a put-down—honest, Maggie." He reached out, needing to touch her, but before he could caress her cheek, she stepped back.

"I thank heaven I'll never have to experience your version of a put-down, as I doubt we'll ever meet again. I think it's time you went now. Don't you?" Turning on her heel, she walked away, hoping Max would follow her. He was too big to throw out.

He followed in her footsteps, then slipped in front of her before she reached the archway. "Look, Maggie, the way I see it, you've got a history and I've got a history and we haven't got time to go into them tonight. But what's between us could be bigger than all of that, if only you'll give it a chance."

"And I think we used up all our chances long before we met. Everything we have going for us is on the debit side, and I can't stand being in the red." She moved around Max and headed for the door before he could attempt to change her mind.

Maggie gripped the handle tightly, ready to close the door the instant he walked through it. She supported herself with the doorknob and raised her heels from the floor. It wasn't fair; Max's height put all the advantage on his side.

"I want to hear you lock this door behind me," he said, moving closer. "I don't trust that security guard. He's probably asleep behind his desk."

She tilted her chin, refusing to be cowed. "Don't worry, I'm going to make sure you can't get back in."

Max laughed and took her stubborn chin between his finger and thumb, then gave her a kiss meant to curl the toes she was standing on. When he lifted his mouth it was with reluctance, and as he straightened he could swear Maggie was swaying on her feet.

It didn't stop her trying for the last word. "So, goodbye."

"Wrong, Maggie. I'll never kiss you goodbye. Only hello."

"I wouldn't bet on it."

"I won't. I'm not a betting man. So I'm going to count on it."

Maggie leaned her back against the door after she'd locked it and a rap of Max's fingers on the outside told her he was on his way.

Why did life have to be so complicated? She had enough problems without Max adding more. Despite his confidence, Maggie knew things could only get worse.

Without Max's presence the apartment closed in on her and the air grew thick with memories of past apparitions. She shivered as she thought about going to bed. The last thing she wanted was to cushion her sleep and dream.

Chapter 3

The baby was fussing again. For almost a week now, it had kept Maggie awake. Fussing and fretting, fussing and fretting, driving Maggie mad as it brought her maternal instincts screaming to the surface. Instincts she could do nothing to quash, as the source of her dilemma hid in the center of her mind where no human hand could find it. There were no ear-plugs or sleeping pills to fix what ailed her.

A baby fist reached inside her and twisted her gut, more tightly than any man's could, with its demands for succor. She wanted, needed to find it, to comfort it and relieve herself of the torture her nights brought.

Maggie slammed her fist into the pillow, displacing the feathers. Hands above her head, she twisted and turned while attempting to cover her ears with the soft, insulating sound barrier.

There was no hiding from herself.

"Go away! Go to sleep and leave me alone...leave me alone."

She didn't want to cry. It was exhaustion, not self-pity, that spilled tears from her eyes. She tried unsuccessfully to focus on Max, anything but the plaintive cries in her head. Max wasn't the answer. How dare he or any damn cop think she'd wished this on herself?

Pulling the pillow off her head, she slapped it a few more times and threw herself on top of its downy softness. She lay partly on her stomach, twisting sideways as she brought her knees up to ease the ache pulling at her insides. It was 11:02 p.m. by the bedside clock when the baby stopped crying and Maggie fell asleep.

And began to dream.

He stepped back from the bed to admire his handiwork and frowned. Under the heels of her shoes the duvet wrinkled slovenly. With care he slipped the shoes off, set them neatly at the side of the bed, then smoothed out the creases.

He sighed, thinking, I'll bring my camera next time. Definitely. A ripple of pleasure caressed his senses. The way the red scarf picked up the flecks in her suit, she could almost have dressed for the occasion. Even the bedcovers, sprigged with roses, added to the overall effect. She had good taste. They made a beautiful picture. He'd arranged it just right. Madonna with child.

And the baby! So good, so angelic. No more crying now it had found its mother. The effort it had taken to tuck the babe against its mother's breast had been worthwhile. Luckily she was a full-busted woman, ample. The child would never have to go without again.

He walked to the door. His surgical gloves snapped as he rolled them tighter across his knuckles. He touched the light switch, then hesitated. He couldn't bear to turn the light out. One more look, just one, and then he would go.

He smiled the smile of an artist who knows when to paint the last brushstroke. So perfect. To leave them in the dark would be a crime.

Quietly, he slipped out of the house into the night. As he

*vaulted the back fence his head spun with pictures of blond
hair arranged across a pillow scattered with rosebuds.*

*And two pairs of matching blue eyes staring sightlessly at
the ceiling.*

Maggie parked her car in the civic car park and walked up
the slope of Mayoral Drive. Auckland Central rose six stories
above her. A patchwork of earth-colored scoria blocks some
volcano had spewed up millions of years ago formed the base-
ment wall. It opened halfway along its length, a gaping black
maw indiscriminately swallowing cop cars, cops and prisoners
alike. Dim, hollow, a place where slamming metal doors and
screaming sirens echoed in air heavy with disinfectant, vomit,
fear and defeat.

Maggie took the last few paces at a run, turning into Cook
Street and up the steps to the entrance as if the devil nipped
at her heels. Time, precious time didn't allow for a meeting
on neutral ground and had driven her to this place against her
will. On the top step she paused, her heart in her throat. Hadn't
she vowed never to cross this threshold again? And here she
was doing just that.

Conscience drove a hard bargain. Hers had been up and
running from the moment she'd opened her eyes. Three
women dead. Three too many. A single thought, blinding in
its simplicity, had forced her out of bed, into the shower, and
sent her in search of paper and pencil.

Maybe it's not too late.

This, the first dream of death she'd had in Auckland, had
been clearer, more edgy in its intensity. Pathetically, she shied
away from the word *murder*. It was too out there, too in her
face. The word *death* was easier to swallow, if it stopped her
wanting to run to the nearest bathroom and throw up. And if
living the dream slammed her with a knockout punch, the
flashes, images, caught her off guard, winding her with short,
sharp jabs to the solar plexus. What could be worse? Noth-

ing—except maybe the ridicule she knew waited on the other side of the door.

She'd been directed to the fifth floor. Reception was empty, though a light, electronic hum issued from a double-doored office. Her muscles tightened, screaming with tension. Maybe she should barge in and sing out, "Can anyone tell me where to find Sergeant Strachan?"

Impatience gave in to need. Fists clenched, teeth clamped over her bottom lip, she stepped toward the office.

Maybe it's not too late!

A huge, tawny-haired man dressed in uniform blues preempted her decision. Doors swinging in his wake, he asked, "Need any help?"

He had a look of authority, of reliability, and a badge with the legend Sergeant McQuaid sitting squarely on his massive chest. A cop she could trust, thought Maggie, taking in his attractive, craggy features. If only he was the one she had come to see. "Yes, could you show me to Sergeant Strachan's office?"

"Sure thing." Warm, teasing hazel eyes gave her a quick, speculative once-over. "Follow me," he said as he walked on, keeping her pinned with his inquisitive gaze.

Since he hadn't asked her name, she didn't have to suffer a swift change in his attitude. Taking two steps to his one, she kept pace with him, keeping close to the wall; the sergeant's shoulders needed all the space they could get.

They passed two interview rooms before they reached the corner office. Knocking once, Sergeant McQuaid opened the door. With her view blocked by his bulk, Maggie listened for Max's voice with her nerves prickling her skin like an invasion of ants.

Maybe it's not too late!

Max looked up as Rowan McQuaid invaded his privacy. "What's up?" Although McQuaid was slightly younger than Max, they'd been in the same year at Trentham Police College. Jamie Thurlo, the other member of their trio, had been a hel-

icopter jockey when he signed on and now rode the skies in
a blue-and-white beauty. Their friendship had survived the
years and been tempered by them. The young hotheads were
long gone. Rowan, the more methodical member of the group,
had stuck to the route where the donkey work lay, the papers
and reports that Max hated. Like the ones littering his desk.
After eight agonizing hours of constant arousal, while his mind
reran in a constant loop every second spent with Maggie, he'd
woken up feeling as if half his brain had shut down while the
rest worked at half speed.

"Visitor for you, Max."

Secretly glad of the interruption, he grumbled, "This better
be important. I'm busy." Anything was better than reading
each line three times over without taking it in. The hell with
it. He needed something, someone, to take his mind off Maggie. "All right, show them in."

"I'm sure you'll want to see this one," Rowan said, grinning, and he moved out of the way, giving Max his first
glimpse of his visitor.

"Maggie!" Max was halfway out of his chair before she'd
stepped into the room. He caught the conjecture in Rowan's
glance as he rounded his desk. "Maggie," he said, "this is a
friend of mine, Rowan McQuaid." He watched her offer her
hand as he finished, "Rowan, meet Maggie Kovacs." But her
eyes were on him.

Max took in Rowan's recoil without surprise. The trouble
with friends close enough to know your whole life history,
preferences, prejudices and the kind of breakfast cereal you
ate was they took a personal interest in what you were doing
and with whom. They stood up with you at your wedding and
cried with you over your divorce, and because of the last two,
this meeting with Maggie wouldn't make any sense to Rowan.

Max cut off the question forming in Rowan's eyes with a
meaningful glare and a nod that said he should leave.

"I'll leave you to it then." Rowan started to turn away,

speaking over his shoulder as he left. "Good luck, and don't sweat it, mate. I won't tell a soul."

Max brushed past Maggie and closed the door, shutting out his friend and the rest of Auckland Central. He'd no idea why she had come, but he wasn't sharing. A pulse throbbed in his temple as fantasies born in the dead of night flooded his memory. At the mere sight of her, his palms itched to touch and the fire in his groin as her scent filled his head warned him to keep his distance if he was to maintain control.

"Take a seat, Maggie."

"I won't, thanks." Turning her back on him, she walked over to the corner window and stood looking down.

"If all you came for was the view, there's a better one from your apartment." Drawn by the vulnerable picture she made, Max followed, but instead of dropping a kiss in the unguarded hollow at her nape to appease his craving, he turned her to face him. All his good intentions crashed and burned the moment he searched her eyes. They shone darkly, sparkling with unshed tears that made his breath catch. "What are you doing here, Maggie?"

"Maybe it's not too late!" Emotion made her voice crack as she uttered the words chasing through her brain in a monotonous litany. "It doesn't have to be."

"Too late for what? C'mon, give me a clue, babe. I need more." His hands tightened on her shoulders.

Dammit, he needed Maggie!

It had happened so swiftly, this blinding need for the one woman who should be anathema to him. Steady boy, steady. Max drew a deep, calming breath and compounded his dilemma with her womanly scent. The perfume she favored blended subtly with her own secret essence. It had lingered on his hands and driven him crazy replaying the pleasure derived from touching her. Tasting her. Crushing her against—

He had to stop punishing himself. He couldn't.

Her warm camel coat, the same one she'd worn last night, seemed to melt away beneath his palms as her tight muscles communicated with him. Could Maggie feel him through it? Feel the heat generated by the burning ache in his groin? Hell! No wonder. Being close to her was playing with fire. And he knew it. Sliding his palms from her shoulders to her hands, he pulled her away from the window before he could set her on the ledge and take her there, for all the world to see. He forced the words *"Let's sit over here,"* past the stricture in his throat, and settled Maggie in a chair, pulling the other one close. "What's got you so upset? Are you still worried about Jo?"

"No, not her!" She felt Max's hands caress hers as if he would rub her cares away. How would he react when she told him her reason for searching him out? He looked tired, and a strange longing to hug him tightly shoved her other emotions aside. Not that she wanted to mother him. How could she? He was so big, so handsome. And the rakish silver blaze in his hair curled on his forehead and fought with the tenderness in his eyes.

Any second now, all that would change. Preventing it was beyond her control.

She wished this small section of time and space could be set aside for herself and Max. Wished everything standing between them to the farthest ends of the earth. And knew there wasn't a snowball's chance in hell of it happening.

What would Max think if she told him she didn't want him to make her dreams come true? She wanted him to make them go away!

But all this heart searching could only delay the inevitable. Time he faced up to who she was, even if it drove him away.

Pulling her hands back, she reversed their positions, holding his long fingers and taking courage from their strength. "Max, I had another dream last night."

His withdrawal was more spiritual than tangible. The heat drained from his hands. She gripped tighter. His eyes iced over, still true blue, but cold, icy cold, and although she'd expected his reaction, it still hurt.

"Sure you did, baby. So did I. You were there, hot as hell and pure, freaking magic." Max's lips curled without showing his teeth and his gaze stripped every stitch from her body.

Maggie had known it was coming, so she didn't flinch away, didn't try to retreat or shield herself. Nor would she essay an apology for who she was—especially to Max.

"Dammit, Max! This isn't about me, or us. It's about some poor woman who's going be killed, who may already be dead. I pray she isn't. But I can't fix this on my own. You have to help me before it's too late." She let go of his hands. His skin was red where she'd gripped them. She got to her feet. Max stood, too, and then sat on the edge of his desk, sweeping the silver strand of hair back from the harsh red of his scar.

"You have no idea, Maggie. None at all. I'm the last person to ask for help. I'm a nonbeliever from way back." His lips stretched in a grimace. "Hell, Maggie, I still want you, don't want to lose you, but all this psychic nonsense will be the death of any relationship before it's had a chance."

"We never had a chance, never will. Not if you can't at least try to believe. You make me feel, make me wish." The fist she wanted to pound him with hit the arm of his chair. "Even without Jo's wanting you, we never had a future. All we ever had was the possibility of a quick affair...." *I could have settled for that.* Maggie sighed and pushed her hands up under her collar. The touch of cashmere against her face felt good in a room where all warmth had been depleted. She straightened and looked Max straight in the eye, her decision made. She would go home. "We haven't a hope in hell if you can't even bring yourself to listen."

"Lady, I wish to hell you'd never shown up today! I warned you last night: failure guaranteed. I already lost a marriage to all this psychic garbage. I won't get mixed up in it again. No way! Never!"

"I didn't expect to win, but I knew I had to try." Maggie retrieved her purse, and as she stood, undid the clasp and took out a folded paper. "You see, I was damned if I did and she's dead if I didn't!'' She tossed the paper on his desk. ''I know you won't make use of this, but hang on to it. I think you'll be surprised at the likeness.'' Maggie's ironic laugh came out as a sob. ''I even surprised myself.''

Max watched her walk away, amazed that for all the anger between them, he still had the same gut-wrenching reaction to the view of her slim ankles showing through the slit in the back of her coat. He closed the door, sat behind his desk with his elbows braced on it. ''Jerk,'' he muttered, cursing his inability to embrace the concept that would give him Maggie. The folded paper glared at him, challenging him to pick it up. He reached over and unfolded it.

The notepaper was Maggie's father's. Frank Kovacs, Kereru Hill Winery, Pigeon Hill. Max's gaze skimmed the header to study the head-and-shoulders pencil drawing of a woman.

He didn't recognize her.

The bow tied at her neck was another story. He knew for a fact it was red, tied with precision, each loop and tail the exact length of the one opposite.

It was scary the way Maggie had caught the eyes. And notwithstanding the simplicity of the medium, a cold chill slithered up his spine at the complete lack of life in them.

She'd got halfway to the civic car park before he caught her.

''Well, Sergeant, come to finish the job you did on me?'' Her bold question was at odds with her grim expression.

An urge to rub away the hurt he'd caused stirred his hands. But only turning inside out and remodeling himself could achieve his aim to redeem himself in her eyes. Deep within him a wish flickered like a candle on one of the birthday cakes his mother used to bake when he was young, but even he could see it wouldn't take much to blow out the flame.

''We need to talk. Let me buy you a cup of coffee.''

''I gave us a chance to talk not five minutes ago—I've changed my mind now.''

"Don't be like that, Maggie. I'm not saying that you're right and I'm wrong. I just want to discuss the possibilities." He caught hold of her sleeve, wary of actually touching her skin. Of what it would do to him. "I've got the drawing with me," he said persuasively. "We can go to the Blues Café in the Aotea Center. It should be quiet this time of day."

"All right, but don't think I intend spending the whole day in Auckland. I have work to do."

"See, I told you, practically empty," Max said, lowering his voice to prevent it bouncing off the hard surfaces of marble floors and avant-garde chandeliers. "Let's sit by the window."

Thickly padded tub chairs softened the starkness of the rest of the room. But the only warmth Max felt came from the body heat Maggie generated under all that cashmere. A part of him hoped she'd slip her coat off, the rest wanted to hide her lush curves from everyone but him. Dragging his mind back from under her coat, he asked, "This spot do?"

"Yes, fine…okay, I don't mind." She listened to herself agree every which way and do it twice over. Boy, Max was in for a shock if he thought her compliance normal.

"What will you have? Cappuccino?"

"Latté, please," she said as Max headed for the counter. Decaf was her usual brew, but she needed a caffeine jolt. She'd begun the morning on an energy high that now fizzled from lack of sleep. Or maybe she had a touch of the Mary, Mary's, letting contrariness be her guide in spite of his change of heart.

Or maybe she was just plain scared.

All along there'd been a small niggle working away at the back of her thoughts until it dug a hole big enough to climb out. But she wouldn't voice it just yet. Time enough to hit him with it when he discovered this wasn't just a case of her imagination playing up. Blast, she didn't want to be proved right. But the odds ran against her being wrong. No, she wouldn't mention her suspicions to Max yet; one small step at a time. That way when Max threw his doubts in her face she wouldn't run into them.

"Any leads on the Khyber Pass Killer, Sergeant?"

Startled, Max spun around and spilled froth over the side of the cup, saucer and his fingers. Damn! Couldn't he get a minute's peace? A sinking feeling gripped him as he recognized Babcox, crime reporter with the *Tribune*. A man with the fierce animalistic tenacity of the weasel he resembled, all ginger hair, sharp features and canines. Young and eager, Babcox made up in effrontery for what he lacked in years and inches. Like the way he'd slapped the name the Khyber Pass Killer on the man they were after. A name that stuck once the other papers ran with it, though only the first victim, a young prostitute, had lived in Khyber Pass Road.

Apart from the killer, all three had only one thing in common. The police team's latest clue, unearthed after the last murder. Certain aspects of the case needed to be kept secret, and if Max had his way Babcox would be the last to know.

And that was only one of his problems.

What he needed was a reasonable explanation of why Maggie Kovacs knew details that had Detective Inspector Henare threatening a stint in the Chathams for anyone who spilled his guts to the media.

Max turned his back on him. "No comment."

"Come on, Strachan. Things must be progressing well if you can afford to take a coffee break in the middle of the morning."

One glance at the waitress told Max she was agog with speculation. "Here," he said, pushing the cup and its saucer full of milk toward her, "can you fix this for me?" Then he softened his demand with, "Thanks," when she took it away. That done, he told Babcox, "You know all statements have to come through Detective Inspector Henare's office. Call him."

Max felt the reporter back off mentally if not physically. It took a brave man to approach Mike Henare. He wasn't any taller than Max's six-five, yet the inspector could make two of him, and the Maori half of his ancestry lent a fearsome cast to his features that intimidated felons and scared the crap out of journos. It was a skill Max hadn't mastered, one that needed cultivating, seeing that Babcox still took up space beside him.

"Why bother with the ringmaster when I can get it from the horse's mouth? Doesn't it worry you that women can't sleep at night without wondering who's going to be next?"

Max glowered at him and swallowed a curse as he heard the waitress set the coffee down on the counter behind him. The nerve of this guy! Hell, it was his embroidering of the facts that kept women awake at night. "Take it up with Henare."

"Who's the babe? Any connection with the case?"

Damn! Max didn't want this jerk sniffing around Maggie. "Give me a break, mate, I do have a private life." Maggie'd be sure to clam up if she caught on to Babcox's line of work.

"Can't say as I blame you. Wouldn't mind a piece of that myself."

Max stiffened and his hands fisted as he fought back the urge to plant them in Babcox's filthy mouth. His nostrils flared with loathing as he sucked in a breath and held it.

With a nod of his head he drew Babcox's attention to a poster advertising *MacBeth.* "If it's more bloody murder you're after, try backstage. You'll learn more there than you'll get out of me."

"Yeah, real funny, Sergeant. But at least they know who did it." The reporter put a couple of paces between himself and Max, then added, "Never let it be said I couldn't take a hint. I'll be seeing you, Strachan."

"Not if I can help it. Listen good, Babcox, keep out of my face or I'll get you banned from media releases."

Max set Maggie's coffee down in front of her. "Here you are. I hope it's not cold. I got held up. Did you want something to eat with it? I didn't think to ask if you were hungry."

"No problem, coffee's fine. Who was your friend?"

"*Friend*'s the wrong word for a lowlife you wouldn't wanna be caught dead near," answered Max, and realized his mistake as he saw Maggie's expression tighten. He took the tub chair beside her, keeping his back to the window so he could see the whole room. He didn't trust that guy one inch. "Anyway, he's gone and the air's fresher for it."

"I suppose in your line of work you meet more people you dislike than not."

"That just about sums it up."

Maggie didn't reply; instead she tore open three of the small packs of sugar and tipped them one after the other into her coffee. Caffeine was what she needed but a little sweetness wouldn't go amiss.

"Maggie Kovacs! It *is* you."

Suddenly Maggie found herself smothered in a soft, pillowy chest and a designer fragrance.

"I could hardly believe my eyes, it's been so long."

Once she'd been released and could breathe again, Maggie recognized Carla Dunsmuir. "Carla, how are—?"

"Oh, my dear! I'm so pleased to see that at last you've come out to play. And is this the man who's rescued you? Your father would be so pleased." Ever flamboyant, Carla gushed over both of them in warm, scented waves, eyes flashing and hands keeping time with her mouth.

The direction of Carla's thoughts was all too obvious. She rushed on, not waiting for introductions. All Maggie could do was let her run her course. Nothing and no one ever stopped Carla once she'd hit her stride.

"I haven't seen you since Frank's funeral. So sad, so sad, but it's thanks to him that I'm here today." She smiled gently. "You know what they say about ill winds."

"I do?" What was the woman talking about? Here because of Frank? Maggie needed help keeping up with her. She needed coffee.

Max stood with his hand on the chair next to him. "Care

to join us?'' he asked, hoping like hell the woman would say no, yet interested in spite of himself in what she had to say on the subject of Maggie's father.

"No, thanks. I'm just passing through. That's what I meant, Maggie. I needed something to do. I was lonely without Frank—you know what I mean. You must miss him more than me. Such a beautiful man.''

For a moment Carla's face crumpled and Maggie braced herself, but thankfully she carried on with her explanation.

"So I ended up getting involved with the opera company and now I'm on the board. We're doing a short season of *Turandot,*'' she said, as if she personally would appear on-stage. "It starts tonight with a gala opening,'' Carla chiruped, her hands fluttering and chest quivering in excitement. "So much to do, so little time.''

"I'm happy for you. Very happy.'' Maggie felt positive Max must have realized by now that Carla had been her father's lover.

"Such a tragedy.'' Carla looked over at Max, sighing gustily. "I'm sure Maggie's told you all about it.'' Max nodded, but still she carried on. "So unexpected, too. I mean, these things always are, but it's just that Frank was always so careful, checking everything before we took off. I often went with him, you know, but not that day. He refused to take me....'' Carla trailed off, then looked at Maggie apologetically. "You mustn't think he didn't believe in you—I'm certain he did. It was just that being the sort of man he was, he wouldn't let it rule his life.''

Max reached under the table and took the hand he knew Maggie had clenched in her lap. He undid her fingers and wrapped his own around them, rubbing the back of her hand against his thigh. Blasted woman! Why wouldn't she leave? Would nothing go his way this morning?

"Anyway, Frank saved my life, but I never understood how it happened. I mean the plane was only six hours past its last fifty-hour check.'' Carla looked at the jeweled watch circling her plump wrist. "Heavens, I must run!" She leaned forward and planted a kiss in the air near Maggie's cheek. "Look after yourself, dear, and remember," she said with a wink, "don't let life grind you down!"

"Phew! I'm exhausted. How about you?" Max asked as he watched Carla's departing figure disappear into the auditorium.

Maggie felt drained, which wasn't unusual after a meeting with the woman. She shook her head. "It's all right, I'm used to her." She laughed out loud at a joke she'd thought long dead. "I never understood her and my father. I mean, their personalities were so different it was like combining candy floss with a lit match, yet I'm sure he loved her. In fact, I always thought he would marry her one day, but they never even got engaged."

"They say opposites attract. Look at us." Max dropped the statement into the conversation, reminding her their relationship wasn't all-business. Truth be known, he'd rather it was pleasure that had brought them to this stage, where Maggie was easy with him holding her hand, and trusting enough to let him warm it against his thigh. He looked at the lush redness of her mouth and wondered how long he would have to wait to taste it again.

But anytime now he would have to get back to the folded paper, and the drawing burning a hole in his pocket.

"At least my father and Carla had some common ground, like opera, flying and wine." There were questions in Maggie's eyes, thousands of them floating around in the dark brown depths.

Max didn't know the answers. He wished he did. All he could do was work his way through them and pray for a miracle. For one clue to jump up and hit him in the eye.

"I like wine, but as for the rest…" Max shrugged. "…I can't tell *Turandot* from a tarot card. But tell me, what really did happen to your father?"

"I believe he was murdered!"

Chapter 4

Maggie blinked. Max hadn't disappeared, which surprised her as much as the words she'd uttered. *I believe he was murdered.* She'd hardly dared think it before, never mind give breath to such an outrageous idea. A few moments with Carla, a woman as irrepressible and gregarious as she was generous, and suddenly Maggie had deviated from her rules. Rules that kept her safe from people like Gorman.

Now Max really would think she was nuts.

And maybe he wouldn't be far from wrong. She probably came from a whole line of nutcases. Look at her father. A rational man would have at least taken some heed or precautions after she'd warned him. The surprise, in what was rapidly becoming a day of them, was that he *had* listened, and saved Carla from certain death, if not himself. Dumb! Maggie would never understand men.

"There was no mention of murder in the notes, from either you or anyone else who was—"

"Notes!" She gasped at this revelation, "You checked up on me?"

"Did you expect anything less? I'm a cop, Maggie. I take no one at face value, even with a face as beautiful as yours."

"Is that supposed to make me feel better? That you think I have a beautiful face? A shop window dummy is beautiful, but there's nothing inside." She quivered with anger and stared at the frothy latté in her cup. No wonder he hadn't wanted to listen. Gorman had done it again.

Courage don't fail me now!

She set her cup into the saucer with a clatter and searched blindly for her purse. "Sorry I wasted your time. But don't worry, I'm out of here. Me and my beautiful face." She lashed out at him in her disappointment. She'd expected the moon and been handed a false coin.

Hurt tears distorted an image of the woman from her dream. *I tried. I really did try!*

Max's fingers circled her wrist as she pushed up from her seat. "Maggie, don't go! Stay. Please." His voice exerted the same light pressure as his hand. "Take it from me, nothing in Gorman's notes made me think any less of you."

"What does it matter?" She shook off his hand and slung her purse over her shoulder, determined to leave.

"What do you want from me? Blood?" Max blocked her way and the world shrank to the width of his massive chest and shoulders.

She fixed her gaze on his chin. Any higher and his blue eyes might be her undoing. True blue as they say, she couldn't bear to see them lie. Teeth clenched, she muttered, "That would do for starters, then you might try relying on your own judgment instead of that mouth of Gorman's!"

Blast! Forcing her eyes wide hadn't held back the liquid frustration in them. Now a tear hit her cheek, and to cap it off, she probably had a drip at her nose. Typical—it never rained but it poured. Maggie dug in her pocket and drew out a tissue.

Drowning was too good for him, unless he could do it in that tear. That's all it took: a little salt water and he felt like a jerk. The rest of the coffee bar patrons probably thought so, too. Max and Maggie had drawn a small audience, and the waitress seemed ready to get on the phone and call the cops. She'd scream police brutality if he showed her his badge.

Maggie's tears gouged a scar inside him deeper than the bullet had done when it seared his forehead. "Hey. Why don't you sit down, blow your nose and tell me about Frank?" He swiftly scanned the coffee bar. "People think we're fighting." The brusque heartiness of his words didn't have the desired effect.

Discomfort was written all over Max, and a newer, more tender emotion crushed her resolve. This huge man handled the worst the criminal element threw at him, but a crying woman cut him off at the knees.

"They'd be right then, wouldn't they?" Her question spilled out, wrapped in a mixture of sobs and pent-up laughter. Then Max's arm came around her shoulders, and the feel of him, firm and strong, holding her, stole the rest of her resolution.

"C'mon, honey, let's go outside where we can find some fresh air and privacy." Quickly! Before he pulled her into his arms and kissed her senseless. Wouldn't that give everyone something to stare at?

Wide steps flowed onto Aotea Square, and at their base he steered Maggie toward a convenient alcove. A curve designed for elegance would keep them private and would shelter them from the wind. He'd sweated it out back there, thought that Maggie would turn and run. But she'd capitulated, and he didn't know who was happier—the cop or the man. His baser, more selfish, hormone-driven instincts howled at the thought of losing something they'd decided was theirs by right.

Maggie.

Base, because even while he offered comfort, dried her eyes and soothed her with gentling sweeps of his hands, those same hands wanted to rip open her coat and push her against the wall. He wanted her to feel his pain. Pain that wouldn't sub-

side until he'd had her, until he'd felt her hot wet flesh sur-
round his needy hardness and welcome his seed—and still it
wouldn't be enough. He'd want her, again and again and
again....

Who was he kidding? He needed her. Needed her to make
him feel alive.

Whatever it took!

But the cop had his own agenda. The kind that pricked up
its ears at the mere mention of murder. However implausible.

Max felt her breasts swell and subside against his chest as
a sigh travelled through her. He restrained himself from increasing the contact. From gluing them together from breast
to thigh. "Feeling better now?" he asked, pushing his Maggie-
moistened handkerchief back in his pocket.

With another sigh, she murmured, "You must...think...I'm
nuts."

"Not really. Slightly kooky maybe." That was better; he'd
raised a smile big enough to play havoc with his good intentions. Much as he lusted after the feel of Maggie in his arms,
it was time to get back to business. "Listen, Gorman never
wrote that you'd warned Frank not to fly, and there was no
mention of dreams in his report. Nothing. He saved all that—"
Max bit back the word *garbage*. "He saved it to humiliate
you in the media. I'd never treat you that way." His finger
tilted her chin toward him. "Look at me, Maggie. Know this.
Anything you say to me is completely off the record. I'm no
more crazy about journos than you are."

Maggie didn't answer. Instead, she stared at him and
through him, as if she could see forever. A worm of apprehension crawled up his spine. His hands dove for his pockets
and his feet wouldn't stop fidgeting. He had an urge to shut
his eyes and hide his thoughts of Maggie, way back in his
mind. It showed that his natural skepticism could only stand
so much. What the situation wanted was lightening, before the
tension between them snapped like cheap elastic and he was
the one who got stung. With a couple of quick swipes of his

finger across his chest, he said, "Cross my heart and hope to die."

Bad move!

What he hadn't said—might never say—had screwed him up.

"That was pretty facile even for a cop." Maggie shrugged inside her coat as if she might shed him like water. No such luck. She'd started this and her impulse might have washed out any credibility she had left.

Reluctantly, she laid her thoughts out in front of him. "Five months before my father died, another Creighton aircraft, the same model as his, crashed in the Pacific somewhere near Hawaii. The accident report on that plane said it had been caused by a fuel leak in the engine. The sensors malfunctioned, so the fire extinguishers didn't come on.

"As soon as the report came out, Dad had his plane checked from nose to tail. Knowing my father, I'd bet that engine was clean enough to eat off." Max frowned down at her, but she insisted, "Dad wasn't stupid, just stubborn. He didn't take risks." Max *had* to believe her, even though all she had to go on was intuition. She *had* to convince him.

"I was wondering about what Carla said. How it was only six hours past a fifty-hour check. Is that the one she meant?"

"Yeah, it would have been more only we'd had a lot of building done at the vineyard and then Dad took a holiday in Australia."

"From the account I read this morning, your father's plane went up in flames. Am I right?"

"The scenarios were identical, though the air-accident inspectors tried to make out that the fuel line fractured near the intake. Yet the engineer swore the fuel line was new and the extinguishers should have controlled the fire, from the amount of leakage there was. I believed him. He wouldn't have short-changed my father—not a valuable customer like him. If he'd been shoddy in his work, Frank Kovacs…" she tilted her chin at Max as she said her father's name "…wouldn't have kept

going back. Dad expected the best and he usually got it. That's
why he laughed when I told him about the dream, the warning.
He didn't need it. All the angles had already been covered and
he thought nothing could go wrong. Now I find he wasn't as
confident as he made out, otherwise he would have taken Carla
with him.''

"Why didn't you tell someone?" he asked, then shook his
head. He already knew Maggie's answer. He didn't need to
be a mind reader for that.

"Just who do you think would have listened, after the number Gorman did on me?" She hung her head, and her voice
when she spoke again was gruff and teary. "Besides, I had no
proof. Nothing to give anyone except that it was too much of
a coincidence. Too easy. You can see it, can't you? The ditch-
ing of the other plane made it the perfect setup for anyone
who wanted to harm Dad.''

Max was no great believer in coincidence. More often than
not some manipulation was involved. "What about enemies?"

Maggie lifted her head a little, looking at him from under
her lashes. There was a softness in her eyes he'd never noticed
before. They reflected hope and displayed a vulnerability he
hadn't expected, just because he'd taken a little interest in her
theory.

"He had none, that I know of. But then, nobody gives away
all their secrets. And Dad played his hand pretty close to his
chest." Unconsciously, she grabbed Max's lapel, as if hanging
on to the shred of hope he'd given her.

Max knew he was going to let her down.

He felt a sudden compulsion to kick ass. Gorman's in particular. For the sake of a laugh Gorman had let a case go
begging, left it incomplete. Max laid his own success as a cop
on his instinct for sniffing out things that weren't quite as they
appeared. He'd caught a scent as Maggie spoke, a faint one.
What good would it do to inform her there was a chance she
could be right? Fifteen months down the track they were look-

ing at a trail that was cold as ice and had been trampled so heavily it would be unrecognizable.

Much as he'd love to help Maggie out by digging into the particulars of her father's death, he had more immediate problems. Like the woman in the drawing. Did she exist? If so, who was she? And was she alive?

It was Maggie who'd said, "Maybe it's not too late." Well, he'd have to see about that. An idea clicked into his mind as quickly as fingers snapping. Damned if he hadn't come up with a way to knock off two birds with one stone!

"Any minute now," said Jo, swiveling around to face Maggie. "It's just coming up, next street on the right."

She'd picked them up at Aotea Square in an unmarked police car. Speculation was rife in Jo's eyes. They'd narrowed when Max and Maggie strolled up together, but she'd made no comment. She'd just handed over the driving to Max and taken the seat beside him.

"Where are we? I don't recognize the area." The inner city suburb they drove through boasted a plethora of older houses, mostly standing in large gardens untrammeled by the recent rush to subdivide and squeeze in another house. The area looked like old money and the professions.

"It's just off Mountain Road. Haven't you been this way before?" Max asked, in an offhand manner at variance with the glitter in his eyes through the driver's mirror.

"I once went to a hospital there."

Max signaled, took a right and slowed down at the second building on the left. "This one?" He nodded toward the large squat villa, glowing in a mixture of pastels that aped the latest trends.

To Maggie it looked like a blowsy old tart had stopped by to chat up the regimental lines of hedges and flower beds standing at attention in front of it.

"No, I meant the—" Maggie broke off the instant an overwhelming feeling of dread filled her. She touched her face as if that would ward off giddiness. It felt bloodless, as if it didn't belong to her, but it wasn't as cold as her hands. "The Mater Hospital. I went to visit a friend there years ago." She looked at Jo. "What is this place?"

"It's a maternity home," answered Jo.

Max flashed Jo a sideways glance with "keep quiet" written all over it. What was his problem? Was this some kind of test? Maggie could tell him he was wasting his time. She couldn't kick start her abilities on a whim. All she had were her dreams.

Only the dreams!

"So, you don't recognize the place, huh?" he asked, sliding the car into a parking spot facing a flower bed in front of the building.

Her earlier relief at escaping the interrogation she'd expected before Jo picked them up died swiftly. This was a test! "This is one that arranges adoptions, right? No! I've never been here. I *think* I might have remembered."

Jo gave Max a look that should have made his hair curl. "This is all his idea. I could have told him it wouldn't pan out."

"Quit arguing, you two! It won't solve anything. Maggie, you remember what you said to me this morning? 'Maybe it's not too late.' Well, this might be the place to find out just how late it is. So far, this hospital is the only link to all three murders. The victims each left a baby here for adoption at varying times. Four months ago this place had a break-in. The office was ransacked. One month later we had us a victim.

"So far we can't tie anyone to it. We're looking at people who've been refused a child or a father whose child might have been adopted without him knowing. Frankly, we're floundering, and ideas aren't coming thick or fast. Some sicko has these women in his sights and is sticking to his own twisted agenda. The trouble is the killings are too stylized and don't follow any of the patterns we've been taught to look for in serial killers. There's been no escalation in the violence, no mutilation.''

"Can't you give the women who come here protection, or warn them?''

"There are too many, and not enough cops. Issuing a warning could start a panic, and because of the privacy act, the hospital isn't keen on giving us any more names than we need. Some people wouldn't be too happy about everyone knowing their business. What we're gonna do now is show the picture you sketched around to the staff. See if anyone recognizes her.''

"But—''

"No worries, just sit tight. Jo and I will see to it all. C'mon, Jo. The sooner we're in, the sooner we're done.''

Maggie hadn't expected an invitation. What could she do? She watched them exit the front seats and Jo walk around the car to join Max. They made a handsome couple, both tall, dark, attractive. Two sides of a triangle, with Maggie making up the third. Not the best shape for relationships to be in, no matter how Max made her feel. The confidence in his touch, as if he had no doubts; the way his mouth had covered hers; the taste of him... For once she really wished she could see into the future.

Sometime soon she was going to have to tell him her other secret. The one that had been tormenting her since the dreams began. The one she hadn't dared voice.

No, there'd be time enough once he realized her dreams did come true. She had no family and few enough friends, since she'd neglected them to immerse herself in running the vineyard. Max hounding them, when he discovered she only had premonitions about people she knew, wouldn't win her a Miss Popularity crown. Yet all the women had been strangers, which left only one conclusion. The man perpetrating these murders—whose face never appeared in her dreams—was a friend of hers.

* * *

"What's this about a drawing?" Jo demanded. "Let me in on why we're here and what it has to do with Maggie."

Max handed her the drawing. "Here, take a look." He waited, silent while she studied the sketch. Her eyes widened. Hopefully, Jo was man enough to get on with her job like a good cop, without giving him any hassles. He took no pleasure in what he was about to do to Maggie. Hell, he'd already pushed the wrong button by snooping in Gorman's report. And just as Jo shouldn't let friendship get in the way of her job, he needed to clamp down on what he felt for Maggie till this was out of the way.

"Something catch your eye?" he asked, as Jo still hadn't spoken.

"Do you need to ask?" She straightened and stepped back, then nodded toward the clinic. "They're not going to be jumping for joy to see us again."

"Tough! I want you to show the picture to the staff, check everyone on duty, even the tea lady. I'll do another search of their records to see if they have Maggie's name there."

"Max! You can't do that. I know Maggie. Besides, how could she get away with it? If ever you had a wild idea, this is it!"

"We're professionals, Jo. Deal with it!"

Max repeated the words in his own mind, reinforcing his decision. Like it or not, it came with the territory. He watched Jo stomp away from the car, leaving angry marks in the newly turned black earth of a flower bed as she cut across it to the front entrance. Uh-oh! The old gardener working at the far end of the bed got to his feet, following Jo's progress with his eyes. If Max was a gambling man he would bet the guy was really pissed off. "Sorry, mate." Max tossed him an apologetic wave and strolled after Jo, taking the longer route. He wasn't in any hurry to be proved correct.

Being the eldest of a big rough-and-tumble family of four boys and two girls, he could see why people wanted to adopt kids. He had nothing against a kid getting a good home. Now they'd met, he was certain Jo had it right—Maggie had never been here. But this was his only connection, and he still needed to check her out.

This place made him uptight. Somehow every time he came here he was reminded of Lisa, his ex-wife. Not that she'd ever had a kid adopted; she'd flatly refused to start a family. With him, that was. Last time he'd seen her, she'd been walking arm in arm with her new man. Max didn't know if they were married or not and didn't give a damn! She'd looked happy as a pig in mud and twice as big. That's what had really gotten to him. The ink on their divorce papers hadn't had time to dry and she looked ready to pop any minute.

The scar on his forehead began to tingle as it always did when he thought about Lisa. When they'd first married, starting a family hadn't been top of their list of things to do. There'd been buying a house, a nice car, taking holidays—all the usual ways to spend money. Then suddenly he was thirty and the fuse on his biological time bomb got shorter. He'd wanted a family and all the values that went with it since he was a young boy. Values missing from the people his job brought him in contact with. Lisa hadn't been overjoyed. And the idea went down the tubes after he'd been shot. Not that it had been bad—a bit of skin and hair missing, and a mild concussion from how he'd flung his head back and hit the wall.

Maybe if he'd made her have counseling afterward, the way he had, they might still be together. Maybe? She'd said she was okay with it. But it was then she'd started bingeing on 0900 clairvoyants, and he'd been too caught up in the job to notice, until the phone company darn near cut off their service for nonpayment.

With the clarity of hindsight he could see why it had happened. But it had taken him over two years to work it out, and the part about psychics still needed attention. No. Lisa had been after reassurance she couldn't get from him. Reassurance that next time someone pointed a gun at him, he wouldn't end up dead.

It was easy to rationalize their relationship in the cold light of day. But there were times when he woke in the dead of night, alone with no one to hold, and he hated Lisa. Hated her for robbing him of a stake in the future. For turning him into a man who'd never be able to accept Maggie as she was, without remembering what Lisa had done to him.

Max took out his ID, let the door swing shut behind him, and walked up to the reception desk.

The tangle of fingers in her lap was a dead giveaway of her feelings, but having them explained wasn't enough to get rid of the bogeyman crouching on her shoulder, ready to shout "Gotcha!" in her ear. If the gardener hadn't been crouched in front of it, she could have left the car and walked off her nervous energy. She just prayed Max wouldn't leave her sitting there too long.

The gardener rose and walked away from the car, though his khaki overalls still hovered on the edge of her vision. *Stay put. Stay put.* Maggie concentrated on the entrance door. She wasn't naive; she knew Max was checking her out.

He had no faith in her and it hurt.

Less than twenty-four hours she'd known him, and in that short time he'd used up every chance she'd given him. Soon he'd be back again with his hand out, and this time she'd give him her friends. Some of them she'd known forever and couldn't imagine perpetrating such heinous acts.

And the people she worked with. Good people. People who'd labored in the vineyard season after season since she was a child. Her mind couldn't encompass any of them being guilty.

And the ones she worked with every day…Grant, her marketing manager, was all right; he was in Britain. And Alison and Gwen on the retail side? To point the finger at them would be blasphemy. Then there was Steven, the new wine maker she'd hired when she'd first taken over. A nice quiet guy, certainly intense about wine, but then that was the only level they met on. She'd watched him one day out among the vines. He'd been on his knees, his hands in the earth, running it through his fingers, and she'd known she'd hired the right man, one who appreciated the meager soil the grapes preferred, the way her father had. She liked him. How could she set Max on a man like that? It wouldn't be right.

Max appeared at the entrance. He looked pleased with himself. Well, not for long. She swung her legs out of the car as he approached. "Find any skeletons in my closet?"

"Not a one." He smiled like a cat contemplating cream.

"You're the darnedest man, Max Strachan. One day you tell me you intend getting into my panties, the next you're checking to see if I've given any babies away. Well, if I ever do, you can bet they won't be yours!" Maggie took a step toward him with her purse swinging. She'd never known anyone to make her get so mad before. The heel of her shoe hit soft dirt and her purse went spinning.

Max caught her, gathered her into his arms and held on.

The problem was she felt safe. As though nothing bad could happen with Max here. The rhythmic thunk of his heart sounded in her ear, and with each raw breath she sucked in, she tasted the sharp male muskiness of his scent.

That was when she knew she would give him another chance.

As many as it took.

Max pressed her face into his shoulder. He could imagine the razzing he'd get. If the cops at Auckland Central discovered what he was up to he'd never live it down.

Max held her away from him. It was either that or let her find out that her nearness turned him hard as a rock. "You all right, Maggie?" His eyes sought hers. For a woman who'd seemed intent on hitting him with her purse just seconds ago, her eyes glowed with a soft dreaminess that made it tough to keep his mind on the job. "You didn't hurt yourself?"

"No, I'm okay. Just shaken." She took a deep breath, squared her shoulders and blinked sheepishly. "I guess I need to look where I'm walking."

Jo strode down the path toward them. If his Detective Constable had done her job, they could kiss this place goodbye. He didn't have long to wait.

"What's up?" Jo asked.

"Maggie lost her shoe in the garden. She's all right, though." He looked over her shoulder at her now empty purse. "I just caught her littering."

Maggie pulled back from him. "I'm still capable of speech." Self-consciously, she exhaled a sharp puff of air that lifted her long black fringe.

Jo grinned at her. "Geez, Maggie, how d'you get all those things in that little purse?"

"You get a result in there, Jo?" Max asked. "If not, get on with it. We haven't all day to muck about. Maggie wants to get out of here."

Jo waved the paper in her hand above her head. "I got a result!" Turning to Maggie, she said, "I didn't realize you were so talented. They recognized her straight off. I've got the address right here." Her eyebrows quirked wickedly at Max. "How'd you get on?"

"No result."

"Good one. We can go then," said Jo, circling around them and heading for the car.

It bugged Max how Jo seemed to accept Maggie's psychic abilities as the norm. Even with the leads they'd just gotten, there were still questions that needed answering.

It was all right Jo feeling cheerful. The problem was, now that Jo knew where the woman lived, what would they find when they got there?

Max took Maggie's elbow, but she shrugged him off and began picking her gear out of the garden and grass. She hunkered down, grimacing in disgust when she saw some of her business cards smeared with dirt.

* * *

Maggie didn't want to face this woman, dead or alive. Once was enough. She'd been there, done that, and she didn't need a T-shirt to remind her.

"This is the street, number twenty-three," Jo directed.

It was a pretty suburban street, with small weatherboard houses in neat gardens. The few that needed a little TLC stood out from the rest.

Number twenty-three was one of those.

But it wasn't the type of place where you'd expect violence to be done. It was ordinary. A street where men worked eight-hour days, with overtime twice a week, and were happy to kiss their wives when they got home, and crash in front of the TV. Not a place you'd expect murder to be done.

A garbage truck hogged the middle of the road, and Maggie wanted to scream at Max to drive around it. Their slow progress knotted the cords at the nape of her neck. She was dreaming of a backrub to ease the ache when the first cry sounded. Neither by look nor word did Max and Jo signal they had heard. The noise grew swiftly from attention-seeking whimper to a full-blown yell.

The baby was awake.

"This is the place," said Maggie.

"Yeah, I know. Pull over here, Max."

"No! I mean this is the place! Can't you hear it? Can't you hear the baby?" Cold sweat broke out on her top lip and a feeling of clamminess crept down her spine. A swipe across her mouth with the back of her hand took care of the sweat. Erasing the words she'd uttered wouldn't come so easy.

Max studied her through the rearview mirror, then cut the engine and turned around. "Baby? You feeling okay, Maggie?"

"No, I'm not, Max. I'm scared." She shuddered. The quest she'd initiated this morning was about to reach a conclusion.

One way or another.

"You look it," Jo commented.

"I really don't want to go in there."

"Don't worry, Max won't make you go inside. He'll just go up to the door and speak to the woman. She has to be home—her car's in the drive."

"Oh, I know she's home." *But he won't be able to speak to her.*

"Let me deal with this, Jo? And for heaven's sake, Maggie, don't go all weird on me!"

Max sounded exasperated, unlike his usual self, as if he was reflecting her own tension back at her. A frown pulled his eyebrows straight, deepened the crease between them and crinkled his scar. He only needed an eye patch to complete the picture. How would a man who looked as if he'd as soon throw a baby overboard as put up with its noise react to the crying in her head? He'd lock her up, and it wouldn't be in jail. Maggie folded her arms and sank deeper into the car seat, as if a few inches could make any difference.

Max felt certain the hollow sound as he rang the doorbell was a result of his imagination. He waited a few seconds, then tried again.

"Maybe she's gone out with someone else," said Jo.

Her voice was so low he had to strain to hear her words. It seemed he wasn't the only one spooked. Maggie watched from the car. Even at this distance her lips looked white and strained, and though he hated to admit it, this whole business had taken on an otherworldly feel.

Damn! He wanted this settled now. Not when the woman who lived here came home from work—if she even lived at this address. She could have moved. He gave the bell another jab, letting it ring long and loudly, but he still heard Jo's impatient fingers drumming on her leather jacket, where she'd hooked her thumbs in her pockets.

"No point in standing here any longer. I'm going around the back, you wait," Max ordered. Anything was better than letting the situation freak him out like the other two. Women!

The rear of the house was fairly secluded, with a six-foot fence, a few straggly shrubs and an untidy lawn.

He'd kept pretty quiet on the way over in the car. His beliefs had taken a kick where it hurt most, and he wasn't dealing too well with the pain. A man couldn't change his ideas without mulling them over in his mind, and Maggie had given him a lot to think about. Most of his conclusions would depend on what he found when he got inside the house.

A couple of towels flapped noisily on the clothesline, and paper blew around the lawn, most likely from the red plastic garbage can by the back door. The lid had popped open and animals had scavenged the contents.

From his pocket, Max retrieved a pair of latex gloves and slipped them on. He tried the door handle and sighed, thankful to find it unlocked. Under his breath he whistled a tuneless melody more than half a tone off-key. That way anyone inside would hear him coming, and hopefully he wouldn't scare them spitless. So far his luck was holding. But the portents weren't good. The brush of air on his face was easily as cold as the temperature outside.

The door opened into a galley-shaped kitchen with a dining room at the far end. Both were empty. Ditto the lounge. Max's mood perked up slightly when he saw there was no sign of struggle anywhere. Inside, the house was neat as a pin. Not what he'd expected when he'd seen the garden.

Dear Lord, don't let this woman come home from drinking coffee with a neighbor and catch me peeking around her bedroom door.

The layout looked standard, so he bypassed the laundry and took a quick gander in the first of the front-facing bedrooms. Zilch. The master bedroom should be on the front corner. A floorboard creaked. Max froze with the door open just enough for a beam of artificial light to pierce the darkened hallway.

What if she was in bed sick? There could be a hundred and one reasons for the door to be unlocked and the garbage forgotten. He steadied himself with a deep breath, listening. Any second someone might call out, "Who's there?" Gradually, he relaxed, and with two fingers on the handle, he let more and more light spill into the hall until he could see through the opening. The curtains were still drawn. A pair of shoes stood lined up like little soldiers by the side of the bed. Two nylon clad feet pointed from a rose sprigged duvet. They didn't move. Not even when he swung the door wide.

She was too engrossed in something on the ceiling.

Chapter 5

Good. Someone had put the coffee on. Maggie grabbed a mug, filled it with steaming black coffee and added two spoonfuls of sugar. She'd give cream a miss today. Last night she'd been so tired she'd gone to bed early and slept like the dead. No, retract that; her thoughts were becoming imbued with death. She'd slept so deeply last night she'd had to dig herself out of the mattress this morning. Much better.

Better still, there'd been no crying to keep her awake.

She took a long slurp of coffee. It almost took the skin off her tongue, but at least she knew she was alive. With the mug in one hand, her briefcase and some files she'd had up at the house in the other, she made her way into the office. After playing hooky yesterday she'd have twice as much work to get through today.

Laying her files and coffee mug on the kauri desk that had been her father's, she slipped off her jacket, hung it up and sat down. The mellow grain of the desktop glowed in the pale winter light, and smoothing her hand over its surface, she sighed, "Home again."

Until she'd stepped into her office she'd had no notion how much she craved normality. After a week of sleepless nights, the thought of getting back to her everyday routine was like a glass of their best sparkling wine after a surfeit of vinegar.

Maggie let her gaze roam over all the dear, familiar possessions of her father. In the light from outside, the framed, gold and silver medals he'd hung above the antique chiffonier glowed—his awards for prize-winning wines. Before her father died she hadn't known she loved all of this. She'd simply thrown herself into the deep end of the business, and when she'd come up for air, realized how much it meant to her.

Out of habit Maggie's eyes turned toward the office window. Dead season or not, the view filled her with a pride of possession the stark symmetry of the scene couldn't diminish. It had rained earlier and the bare vines glistened black and slick, like supplicants to Allah, arms raised, praying for his mercy.

In the distance, light gray smoke danced over and through the vines where the pruners worked, trimming and burning the remains in large metal wheelbarrows. Cleaning up as they went meant no disease could travel from one part of the vineyard to another. It was a job she always found soothing, with the spongy leaves underfoot, the scent of moldering dampness released with every step and the smell of wood smoke and rain in the air. She loved the basic earthiness of the season. It reminded her that winter wasn't an end but a beginning, and next year these preparations would mean a better crop, God willing.

One day she'd have someone to share this with—a man who'd love the place the way she did. When Steven Dexter, the wine maker, had first joined them, she'd thought it might be him. But though she liked him, a relationship with wine instead of sex holding it together would soon turn sour and unpalatable. No, she wanted more. She wanted someone who would rouse the feelings that Max wrought in her with a touch or a glance. She could picture herself with him next spring, walking through the vines as the soft green, crumpled buds opened to the light. The vineyard looked like a whole different world then.

"Max." His name echoed thinly. Loneliness filled the quiet office, and the leafy vines in her mind's eye disappeared. There were bigger hurdles between them than the taut strands of fence wire whistling in the wind. And Jo wasn't the least of them. Maggie could never see her friend settling for an unrequited love. A bigger leap of the imagination was that Max might lose his bias against a gift Maggie had never wanted. Would gladly rid herself of.

If only it were possible.

Maggie pushed her mug out of the way and opened one of the files she'd brought down from the house. She'd promised herself not to think about Max this morning. But the figures alone weren't enough to snag her thoughts and keep them away from both him and that poor woman they'd found yesterday.

When he'd returned to the car, one look in his direction told her they'd been too late. His body language as he'd walked briskly toward the car showed his eagerness to get started. In contrast, the tightness around his mouth whispered of resignation and going through the motions again, hoping against hope the killer had slipped up.

From the moment she'd exited the car and hurried toward him, he'd been distant, unapproachable. "Take Maggie to her car and come back ASAP," he'd practically snapped at Jo.

Then he'd shocked the hell out of Maggie.

Jo, too, had stopped, watching, with the car door partially open.

Maggie's eyes fluttered closed. She could still feel his touch as he'd skimmed her cheek with the back of his fingers. There'd been a tenderness in the contact that was almost blasphemous, considering the situation. Her heart had leaped in her chest like a crazy thing, and she'd held her breath, hardly daring to release it lest the heaviness of her sigh took him out of reach again.

Half-closed, his eyes had glittered with secrets he had no intention of sharing. Yet the slight droop at the corner of his eyelids spoke of his confusion.

Nothing had made sense to her, either.

"Jo will take you back to the city. It might be a while, but I'll be in touch." She'd started to speak, but he'd halted the words, rubbing his thumb slowly across her bottom lip in lieu of a kiss. "Later. You shouldn't be here now. I'll give you a call when I can."

If she'd tasted him, let her tongue glide sensuously over the pad of his thumb the way she'd wanted, how would he have reacted?

Neither she nor Jo had spoken on the drive back to the city. To do so would have shattered the tense atmosphere into ugly, hurtful pieces. Instead she'd used the time for her own thoughts. The twisted fragments of hope she'd tied up with doubts. And those she'd left behind in the police car.

Maggie picked up the phone. She'd deliberately avoided TV last night, but she'd never be able to get on with her work now until she'd checked out the newspapers. Gwen answered it. "Hi, Gwen," said Maggie. "Did the newspaper arrive yet?"

Gwen's voice squeaked unsteadily as though her throat hurt when she asked, "Do you want me to send it through?"

"Thanks, I'll read it while I drink my coffee. You be sure to take something for that cold—your voice sounds awful. And when Steven arrives, send him straight in."

Suddenly it dawned on Maggie how chilly her office had become. The coffee had warmed her inside, but the surface of her skin felt goosey, so she turned on the heater. Soon the office would be warm as toast. She'd worn an almost-brand-new angora sweater in a deep mauve that was a kissing cousin to indigo. It matched her slacks, and underneath she wore a lilac silk blouse to keep the rabbit's wool from irritating her skin. She knew the color suited her dark hair, and wearing it gave her an assurance she badly needed today. An assurance that she looked like any ordinary, attractive, red-blooded woman.

Normal, in fact.

Her office door rattled in its frame thanks to a few solid knocks on the outside. "Come on in, Steven," she called, without looking up from the spreadsheet of sales figures she'd laid out on her desk.

"It's not Steven, it's me."

"Gordon!" She smiled. "I hadn't expected you today. How's it going?"

A wide grin split her landscaper's ruddy features as he looked at Maggie from the doorway. Not moving, he stood with a roll of papers clasped in one hand. Gordon wore heavy boots topped by faded jeans under a woolen *Swanndri* in a red-and-black check that clashed marvelously with his hair. Thick strands of ginger curled out from under the brim of a battered felt *Akubra* that had seen better days. But not many of them as good as today, judging from the delight on his face.

He waved the roll of papers. "I've finished them, subject to your approval, of course." He almost quivered with excitement, but still didn't advance into the room. Instead, he lifted one foot to show the sole of his boot. "Do you mind these? They're clean."

Sometimes Gordon was just too reticent. Maggie sighed and signaled for him to enter. As if the pair of them hadn't already spent hours in here, going over the sketches of the garden designs. "What's a little dirt compared to the goodies you've brought me? I can tell you're pleased with the finished plans. Don't keep me in suspense any longer."

"I think it's the best thing I've done, and I'm sure you will, too."

Maggie smiled at his obvious pleasure. "Well, spread them out on the desk and we'll see," she said cheerfully. Gordon's good humor had a habit of infecting others. This was going to be a good day; she could feel it in her bones.

A feeling that faded abruptly when she remembered Gordon would be one of the people whose names she was going to throw Max's way.

Like a human sacrifice.

Work benefited the soul, so Maggie concentrated on the landscaping plans in front of her, while Gordon's finger traced the layout from driveway to retail entrance and from water garden to pergola. "I particularly like what you've done with the picnic area. It'll mean buying new fridges to stock cheese and pâté in the wine shop, and finding a local baker who can supply French and Italian breads daily. But I'm getting carried away with my enthusiasm. This is only the beginning of the adventure." She pointed out a detail on the plans. "These open lawn spaces are good. It gives us a place to put up extra open-sided marquees during the wine fest. I've discussed purchasing some with our logo on them, but I need sizes from you before they can go ahead."

"I can let you have them today."

"Good, and you really think you can accomplish all this before Labour Weekend? When I look at all these plans, the end of October doesn't seem that far away. It's a big job." She was counting on this wine fest to launch the younger wines, the first of Steven's vintage. To back the others up, she'd held on to some of her father's wines, full of his expertise and flair, to release at the same time. The venture was bound to be a success. It had to be.

"Did someone ask for a newspaper?"

Maggie looked up and smiled. She hadn't heard Steven enter. He was a quiet man in more than his manner. Soft-spoken, soft-footed and sure-handed when he handled the wine. The bottles never rattled when he held them.

"Hi, come in and have a look at Gordon's plans for the gardens."

Gordon moved away and let Steven take his place, answering his swift, intelligent questions. Steven was the younger of the two, sleeker and with none of Gordon's chunky, almost teddy bear qualities. Instead of in curls, Steven's brown hair grew straight, and was lighter at the tips where last summer's sun had bleached it.

Finally Steven said, "I approve, Gordon. This layout is a fitting setting for my wines."

Maggie cocked an eyebrow in Gordon's direction and shared a smile with him. "Well, since we're all happy, I'll let you get on with it, Gordon. Get those measurements to me later." He was almost out the door when she called after him, "And take care, Gordon. I'm depending on you."

He just waved the roll of plans at her and nodded.

"I see you've started the pruning, Steven. Not too early?"

"No, the wood's just right. I've been down there and shown the men exactly how I want it done," he said. Turning toward the window, he stood with feet apart and hands on hips, watching the spiraling smoke at the far end of the vineyard, where the work was going on. Nodding, he said, "This office has a wonderful outlook."

"I like it. My father spent a lot of time in here. But we're wandering off the subject. Most of these men have been pruning our vines for years. You do know that, don't you, Steven?"

"Yes, I just like to be sure they're pruned for optimum growth. No offense, but last year most of the pruning was done before I started. This year it will be better." And though he smiled, his statement brooked no argument.

How uncomplicated his life must be to have such confidence in himself. Unlike Maggie, who planned for the best, and if it actually came off, considered it a bonus.

"We ought to look at getting rid of those wheelbarrows. There are newer, more efficient methods."

"No! I like them," Maggie said emphatically. "Sometimes it's the little traditions that make a vineyard. Let's get down to business. How is the bottling going?"

Half an hour later, she was ready for another cup of coffee. Working closely with Steven got to her that way, but she honestly couldn't complain about his input, and if something was good for Steven, it had to be good for the vineyard.

Steven was almost out the door when she opened the paper. "Oh, no!"

"What's the matter? What's wrong?" He came back quickly, took the paper from her white, numb-with-shock fingers and scanned the front page. "You look dreadful, Maggie. Sit down."

She knew the exact moment his gaze hit the headline "Psychic Helps Police with Khyber Pass Killer Inquiry" and landed on the photo of her and Max beneath the banner.

"This is you!"

"Yes, it is. I could kill him for doing this to me!"

"Are you really helping the police?" he asked, lifting his gaze from the newsprint. His eyes narrowed as he looked at her, yet he didn't seem surprised. She'd have thought Steven placed himself above listening to gossip, but someone had informed him of her last fiasco.

"Yes…no, not really. I've had these dreams about women being killed with red scarves around their necks and—omigod! Forget I said that, will you?" She clutched at his elbow and rolled her eyes, making light of her mistake. "Mum's the word, Steven, I'm not supposed to discuss it with anyone. Just do me a favor and forget I even mentioned it."

"For you, dear Maggie, anything." He picked up her hand and, in an exaggerated gesture, kissed her knuckles. He grinned and said, "Your wish is my command."

Maggie laughed, the little piece of byplay shifting her thoughts away from what she intended doing to Max when she got her hands on him. "You're a fool, Steven, but you've cheered me up. I command you to tell Gwen to man the barricades and prepare for an invasion. She obviously chickened out on telling me herself, but she knows what to expect. We've been down this road before. Meanwhile I have an extremely urgent phone call to make.''

Mike Henare fixed Max with the kind of glare usually reserved for D.C.s and under. The newspaper he'd been reading fell from his meaty hands and dropped in an untidy shuffle on top of his desk. "What the hell is this?" he bellowed, using his clenched fist like an exclamation mark. "You've got some explaining to do, Strachan."

Max read the banner headline upside down. "I've got to hand it to him. Babcox got it right and scooped the rest of the papers."

Max had been observing the autopsy with Jo, who was Officer in Charge, of Victim, when his pager went off. Brief and to the point, the message said, "Get your ass up here." Mike wasn't known for his subtlety.

If there'd been anything out of the ordinary happening, Max might have chanced it and let Mike stew for a while, but with this particular case it was same old, same old. He was sick and tired of guys who repeated themselves!

The victim, one Mavis Johns, had died of a broken neck, the way the other three victims had met their end. Arm across the throat from behind, a quick jerk, a snap, and it was all over before they had time to panic. Very neat. Too neat. Like everything else about the crime scenes.

Every time he thought of the latest victim lying there with that doll tucked in her arms, his skin crawled.

"You didn't have to make an issue of it, Chief. I was gonna see you and explain," Max said at his most laconic, and benefited by seeing the color come and go in his chief's face.

Henare made a lot of noise about folding the paper. "Did you make that decision before or after it appeared in print?"

"After."

Max's admission did nothing to soften his senior's mood. Babcox had set it up for the day, and nothing Max or anyone else could say was likely to shift it. "And before that? How did you think you'd pass it off?"

"Well, I'd considered listing it under information received."

"Did you pay this woman money?" Mike's eyes zapped him with a flash of pure green indignation. As green as the digits of a calculator adding a sum to the total costs of this case.

Max shook his head.

"Is she getting paid by the *Tribune?*"

"Hell, no! None of those. It's quite simple. She came to me. I met her for coffee, but Babcox was sniffing around like a ferret in heat. I thought I'd nixed the scent and thrown him off, but the little weasel must have followed us. I guess he recognized Ms. Kovacs from last year's incident. Right about now, I imagine she's howling for blood—mine! Seeing as how I made a promise not to give her to the media. She's almost paranoid about them." He took the drawing Maggie had done and threw it down on the desk in front of Henare. "This is what she brought me. I think you'll recognize the likeness. You realize, if it hadn't been for last year's business, she might have come forward sooner."

Max caught the astonishment on Henare's face, and added, "I know, I know, this is Max Strachan speaking. The world's greatest skeptic, who'd as soon break the balls of any psychic as let them come near me." He grinned ruefully as Mike rolled his eyes. "Well, let me reassure you, Maggie doesn't have any."

"Maggie?" his chief squawked.

"Ms. Kovacs. But never mind that. The way I see it, I'll look at anything, even if it goes against the grain, if it's going to help us catch this maniac. If it hadn't been for the other business, Ms. Kovacs might have come forward sooner and we could have saved lives." Max listened to himself mouth the words and didn't know if he really meant them. Would he have listened to Maggie if she'd come to him earlier? It was doubtful. He'd as soon have sat down and supped with the devil. Desperation makes liars of us all, he thought.

Leaving Mike brooding over the drawing, he hitched a chair over to the desk and sprawled in it with one ankle supported on the opposite knee. That was as much as he dared relax. If he'd gotten three hours sleep in the last forty-eight he'd be lucky.

The drawing spun across the desk to him while the chief harrumphed under his breath. "I take it you checked this alleged psychic, this *Maggie* out?"

"The boffins estimate time of death between 10:00 and 11:00 p.m. I was with Ms. Kovacs till 10:00 p.m. She wouldn't have had the time, nor the motive as far as I can make out. D.C. Jellic and I showed the drawing around the—"

"What d'you mean, with her till ten?" The desk creaked as Henare half rose from his chair, putting his weight on his flattened palms, his face closing in on Max.

"She's a friend of Jo Jellic's. We met in the pub, she dropped her scarf and I returned it. She gave me a drink and I went home. Simple as that."

If only that were true. Nothing about the last three days had been simple. Not one solitary thing. There were dozens of issues between Maggie and him that needed seeing to. He'd have to put them on hold till this case was over.

"And you didn't say anything or do anything to prejudice the investigation or yourself?" Mike asked. His pale green eyes, which looked so out of place against his bronze skin, narrowed and caught Max in their beam.

There was only one thing to do. Fudge it!

"Not a thing."

"I gather it's just the angle of the camera that makes you and the Kovacs woman look so cozy?" Mike asked almost coyly. If a man as cunning as him actually carried an ounce of coyness in his enormous body.

Max knew the solution to shoving Henare's shrewd nose

out of his business and back where it belonged. "Take a look at this. I think our guy made a boo-boo."

Max eased forward in his chair as he pulled a small plastic bag from his pocket and dropped it in front of Henare. It contained a single silver metal button.

"We're still working on the fingerprints, but it didn't come off anything of Mrs. Johns's. Henry Johns is a merchant seaman and away for long stretches. He's flying in from Perth today, and Jo will meet him at Auckland International."

"At first the scene looked clean as a whistle, the same as always. You'd think this guy was after a good-housekeeping award. Then, wham! One of the forensic crew found this in the toe of Mrs. Johns's shoe." Max twirled the plastic bag between his thumb and forefinger. "The button may be tiny, but it's big enough for a partial print." He slipped their find carefully into his pocket and said, "I'll leave this with the boffins when I go."

"Tell me you didn't break in to her house."

"Would I do that?" Max pretended to look shocked at the suggestion. "No force was necessary. The back door was open. A lucky *break* you might say. It could have been three weeks till her husband got home. After that long, I wouldn't have fancied handling Mrs. Johns, even if it is midwinter."

"And the doll? Like the others?"

"Blond hair and blue eyes just like its mama. The crew is still checking it out, but I'd say it was handmade like all the others. Bloody funny how someone could make it without leaving a print inside or out. I know he'd have cleaned up the outside after he bought it, but the inside? And Mrs. Johns's prints are bound to be all over the damn thing. I'm still betting on the doll being his entrée to the house. What woman could resist one of those googly-eyed things, when it looks just like her?" Max glanced at the door, ready to leave.

"All right, go. Just do me a favor," Mike chortled wheezily, in the way he had of laughing at his own joke before he'd given the punchline. "Try and keep that ugly mug of yours out of the papers for a while."

Max's shoulders straightened as he walked along the corridor. The meeting with Mike had gone better than expected. The old guy must be feeling his years, letting him off so lightly. Though for the next few days Max would be careful about turning his back on him in case of unidentified flying objects, like the nearest thing Mike had to hand. Frustration was hammering at all of them on this case, and Mike was the man in the middle, copping most of the flack, from the commissioner above and the media below. It was enough to make Max think twice about taking the D.I. exam scheduled in October.

Max had always been sure that somewhere among the tangle of information, a thread dangled. One that would link all the victims together. All he had to do was grab it and pull, then everything would unravel.

It had taken the third murder for the knot to begin unwinding. Plus a willing informant. A friend of the third victim, a woman for whom gossip was the staff of life, had mentioned she'd had her baby adopted, and they'd taken it from there.

One of the things bugging him was the cycle. Twenty-eight days was a long time between highs for someone feeding off excitement jags, and had some of the team leaning toward a woman as the killer. Not Max. He couldn't see one being strong enough. No, his pick was a man.

Each killing had taken place just far enough apart to let his team relax, think they'd seen the last of them. Max had either been too relaxed or too stupid and stubborn to connect the date with what Maggie—

Oh, God, Maggie!

The woman had him twisted inside out. Yesterday, after he'd found the body, he'd been exhilarated—sickened for the victim, but optimistic of being a few steps closer to the perp. Maybe he could get the jump on this guy. Yet the moment

he'd looked at Mavis Johns, lying on the bed with her red
scarf tied in a perfect bow under her chin...

Yeah, it was hard for him to contemplate. Each time he
tried, his ingrained beliefs suffered a hard blow to the gut.

She'd looked exactly like Maggie's drawing.

Somewhere there had to be a logical explanation.

Something to make it acceptable.

Knowing where to look was the problem.

Once he'd dropped the button off at forensics, he'd better
answer all the messages Maggie had left with his service. And,
with a bit of luck, she wouldn't be home.

Maggie jumped when the doorbell sounded. No matter that
she'd been twiddling her thumbs for almost an hour, waiting
on just such an event. Two days had passed since she'd gotten
Max's message on the answering machine she'd been using to
filter her calls. Thanks to the media, she'd been a virtual pris-
oner for those two days. It hadn't done the retail side of the
winery much good, either. People visited them to kick back,
sip a little wine, not fight their way through ravening hordes
of reporters.

Short but definitely not on the sweet side, Max's message
had run, ''I'm unavailable right now. Meet me at your apartment Saturday afternoon. I can give you an hour then.''

She'd considered not turning up; it would have done him
good to wait for a change. A couple of days had cooled her
temper to the level where she thought she might at least listen
to his explanation. Although she still felt justified at being
miffed. He'd used her, then walked away and left her to deal
with the media. Clearly, she'd given him one chance too many.

She'd learned her lesson. It wouldn't happen again.

So why had she sat here a whole hour waiting for him to
show?

It was hormonal. She needed to stop remembering how it
felt to be in his arms. To stop imagining his hard chest without
its covering of soft cotton shirts and silk ties. To erase from

her mind the rush of tenderness that had swamped her as he'd touched her face and said goodbye.

Psyched up by the pep talk she'd given herself, Maggie took a deep breath, flung open the door and tried withering Max with a glare.

It didn't work.

Once there was enough room for both Max and his shoulders to cross the threshold, he stepped through and lifted her in his arms. On the first circuit they made, Max shut the door with his heel. On the second he covered her protest with his mouth in a kiss so hot she felt the soles of her feet frizzle.

Her head spun. Not so much because she was orbiting a foot off the ground, but because Max was the center of the world holding her in orbit.

Maggie's heart thumped painfully against her ribs and her breasts swelled and peaked, crushed against his chest in an agony of delight. All her own advice melted away under the heat they generated as Maggie threw her arms around his neck and went along for the ride.

"God, I needed that," he growled in her ear, and began the gradual restoration of Maggie's equilibrium. Slowly, he slid her down the long length of his body to the floor and rested her head against his shoulder.

As her dizziness subsided, Maggie pushed away from the hard chest compounding her weakness. "If this performance is meant to distract me from the way you dropped me in it with the media, you're only partially successful," she said, clutching at what little shred of dignity she had left.

"Maggie," he drawled, "the media will soon have more to chew on than whether or not you've been helping the police with visitations from the other side. We've got him, babe. Cuffed, cautioned and delivered to jail. It was an orderly named Arnolds from the maternity home. He lost a button in the victim's shoe and we got a perfect match on a thumbprint."

She let out a long sigh. Suddenly it felt like all her Christ-

mases and birthdays in one. Maggie wanted to laugh and cry
at the same time as relief bubbled up through her and released
the breath she hadn't realized she'd been holding all these
weeks. She didn't have to be a snitch and she didn't have to
destroy friendships that might never be mended.

"Thank heavens for that. I thought I was going to have to
give you the names of all my friends. I was so worried about
it. This will be the first time I've had a prophetic dream that
wasn't about someone I knew."

Chapter 6

"Anything else you've been hiding from me?" he asked, restraining an impulse to take her face in his hands and look deeply into her dark, glowing eyes in search of other thoughts she'd hidden from him.

Maggie's smile wavered. "Heavens, it's no big deal." She pushed away from Max and flounced toward the arched entrance to the sitting area, only to be stopped short as he caught hold of her hand and pulled her back. "I was going to tell you today," she protested.

"Why now? Why not before, Maggie?" the query came out louder than he'd meant, even as reason whispered in his ear. This is Maggie, remember, not Lisa. Not the woman who ruined your marriage with her secrets and lies. Get over it and go on from here. With Maggie. She's the reason you stayed up half the night, writing reports, getting them collated, so you could take some time off.

And be with Maggie.

Bringing up her free hand in an act of surrender, Maggie said, "Okay, fair enough. I admit to being a coward. Haven't you ever felt that way? That if you didn't say something out loud it couldn't be true? I know it sounds like I'm trying to justify myself, but I've gone through the list of people I know thousands of times in my mind, and even slight acquaintances I don't much care for came out dressed in white and sporting halos.''

Maggie gave him a cramped version of her former smile. Inwardly he cursed his bullheadedness. Max knew she was waiting, wondering if he would let her get away with passing it off as a joke, or if he would bark at her again. He placed a hand on her shoulder and turned her to face him. Beneath his palm he felt her muscles tense. Heaven help him, he'd lost the knack of dealing with women, and had become a distrustful sorehead. The job did it to you. As well as putting the squeeze on your humanity, it robbed you of all the soft, tender ways that made women fall for a man. It had stripped him bare, leaving only the hard shell a cop needed to survive. But he could learn, he thought, remembering the small moment of tenderness he'd felt when he'd sent Maggie away from the crime scene, knowing it wouldn't help either of them for her to be found there.

As he recalled his emotions he knew that's what he wanted with Maggie. Somehow he had to find the man he'd been all those years ago when he'd first met Lisa. He'd known all the moves then. And looking back at the memories of his early conquests, he took no pride in them. Until he'd met Lisa he'd been slick and practiced. Love had changed all that, but it hadn't lasted. Maggie was different. Though his need for her could hardly be ascribed to the spiritual, he wanted her, body and soul.

Instead of Max rushing her, Maggie needed time to know him. Never mind Maggie, he needed time to know himself— know the new Max Strachan, who refused to let the specters and spooks of the unknown daunt him. He wouldn't kid himself that she had converted him. But now that he'd had a few days to think it over—hell, he hadn't been able to get it out of his mind—in future, he wouldn't toss anything Maggie told him aside. He returned her smile. "Halos, you say?"

"Yeah," she sighed, brightening. "But none of that matters now, does it? You've got your killer locked up, and it's all over, bar the shouting."

"A lot more than shouting, but getting there. I guess I'm still feeling antsy. It's been months since I really relaxed." He grinned and slid his arm around her shoulders. "C'mon, let's go sit down and take a load off. Let me tell you how a partial thumbprint caught our murderer."

As they stepped into the lounge, his arm still around her shoulder, he said with a wry twist to his mouth, "Maybe you've got a CD of a fat lady singing. That would really make my day."

"Before that happens I'll make some coffee. It could be a long session. The first thing I want to know is who told the press about me?"

Max followed her into the sleek, modern kitchen. He watched her gather up the makings for coffee as he leaned back against one of the granite countertops. "Do you remember a guy talking to me when we went for coffee at the Blues Café?"

Maggie nodded.

"Well, let me tell you, there's a weasel you want to avoid."

They spent the next couple of hours relaxing on one of the big, rolled-arm sofas, drinking the hot, fragrant coffee Maggie had made, and discussing the case.

"Arnolds is one of the orderlies at the maternity hospital. We checked them all out when the connection to the hospital first came up. All that showed up on Arnolds was a record for possession when he was a teenager. Nothing since. Funny type, quiet, lives on his own. No family."

"Why did I connect with him? It's so strange." Maggie shuddered in his arms. "What has Arnolds to do with me? Has he confessed, or told you why he did it?"

"Not a word. Maybe we'll know a little more when he's

completed his psychological report, but that won't be before Monday. Meanwhile, we've got him for resisting arrest and assaulting a police officer.''

''You?''

''No, Rowan. There shouldn't be any bother proving the murder charge. The jacket with the missing button was hanging in his closet.''

''We can just be thankful he's off the streets. You're sure it's him?'' Maggie turned sideways on the sofa, drew up her knees and faced Max. ''I just want to say thanks for listening to me.''

A pang of guilt ripped through him, as if he'd accepted her thanks under false pretences. It was all down to the boffins, and the jacket with the missing button that Max had found in Arnolds's closet. Once they'd latched on to that, Arnolds had given in with barely a squeak. It had been almost too easy in the end, and Max couldn't shake the feeling of anti-climax.

Gradually they changed position, going from his arm being around her shoulder to her sitting on his lap. It was good just to sog-out, to talk quietly, say stupid things and speak their thoughts out loud as they got to know each other more and more. He spoke honestly about his association with Jo and told her about his failed marriage and the reasons for it, surprising himself that he did so calmly, with none of the angst he usually felt.

Maggie told him about her childhood, about the death of her mother and brother in a motor vehicle accident while they were on holiday in Australia. She'd been only a baby then and didn't remember them. ''My father brought me up himself and he spoiled me.''

Max kissed Maggie's ear, tasted her neck. ''You don't taste spoiled to me,'' he murmured, letting his senses drown in the feel of her hip pressing against his arousal, groaning at the pleasurable ache in his groin each time she moved slightly in response to his kiss.

Their heads lay close together, pillowed on a soft cushion.

Yeah, after the hurly-burly lifestyle he'd been living the last few months, it was good just to sit and be, be together, enjoying the closeness for itself instead of as a means to an end. They both knew they were going to make love. When the time was right it would happen, but for now just holding Maggie was enough. A bittersweet torture he didn't want to end.

This was one of the things he'd thought never to have again once his marriage ended. There was no place for closeness in the fleeting relationships he'd shared in the past couple of years. With Maggie, sex would be more than the smell of sweat, the thrusting and self-satisfying slap of flesh against flesh. With the two of them, just being would be more, would be everything.

Outside the cozy island they'd created on the sofa, the day had turned gray, and beyond the window the orange lights on the Harbour Bridge gleamed with a golden haze. "Where would you like to go to dinner?" he asked, staving off hunger meantime by nibbling on her earlobe.

Maggie sighed and turned reluctantly from his mouth's attentions to look at him. "Sorry, Max. I can't stay in town. I need to give Gwen a break from work. She's had a lot to cope with this week. Me taking a couple of days off at the beginning of it, and having the media camped on our doorstep for the second half of the week. Sunday is one of our busiest days. People like to go out for a drive and do wine tasting, even if it is winter."

Maggie rolled in his arms and kissed his chin, the corner of his mouth, and began working across his lips with tiny whispers of kisses. Each brief touch of her lips made him harder and he splayed his hand over her buttocks, pulling her closer until he was almost enclosed by the softness of her belly. He groaned into her mouth as the ache in him increased, along with the urgency. The way she replied to his caresses with tiny whimpers of delight told Max he could take her here, take her now. But soon it would be dark, and he hated the thought of her driving all the way home. Driving on roads lit only by the slashes of blinding light from cars coming toward her.

He had this sudden urge to protect Maggie, but he knew she wouldn't thank him for trying to wrap her in cotton wool. "What say I follow you home? I've got the night off, and most of tomorrow is taken up with Arnolds having a psychiatric assessment. I don't have to be in too early."

He bussed Maggie behind her ear and murmured, "We could eat a little dinner and make a little love." Max kissed her deeply this time, tasting all the dark velvet flavors and nuances of her mouth as her lips opened under his. He came up for air, breathing hard. "Maybe more than a little." He kissed her again, and this time the struggle to resurface into the real world was greater. "Definitely more than a little."

Giving Maggie a light pat on her softly curved, little bottom, he said, "Let's blow this joint while we still can."

Maggie was on her feet and holding out a hand to help him escape the softness of the cushions when she said, "Max, after this case is over, will you help me find out what happened to my father?"

Twenty minutes should see her home well before dark. Maggie pressed her foot on the accelerator and the spray of dirty rain thrown up by the tires hissed in the wheel arches. It was an almost hypnotic sound, and long stretches of the familiar road passed without her having any memory of them.

Working on autopilot, she focused her mind on Max and what would happen after dinner. She knew making love was almost a certainty. In her imagination, they floated upstairs hand in hand. Or better yet, Max picked her up and carried her, the corded muscles in his arms taking her weight as if she were featherlight. Or maybe they'd just forget dinner and satisfy their hunger right there on the stairs.

Maggie did a mental stocktaking of the underwear she'd dragged on that morning. It would do. In fact, it would do a lot better than the casual jeans and sweater she'd worn to get past the group of persistent reporters still haunting the gate. The BMW kind of gave the game away, but in the baseball cap she'd pulled low over her face she looked more like a teenage boy.

Jeepers! That guy's close! The low black shape filled her side mirror. A quick glance at the speedometer showed she'd slowed down during her meandering, and there was no place on this stretch of road for the car to pass. Putting her foot down again, she accelerated and let the needle climb steadily to ninety, ninety-five, one hundred kilometers per hour.

The car behind fell back as she increased speed. Yet now that she was aware of it sitting behind her, she couldn't stop her gaze from flicking back and forth between the road and the rearview mirror. In the gray half-light the car was only a dark shape, practically invisible, and she reminded herself never to buy a black car, especially one with tinted windows. Someone would be sure to run into it on a night like tonight.

Maggie couldn't recognize the make or model, but she wished they'd reach a spot on the road where she could slow down and let it overtake her. It was kind of creepy-looking, in a stealth bomber sort of way, with its low, rounded roof like the cockpit, and the wide wheel arches like wings.

"Oh, yeah." She laughed out loud at her absurd imagination. "A stealth bomber on State Highway 1, Americans check to see if there are any kiwi cows lagging behind at milking." Her gaze clipped the rearview. The darn car was sitting on her bumper again.

Maggie stepped on the gas, to one hundred and five k's.

That was better. She had room to breathe.

But the breaths she took were harsh and fast and her heart beat in her throat, threatening to choke her, as the vehicle glued itself to the back of her car once more, and Maggie braced herself for a jolt. Great Caesar's ghost, someone out there had a hatred of Beemers. She'd heard about that. There were still people out there who'd lost money in the last crash, ergo BMW stood for yuppie, which stood for the people who'd robbed them of their life savings.

One hundred and ten k's.

They passed a sign that said Speed Camera Area.

This was no joke. Maggie tried not to panic, but it was harder and harder to keep her gaze on the road and off the rearview mirror. She was tempted to put a little more pressure on the gas pedal.

Suddenly the car disappeared in a glare of yellow fog lamps that blinded Maggie when she looked in the mirror.

Without slowing, she whisked past the first scattering of houses that signaled she was nearing Warkworth, and sped through the edge of the township, giving the first turnoff a miss.

Sheesh! One hundred and twenty k's in a seventy-k zone and the fog lights were still behind her. This was gonna cost her her license.

It took mere seconds to reach the next turnoff, and hallelujah for a gap in the traffic. Maggie swung the wheel hard to the right, peeled off the road to Warkworth and shot up the side one to Matakana.

Two kilometers along the road without any yellow lights appearing behind her, she pulled over to the side, let out a sigh of relief and switched off her headlights. The quiet settled around her, only the rustle of the leaves in the shelter belt breaking the hush. No cars, no engines and no stealth bombers.

Thank heavens Max had stopped to pick up some necessities. At least she'd been spared a speeding ticket.

Grabbing a plastic bag from the hooks at the side of the counter in the wine shop, Maggie opened the small fridge and took out a wedge of Brie and a pot of blue Stilton. Men usually liked the blue, though it was a bit strong for her taste. With both cheeses in the bag, she added a box of water crackers and stood considering a bottle of port.

Was Max the type of man who drank port with his cheese?

What the heck. She'd put a bottle in, anyway. Max should be here soon. He'd promised he wouldn't be more than half an hour behind her, and she'd wasted time sitting at the side of the road waiting for stealth bombers.

Maggie let a healthy chuckle fill the quiet shop. It was easy to laugh after the fact, although it hadn't seemed funny at the time. She felt slightly silly when she thought about it now. There had been so much trauma in her life lately, she'd forgotten there were people on the roads who got frustrated by cars dawdling along in front of them with no passing lane in sight. Most likely it had been a poor, stressed-out business executive, desperate to get home to his family for the weekend, and she'd been holding him back.

No way would she mention her scare to Max. He would think she wasn't fit to be let out on her own. She was an independent woman who could look after herself. Hadn't she just proved that? Yeah, you ran like a rabbit with a wolf on its tail. She definitely wouldn't tell Max. He would soon run shy of a woman who was like a clinging vine, expecting him to be at her beck and call day and night. There was no room for a relationship to grow under those circumstances.

She sighed. How soon would it take Max to get sick of the journey north? He appeared keen enough now, and although she could drive down to the city, they were both tied to their jobs, with an eighty kilometer ribbon of motorway and road between.

Brightening up, she determined to make the best of limited circumstances.

A man like Max didn't enter her life every day or even every year. No, the fire that Max kindled in her happened once in a lifetime and would continue to burn with only meager attention, if that was the way it had to be. Meanwhile, she would make the most of the evening ahead of her. There would only ever be one first time for her and Max.

Hello, had he arrived already? She'd left the electronic gate open so he could follow her through, but he must have gone the wrong way. One of the movement-sensitive lamps down by the storage tanks had come on.

The first light flicked off and another one came on.

He'd started walking in the direction of the bottling plant. Maybe he'd mistaken it for the house in the dark. She'd been too caught up in her plans for the evening, speculating on whether or not they had a future together, to hear Max drive up. Now she'd have to follow him back and show him the way to the house.

The clouds had started to break up, and a half-moon was hiding behind them. If the weather cleared she would show Max around the vineyard tomorrow. It wouldn't happen the way she'd planned, with leaves starting to unfurl and the roses coming into bud at the end of each row, but maybe he would find the same beauty in the scene that she did.

The fourth light down beside the bottling plant came on just as her movements activated the first in the row. Max must have realized his mistake by now. "Max!" she called, but the wind carried her voice back to her.

She cupped her hands around her mouth and yelled this time. "Max, where are you?" Still no reply. Then it dawned on her. Had she seen Max's car as she walked down? No.

Weak laughter skittered from her lips and evaporated in the night air as she chided herself. "Imagine walking down here to chase a stray cat." A family of feral ones lived in the pocket of bush growing in the gully that wasn't suitable for grapes.

Her father had always said, "If they keep down the mice and rats, why bother them?" And she liked to abide by his wisdom. Maybe as a way of feeling she wasn't alone in her enterprise.

Taking a deep breath, she started to return to the retail outlet and wait for Max. The gravel crunched under her feet as she slid to a halt. Was it her imagination or did the raisiny aroma that always hung around the tanks smell extra strong tonight? She sniffed the air, and was trying to decide if she'd imagined it when the light beside her went out.

As did the one by the bottling plant.

Maggie stood stock-still, listening. Apart from the wind rattling in the aluminum ladders and overhead walkways that linked the tanks, she heard nothing unusual. But wait. Wasn't that water running? She let out a tremulous sigh of relief. Someone had left a hose turned on. It must have been streaming out long enough to soak through the cables leading to the junction box on the wall of the bottling plant. Sure, that would be the reason the lights had gone out.

Yes, that must be it, she reassured herself. And now she was going to have to walk down there in the dark and turn the darn hose off.

She'd have the hide off the person responsible. If the water had flooded the area, it must have been running for ages, wasting tank water that would cost money to replace in the dry summer months.

With a bit of luck the moon would come out soon and light her way. Maggie shivered. Things that looked perfectly normal during the day took on different shapes in the dark. Like cars and stealth bombers, she thought, and tried to laugh it off as another example of her wayward imagination. But although she opened her mouth, nothing came out.

She closed her eyes and pictured Max driving toward the vineyard. What if he'd gotten lost? *Max, where are you? Please, please, hurry.*

The noise of running water grew louder and the raisiny fragrance of young wine filled her lungs with every breath. Maggie started to run. The moon slithered out and illuminated the pool just as she ran into it. Her worst fears were confirmed. She'd waded into a huge puddle of wine. Red wine. She bent down and dipped her fingers in the liquid lapping over her feet. Thick with sediment, the wine looked black in the moonlight as it ran across the palm of her hand like blood.

Maggie closed her eyes and sent up another prayer for Max's help.

Please, Max, get here soon. I need you!

* * *

Once Max turned off the main highway, the roads were unfamiliar. Maggie had given him directions, but it was easy to miss a turn in the dark. Trees in need of trimming could easily hide a sign pointing the way, and with the roads much narrower than they were in the city, he could quickly overrun his mark.

After he'd seen Maggie on her way, he'd gone to the nearest chemist and bought a few necessities, a toothbrush included. Maybe he was taking things for granted, but he saw no harm in planning ahead.

He felt himself grow hard just thinking of the afternoon he'd spent with Maggie. They'd gotten close. Real close. It had been almost like the warm, sated feeling you got after making love. When you knew it was going to happen again, soon. And the mood turned slow and easy with no rush, no pressure, and you were happy to just *be*.

Be with Maggie.

Tonight there would be no more holding back, no matter how pleasurable it had been. He was pretty much a man in control of himself, but he was no masochist. Tonight his touch wouldn't just skim the sides of her breast through her sweater.

Max shifted in his seat to ease the tightness in his crotch and make driving more comfortable.

He remembered the way her breath had caught in her throat from that barest of touches, and wondered how she would react when he cupped both full globes in his hands and suckled them. A memory of the dark, treacle-colored peaks he'd glimpsed the first night they met flooded his senses. It seemed so long ago now. Too long a wait to discover if they tasted as good and as sweet as the rich syrup they reminded him of.

There it was! Kereru Hill Winery. He hadn't missed the sign. Only five k's to go till he reached Maggie. Until he held her again.

Even as he thought it, a sense of urgency spread through him, and it wasn't pleasurable. It was tense and edgy, with a ring of fear. The kind of feeling he got when he knew the suspect he was about to face might be armed. He'd always presumed it was a residue from the time he'd gotten shot.

So why was he experiencing it now?

Max gunned the engine. He might not know the cause of the anxiety that made his muscles tense and the hair on the back of his neck prickle. But in his line of work his instincts had saved him many a time, and tonight they told him to reach Maggie double quick. As he pressed his foot down on the accelerator, the moon came out and lit his way.

Maggie thanked God for the inventor who'd thought of attaching screw-in bungs to stainless steel wine tanks with a chain. At least whoever had removed the bung hadn't been able to throw it away. For sure, it hadn't been the work of a cat.

The knowledge sent another shiver of fear coursing up her spine. Knowledge that somewhere around her, maybe on the other side of the tank, someone lurked who intended her harm. Anyone who hurt her winery hurt her. This was no penny-ante crime. The tank held thirty thousand gallons of shiraz wine, the loss of which would make a big hole in the winery's profits. Heaven knew how many gallons had escaped. Although the intruder had opened the lower bunghole, the one they used for draining the lees, the liquid running over her fingers as she struggled to tighten the bung felt clean and clear.

Pure, rich and fruity shiraz.

The style she and Max had shared the evening they met.

Where was he?

Maggie's hackles rose. She didn't want to do this alone, but she would if she had to. The perpetrator of this crime might still be around....

Maggie heaved a final sigh as the flow stopped and the bung fitted flush against the tank. She sank to her knees, careless of the state of the wine-covered ground. What did it matter when she'd practically bathed in the stuff?

With both palms braced on the cold, stainless steel tank, she pushed unsteadily to her feet, as if she'd been drinking the wine instead of only breathing its bouquet. Even in the middle of the crisis, she'd thought, Steven had picked this one at the optimum moment. It was going to be great—glorious, in fact—if only they could hang on to it for a few years.

She stood listening for a minute. No more sounds of wine spilling onto the ground reached her ears. Steven would be horrified when she told him tomorrow. He'd be sure to act as if they'd spilled his life's blood.

Shivering with cold, Maggie pulled the hem of her sweater away from her waist and wrung it out, then wiped her hands over her breasts, the only place still dry enough to clean them. A slightly hysterical giggle escaped the hand she put over her mouth to hold it in. What a way to greet Max. He'd think she'd been bathing in the stuff like a wine-crazed sot.

She shook one foot and then the other as she stepped onto dry ground. The lees had flowed across the driveway to the spot where she hoped one day to build a restaurant, backing onto the driveway and facing the vines. Maggie had grand schemes for the vineyard, and it looked as though the restaurant had been well christened.

Luckily, she'd stuck a set of keys in her pocket when she left the shop. The ring held a master key that opened all the winery locks, including the plant, cellar and shop. Between her and the bottling plant stood five huge storage tanks—ten, if she counted both rows. If she went back, there was only the width of four tanks and a large open space to pass, going uphill to the shop. But the switch for the huge spotlights they used during the harvest, when the men worked all night, was inside the plant.

There would be no place for anyone to hide once she threw that switch.

Including her.

The moon kept sneaking out from behind the clouds, then ducking for cover again. When it shone, its reflection bounced off the tanks and lit up the drive, but only fleetingly. Even so, it revealed Maggie's progress. Instead of walking down the center of the driveway, therefore, she kept close to the tanks, ducking into the deep shadows between them.

The aluminum walkway pinged overhead and she stopped, immobile, listening. There it was again, too loud to be the noise of the wind. Only physical weight would make the light metal creak and sigh in that eerie fashion. Someone was on the walkway above her.

Maggie shrank into the black shadows, flattening herself against the tank. She shivered as the chill of the metal seeped through her sweater. And told herself that was all it was— cold, not fear.

Tilting her head, Maggie looked up into the darkness above the tanks just as the moon illuminated a face looking down at her. She couldn't help letting out a yelp as the cold light shaded it cruelly in black and white—a parody of a human face and unrecognizable to her.

As sudden footsteps clanged past her on the walkway over-head, heading toward the nearest steps down, Maggie dashed through the gap and into the long dark tunnel between the tanks, running in the opposite direction, toward the plant. Harsh gasps ripped from her throat. Gone was the pretense of not being scared. There was a life at stake here. Hers!

Shadowed or not, there had been no mercy in the eyes glow-ing down at her. None at all. Whoever it was, he hadn't come here to spill wine. He had come to spill blood.

Her wine. Her blood.

She knew it in her bones.

Max!

Her heart cried out to him.

Why hadn't she seen this? Dreamed this? Couldn't her mind encompass her own death? The thought had barely reached her consciousness when she ran into something and tripped. Hands outstretched to save herself as she fell, Maggie heard a wine crate smash under her weight. Pain pierced her thigh at the same moment her palms crashed into the gravel and she stretched full length atop the remains of the crate.

Despite the stinging pain, she had to move.

There was no time to assess the damage. No time to lick her wounds.

Maggie dug in her toes and painfully levered her body off the crate. First her knee, then her foot shoved the splintered wood out of her way as she crawled over it, accompanying each push with a curse for the fool who had left it there. Jagged pain stabbed her leg with each movement, and she tried in vain to ignore her palms. She wouldn't let the agony stop her. Couldn't. The only choice she had left was to find somewhere to hide.

If she had her bearings right, there should be an old press stored nearby. With a bit of luck she'd have time to roll underneath it, out of sight.

Yes! There it was. Maggie ducked down, grasped a metal leg and pulled with all her strength, forgetting the pain. Forgetting everything but the need to survive.

One more effort and she'd be there. Hidden.

A hand closed on her shoulder as she went to roll under the machine.

And her screams bounced back at her, off the cold metal tanks.

Chapter 7

The gates stood wide, leaving nothing to hinder Max's sweep off the road onto the drive. His headlights cut a swath in the night and highlighted a pale, gold-washed building, its roof lines scalloped with curved terra-cotta tiles. With darkness blanking out the rest of the scenery he could swear he'd turned the corner and been transported to Tuscany.

He recognized Maggie's car parked in front of the building. All she needed was to swap the little Beemer for a Ferrari to give the picture its final touch of authenticity. From inside the building, light poured down the four shallow steps in front, where green vegetation of some kind cascaded over the terra-cotta urns standing on them. Near her car, a sign read Wine Shop Closed.

He wanted to heave a sigh of relief after his mad dash along strange roads for the last few kilometers. He should be able to relax now. Should, but couldn't. The feeling in the pit of his stomach that something wasn't quite right wouldn't leave him.

With his eyes focused on the glass doors, watching for Maggie to appear, he drew up close to the Beemer and almost sounded the horn, but thought better of it, not wanting to break the quiet stillness of the countryside with the kind of noise pollution pervading the city. Max opened the car door and started to unfold from the front seat.

A scream punctured the stillness! Max hit his skull on the door arch with a whack and grabbed the handle to stop himself from falling.

"Maggie!"

He clambered upright, holding steady a moment by gripping the door. If he had his bearings right, the screams had erupted from the dark slope behind the building. *Still* came from there, unless the blood-chilling sounds were simply echoes in his imagination caused by the bang on his skull.

His most immediate thought was to tell Maggie she wasn't alone. Pressing his hand on the horn, he gave it three loud blasts, then unclipped his gun from under the seat. Then he ran toward the screams, their volume fading even as he raced down the slope. "Maggie! Where are you?" he yelled, as if his life depended on it. If anything happened to Maggie…

The moon slipped out as he ran, gun at the ready, his image distorted by the curve of a large metal tank as he splashed through a shallow pool of incredibly pungent liquid. Wine. The sudden wetness of his feet probably saved him from shooting at his own image like a fool.

Apart from his own rattled breathing, an uneasy hush had fallen on the vineyard. The sound guiding him had died. "God, help me," he prayed. "I don't want to lose her…. Maggie! If you're there, answer me."

No human voice reached him, but a ringing metallic sound, high and to his right, sent him diving into the rows of tanks. A rhythmic clash of footsteps, like a spider running across a metal web, set Max spinning, his eyes scanning the fragile network of walkways above him. "Hold it! Police!" he yelled, pointing his weapon. A blur of movement shivered between him and the moon-washed clouds. Without hesitation, it took off in the direction from which Max had just come. As much as his instincts said, ''Get him,'' his heart said, ''Find Maggie.''

He headed toward where the shadowy figure had come from, but at ground level. He walked carefully, dissecting the rows, sensing his way through the darkness, his gaze skimming overhead and shimmying across patches of moonlight as he checked the openings for signs of movement.

Then the moon disappeared.

Blinded, Max pulled a penlight from his pocket, cursing as his foot caught on an object with the dull thunk of wood.

With a flick of his toe, he cleared his path and sent the wood skittering across the gravel ahead of him till it struck something with a soft, hollow boom. He banged the side of his fist against the tank nearest to him. No echo. Yeah, these tanks were all full. This afternoon Maggie had told him about the bulk wine they had stored.

There it went again! But this time not through any action of his. He directed the small beam of light ahead of him.

''Maggie, is that you?''

''Max…''

His name, whispered low in her husky voice, had never sounded sweeter. He let out a groan of heartfelt relief. She was alive. He homed in on the sound like a fly after honey, and played the light over some sort of machinery.

''Underneath the winepress,'' Maggie moaned. ''By your feet.''

Slipping his gun into the back of his waistband, Max got down on his haunches and reached under the machine. His hand collided with cold, wet fabric covering a shin bone, shining dark red in the light. He tensed. Blood? No, the well-remembered coppery tang didn't catch at his nostrils. Only the smell of wine.

''You okay, Maggie? Can I move you?''

''Yeah, do what you like. Anything. Just get me out of here.''

His gut clenched with palpable relief at the testiness in her tone. She might be hoarse, but she felt well enough to bawl him out.

"Do you hurt badly anywhere or can I pull you out?"

"Don't worry about me. Just go ahead and do it."

Max knelt on the gravel as he slipped one hand under her knees and grasped her arm with the other. Gently, he eased her out of her hiding place, to grumbling yips and moans from Maggie. "I wish I could see you properly, babe. You don't sound as good as you make out." She lay in the dirt, her head supported by his knees, and her ironic grunt of laughter encouraged him to pull her closer.

"I've had better days," she wheezed.

Max ran his hands over her supine body. "I don't want to move you till I'm sure you're okay. Where does it hurt worst?"

"All over, but mainly my thigh, my hands and my throat." She broke down then. "Oh, Max," she sobbed, her voice dwindling to a thin thread. "He tried to strangle me."

"Hush, baby, hush." Max pulled her up in his arms and held her close, rubbing his palm up and down her back, trying to calm her fears. "You're all right now, sweetheart. I've got you and I won't let anything happen to you. I'll get that bastard, whoever he is, and that's a promise." His heart beat like a wild thing, swelling with rage. He had murder on his mind— the demise of the guy who'd dared lay hands on Maggie. She was his, and anyone trying to deprive him of this woman had better be prepared to answer for their sins.

Maggie's head burrowed into the curve of his shoulder, her voice growing huskier as she told him, "I thought you were never going to get here. I kept praying for you to hurry. To come help me."

Max stilled for a second, not moving until Maggie clutched at his lapel, then whimpered and released her hold on him. He held back a curse as he shone his penlight, illuminating the damage. Holding her hand like a precious object instead of gravel-pitted flesh, he put his lips gently to its palm. "I heard you, sweetheart, I heard you," he said, his voice barely above a whisper. The attraction, the wanting, needed no explanation. As for the rest? He had no time to delve into happenings beyond his ken.

Maggie required a doctor's attention; she was cold and damp. What if she caught a chill on top of everything else? His first priority was to get some real light on the situation, then he could get her out of this place.

"Maggie, is there a switch nearby for the lights?"

She sucked in a ragged breath. "There's a key to the bottling plant in my pocket. The board of switches is on your right as you go in. Throw them all—I've been in the dark too long."

She squirmed in his arms, then ran the tip of one finger over his stubbled cheek. The sensation rippled across his nerve ends. Maybe he'd never shave again. At least not every day.

"You're going to have to get the keys. I can't put my hand in my pocket."

"Okay, I'll do it. Which pocket?"

"The right one."

Max propped her against his shoulder, slid his arm behind her and reached into the pocket of her jeans. Her belly felt soft beneath his hand. Trembling, he focused on wiping his mind of lustful feelings. Maggie was in no shape for lovemaking. She needed pampering. A little tender lovin' care to take her mind off the trauma she'd suffered.

Max got to his feet and lifted Maggie into his arms. "I'm just going to set you down someplace more comfortable." He propped her back against the end tank and crossed her arms over her breasts to protect her hands. "Don't move now. I'll be as quick as I can, then we'll get you home and call a doctor, and the police."

"But you *are* the police, Max."

For the first time since he'd gotten out of his car he felt like laughing at the perplexed tone in her voice. "Somehow I think

I might be out of my jurisdiction. But in any case, someone should guard the scene overnight.''

Maggie squinted as the lights came on, but she couldn't miss Max, striding back purposefully in her direction with a grim look in his eyes and determined jut to his chin. Everything seemed larger than life under the harsh floodlights, yet in that instant she knew Max would always seem that way to her. Within minutes he'd carried her up the drive and placed her in his car, leaving her only to put through calls to her doctor and the police from the wine shop. With her beside him, he drove through the vineyard, where the land fell away at the other side of the main building, then climbed the rise to her house.

She cherished the dear familiarity of her house and let out a sigh of homecoming as Max carried her to the teak door set in the gold-washed entranceway.

''I could stand on my own,'' she said, expecting the floor to come up and meet her as he maneuvered both her and the key, while trying to open the door without releasing her.

''No way,'' he said emphatically. ''I'm not putting you down till we reach your bed.'' He swung the door wide, and they crossed the threshold into the tiled foyer with her still in his arms. He looked pointedly at the stairs and asked, ''Up there?''

Maggie nodded. Although she couldn't hang on to him, she did snuggle closer to his shoulder. It was broad, strong and reassuring, just what she needed right now. ''Second room on the left.''

The suite had been her father's. It had taken her a while to come to terms with knowing he would never use it again, but eventually she'd moved in to it. Tonight she was glad she had. Her old room looked sweet in comparison to this. *Sweet* was the last word that came to mind when she thought of Max.

Four strides took him across the room, where he halted. His gaze studied her from top to toe, taking in her wine-soaked clothing, filthy hands and face from rolling under the wine-press. Then he glanced at the pale green bedcover.

"Bathroom," he muttered. It was more a statement than a question and brooked no argument.

"Over there." She indicated the door on the window side of the bed.

Plain cream nylon curtains flapped in the breeze. She seldom drew the heavier green side drapes that matched the spread. A large expanse of glass took up most of one wall and opened onto a private terrace. On summer nights, hot, scented air from the garden would mingle with the fragrance of the gardenias growing on the terrace, and she'd leave the doors wide to let the potpourri of perfumes fill her room.

The curtains grabbed at Max's legs as he carried her into the bathroom. This was going to be a fiasco. How on earth could she deal with buttons and zippers, never mind turn on the shower and soap herself?

Without waiting for directions, Max sat her down on the chair fronting the vanity and went to turn on the shower.

Catching her reflection, Maggie cringed. Dirt and wine streaked her face and hair, clumping her fringe and plastering it to her forehead.

Max stood behind her, his hands on her shoulders. "If the lights had been on, you'd have scared that guy for sure."

Through the mirror she watched him grin. And shivered. The width of his smile didn't match the icy gleam in his eyes.

"Let's get you out of these wet clothes."

Maggie stared at Max as she realized he meant to undress her. Was she traumatized enough to allow this to happen?

"Now, sweetheart, before you catch a chill." Gripping the wet, soggy edge of her sweater, he asked, "Can you lift your arms?" Once he had it over her head, he knelt on the floor between her knees. He'd removed his jacket, and the sudden shudder of his chest was plain to see as he stared at her neck.

Maggie glanced in the mirror to see what held his attention. Her skin blanched, making the mass of red bruises ringing her neck appear worse. There was no pretending it hadn't happened. Her assailant had wanted her dead. And now that the collar of her sweater no longer hid the marks, Max knew it, too.

His hand paused halfway to her throat, then changed course and fumbled with the metal button at the waist of her jeans instead. His fingers on the tab of her zipper shook, and took two tries to undo it.

With his head down she couldn't see what was going on in his eyes. "Max?" she said softly. When he looked up the agony there was plain to see, his emotions bare and unashamed in front of her.

"Ohh, Max." The depth of his torment struck her to the bone. "Don't do this to yourself, honey. I'm here. I'm alive. We're together. Put everything else from your mind." Her hands being out of commission didn't stop her from looping her arms around his neck. The pink-stained, lace-trimmed thermal top she'd worn under her sweater clung like a second skin. She pulled Max's face against her breasts, where the knit fabric was dry and warm from her body heat.

"What if I hadn't gotten here in time? What if I'd lost my way? If you had died...I feel—"

"Hush," she crooned throatily.

The heat of his breath penetrated her thermal top, dampening her skin as, with husky, emotion-filled words he tried to take responsibility for her close encounter with death. Now she had to return the favor and restore his mana.

"It didn't happen...you didn't let it. You're a giant of a man, Max Strachan. I'd back you against the bad guys any day. We've known each other such a short time, but long enough for me to know you wouldn't deliberately let me down." She rubbed her cheek against his thick, crisp hair, then said, "Look at me, Max." Their gazes locked. "I trust you. No matter what."

His gaze never flickered, not for an instant. Not even as his hands forked through her raggle-taggle hair and he angled his head and took her mouth.

His kiss overflowed with emotion as he resurrected all the highs and lows of a hundred lifetimes and poured them into her. It was a kiss to lift souls, break hearts, and it touched all levels in between. It was a kiss for today, for all summers past and all futures to come.

Maggie fed from it and gave herself to it, until sensation filled every particle of her mind, every nook and cranny of her body, pulsing through every vein and capillary till they reached their limit and could take no more.

And still he gave, and took, and so did she. They quivered in each other's arms like taut violin strings, and the music they made was the kind that angels speak of. Music of love and desire.

Breaking away gently, Max moistened her face with tiny butterfly kisses as he lapped up the salty overflow of emotion she'd refused to shed earlier. His breath smelled of wine and tears as he said hoarsely, "This isn't gonna get you cleaned up before the doc arrives." He looked at his watch. "By my reckoning we've got fifty minutes."

Maggie questioned, "Did he say why he'd be so long?"

"Just that there was an accident in the Dome Valley."

"And that was all?"

"Yep. It's not far, but if he takes too long, I'll feed you. You need to build up your strength."

She looked at the red abrasions on her hands. "You might have to spoon-feed me like a baby."

He placed a kiss on the corner of her mouth, his finger tracing the damp paths of fresh rivulets. "For my baby, *anything!* Then it's early to bed for you."

"Please," she whispered meaningfully.

"Cut that out. I need to look after you."

"That was what I had in mind."

By the time the doorbell rang, he'd stripped Maggie down to her lace panties and could hardly tear his eyes from the full ripe beauty of her breasts. They were everything he'd imagined and more. Pangs of frustrated hunger coursed through his veins for what might have been if it hadn't been for the intervention of that murderous cretin. Max inhaled deeply to steady his emotions and set his own needs aside. It proved futile. In the small, steamy bathroom, Maggie's perfume scented every particle of air. "Can you manage the rest yourself, while I go and get that?" he asked, but still didn't move to answer the door.

"Sure. I'm not an invalid, you know."

"Maybe not, but I don't like the look of that spike of wood in your thigh or the dirt in your palms. I doubt if the doc will get it all out at one go." The size of the splinter bothered him. Blood had darkened the end he could see, and it had pierced the muscle. No way would he try to remove that on his own. But he might chance tweezers on the shards of gravel nearer the surface.

He gave Maggie a quick, hard kiss as the bell pealed again. "It's probably the police. Give everything a good soak. I'll be back to help soon."

They'd sent one eager cop with minimal experience. When Max first saw him he wondered how long it had been since he'd looked that young—full of his own importance, yet simmering with excitement underneath. "Big with news," his mother had called it when he was a kid.

Max got back to the house with the lights of the bottling plant still blazing behind him so the kid could see to set up the crime scene tape and not feel too isolated. It would be tomorrow before they could spare more cops, since the other four were attending the scene of the accident that had closed the Dome Valley.

Instead of waiting downstairs for the doctor, Max bounded up eagerly, anticipating Maggie's laughter when he told her who was guarding them. Steam fogged the bathroom even though the exhaust fan churned in the ceiling. "It's only me," he called, and when Maggie didn't reply, he flung open the glass shower door.

Waves of damp heat hit his cold face, but the sight of Maggie, a picture of shock and exhaustion draped against the tiles, with her forehead resting on one arm, hit where it hurt.

Water sluiced down her back, its spray bouncing off her shoulders, pearling her black hair with droplets. She looked completely zonked. "You all right, sweetheart?"

She lifted her head, saw him and pushed herself upright.

Her fingers curled liked unfurled petals as she attempted to cover her breasts, and stood at an angle to hide the dark curls shielding her femininity. Her eyes gleamed like black star sapphires and her eyelashes clung in thick tufts beaded with water, as if she'd been crying. Max pulled one hand away from her breast. She tugged against his grip but he held on, circling her wrist with his thumb and forefinger. "It's too late for modesty, Maggie." His eyes skimmed her womanly attributes. "Please don't hide yourself from me. Your body's beautiful."

He grimaced at the red, raw damage to the skin of her hand. "Damn, I shouldn't have left you to cope on your own." Once again he dropped a kiss into her palm. "I bet it stings, huh?"

Maggie nodded mutely, pulling her hand from his reach.

"Trying to wash must be agonizing," he sympathized. Max made up his mind fast, knowing he would test his libido to the limit. "Give me a sec, sweetheart, and I'll see what I can do."

It took two seconds to shuck off his clothes, certainly no more. As she watched him kick them aside and step into the shower, Maggie's eyes widened and she moved back—not as if he frightened her. Simply to give him more room.

"What say we start with your hair?" he asked, pulling her into his arms and letting the hot water cascade over them. He allowed his senses the indulgence of touching her shoulders and back. Her skin, like pale gold satin, reacted to the light rasp of his caress.

Maggie closed her eyes and with a sigh dropped her forehead onto his chest. His muscles jumped at this unexpected pleasure, then settled down and just enjoyed it. Cupping his hand, he poured a blob of shampoo into it, then began massaging her scalp and hair. He'd slightly overdone the amount, as her hair was so short, and dollops of white foam ran down her neck, temporarily hiding the red bruises. Tension coiled in the pit of his stomach as he tilted Maggie's head back and let the water stream over her head and shoulders. Her breasts thrust toward him, water dripping from their tightly furled, treacle-colored peaks.

His hand shook as he repeated the operation, tipping conditioner into his palm. Her beauty stunned him. What had he done to deserve this woman? It had to have been something special for him to have landed an angel like Maggie. Turning her away from him, he gave up trying to control his arousal. As he worked the conditioner in with his fingers, Maggie stood with bowed shoulders and let him have his way. He could count each nodule of her spine. Although she was tall, he'd never thought of her as fragile before. Suddenly he felt huge, clumsy and very protective of this slight creature life had blessed him with.

When he'd finished her hair, Max picked up a bar of soap and began working it into a lather. Smoothing the scented foam over her shoulders, he added to his personal torture by sliding his palms down her back and painting her buttocks with white bubbles. She was soft and shapely. The curves of each mound fit perfectly in his hands, contracting gently as he squeezed them as if testing ripe fruit. He bit back a groan, letting the soap fall to the tiled floor, and slid his hands up her rib cage to cup her breasts.

Maggie felt no compunction to hide her feelings. As his fingers brushed her aching nipples a primal moan ripped from her throat and started her coughing when it hurt.

He pulled her back against him and held her till the paroxysm subsided and she leaned into him, desperate to run her hands down his flanks and making do with the touch of her skin rubbing against him from thigh to shoulder.

It was misery of the worst kind to feel the partition of her sweet derriere press against his male hardness, and hold her in his arms without his being able to take her fully. Maggie rocked against its turgid length, building a frenzied excitement between them as he slid against the hot, wet crevice. Max threw his head back and groaned aloud while the water sheeted between them and his fingers splayed across her breasts. It was a cold shower he needed, not this warm, steamy heat that egged his senses on until he hardly knew nor cared what he did.

Lifting his hands from Maggie, he flattened them against the wall, making stars with his fingers in the steam, keeping her surrounded by his arms and body. She turned inside the boundaries, openly staring at the evidence of his need. Her hands rose as if to touch him, then dropped to her sides. She lifted her face and her lips parted on a sigh. Blazing passion had burned up the sadness in her eyes.

Max dipped his head in answer to the pure flame of desire and touched his mouth to hers. Her tongue came out to meet him and he suckled it, meeting her demands without force, careful of her bruised throat. Tremors raked her body as she tried to pull him closer, holding him with her arms instead of her hands.

Max shook his head. "No, you'll hurt yourself." Keeping his weight on the wall, he kissed her shoulder. Slowly sliding his palms lower, he worked his mouth around the darling curves of her breasts until the dark buds he craved were his at last.

As his mouth fastened on a tempting morsel, the little mewling cries she uttered found an echo in him. He wanted to throw his head back and roar, "Mine," to anyone who cared to listen.

Reluctantly, he abandoned feasting on her breasts and went in search of a tastier treat. Keeping her locked between his arms, he slid to his knees and gradually circumnavigated her navel with his tongue until her treasure faced him.

Without releasing her he buried his nose in the black wet thatch guarding it. Maggie smelled of scented soap and the honeyed musk of passion. His tongue parted her and licked, sampling a small portion of what would soon be his for the taking. Over his head he heard Maggie cry out as her hips thrust toward him. He laughed in delight and parted her further, snuffling her delicious aroma with his nose and delving further between her swollen lips till he touched the pearl he'd been seeking.

A flush of desire enveloped him and a red mist blinded his eyes. His hard male flesh flexed in agony, weaving like a heat-seeking missile deprived of its target. But Max's mouth had found his goal and his tongue circled the bud till it swelled and rose to meet him.

Maggie's cries filled his ears and the water pounded over them both till he imagined them lost beneath a waterfall. When she forgot her pain enough to rest her battered hands on his shoulders, Max knew he had to end it. Covering her hot, pulsing core with his mouth, he sucked, hard.

Never in a million years would he forget the way she let go, opening up to him till her spasms of release played over his mouth and tongue where they joined her in this most intimate of adventures.

Max stood and held Maggie for what seemed like a lifetime, both of them panting for breath after their incredible experience. The joy of tasting her as personal to him as it had obviously been to Maggie. He vowed there and then that it was one pleasure she would share with no one but him.

When her breathing returned to normal, Max turned off the shower and said, "Sorry, sweetheart. I'm tempted to stay here holding you forever. But the doc will probably skin me alive if he suspects what we've been doing with you in this state. Definitely will if he catches the glow in your eyes. Try and look shocked."

"I am shocked," she said, but her smile was dreamy and secretive, as if contemplating something only she knew.

"The doc was damned angry when I told him what had happened." Max picked up her hands, looked at them and shook his head. "I think we'll leave these to the expert."

"Max, I've never met anyone more expert than you."

"And you never will," he told her possessively as he lifted her out of the shower.

No wonder the inferno had flared between them. Two naked bodies in a confined space...it was only natural. Maggie's only regret was that her injuries made it difficult to make love all the way. She'd wanted to touch Max. Ached to take his length in her hands, in her mouth, inside her, to give him the same pleasures he'd showered on her.

Now she stood on the bath mat and his touch stirred her even through the soft towel he used to dry her body.

It was funny, standing here, letting him look after her so intimately. She couldn't ever remember her mother caring for her this way—patting her dry, being careful not to hurt the sore bits. Maggie had always had to bathe and dry herself. Though her father had stuck the occasional plaster on a skinned knee, even as a two-year old, she'd had to see to her own ablutions. She supposed she'd only missed all this after her mother and brother had been killed, but if she'd known it before, she couldn't remember.

"There, how does that feel?"

Maggie grinned down at him. She felt like giving the silver streak in his hair a playful tug, but it would hurt her too much. The play of muscles under Max's skin revealed the strength in the arms that held the towel. She got a thrill from simply looking at the rise and fall of his chest and the tight mounds of his butt. That's what made it ridiculous to see this gorgeous example of manhood kneeling in front of her, as naked as the day he'd been born.

Men didn't have a modest bone in their body.

She let her gaze travel over the wide scattering of hair covering his chest till it narrowed over his navel and surrounded his male sexuality in thick, black curls.

Even as she watched, it began to stir, thicken, lengthen, making her marvel at the power of her gaze, that she could make him harden with a simple look. "How terrible to be a man," she said sympathetically. "Never able to hide your intentions."

Max stood up and laughed. "I can see you're feeling better, since you're throwing insults around. I hate to disappoint you, madam, but me and my intentions are going undercover for a while."

Maggie pouted. "That's life."

A broad grin creased his face and he chuckled, "But not as you've known it, sweetheart. Not yet, anyway."

"There, I think that's the last bit," said Dr. McCallum, putting his tweezers down in a clutter of wipes and gauze swabs he'd taken from the sterile pack on the kitchen table. "I've some salve here the local chemist makes up for me. It has an antibiotic in it as well as aloe vera and vitamins A and E. It'll heal this lot in no time and help prevent scarring. I'll put some on now, and leave you a tube. In two days time I'll come back and see you, as you won't want to be driving for a while.

"Take the tablets I'm leaving in case your leg develops an infection, though the splinter came out pretty cleanly."

"What about—" Maggie began.

The doctor raised a finger to his lips and hushed her. "And rest that larynx, not too much talking. Take arnica drops to help bring the bruising out, and this tablet to help you sleep," he finished, then looked Max over. "You'll see she does as she's told?"

"He won't be here," Maggie said quietly. "But you don't have to come out here, I can get someone to drive me."

"What, and miss a chance to stock up my wine rack?" He winked at them both. "Just try and keep me away."

"Thanks, doc," said Max. "I'll see she follows your advice."

"At least she'll be able to drive in a few days, which is more than can be said for the other poor beggar I looked after tonight. Broken femur, punctured lung. Rolled his truck, you know. Some lunatic probably cut him off on one of the bends, for he's a local lad, knows the Dome well. They've probably ripped out his spleen by now. They don't waste much time in Auckland Accident-and-Emergency. Gordon will be in critical care for a while, but he's a good strong lad. I'm sure he'll pull through."

Maggie felt giddy. In her mind's eye she could see a truck climbing a bank and rolling over and over while a black car sped away. She shook her head and the vision dissolved. She had black cars on the brain—obviously from the shock of everything she had been through. But she couldn't shake the memory of that shadowy car, tailgating her on the way home. "You said Gordon. Which one?" she asked the doctor urgently.

"Jamieson. Do you know him?"

"Oh, no," she moaned, watching her plans for November dissolve as quickly as the vision had disappeared. "No! Not Gordon!"

"Who the hell is Gordon?" Max growled.

Chapter 8

Max woke with his legs in a tangle, his rock-hard sex pressing something soft and warm, and his arms full of Maggie.

The tablet the doc gave her had put her out like a light. Max had hardly had time to slip into bed behind her and pull her into his arms when she'd fallen asleep with a drowsy ''G'night'' on her lips.

Not much had changed overnight. They'd spent it sleeping spoon fashion, his top leg lying between hers so he could stay close without hurting the thigh the splinter had stabbed.

Maggie had put on a soft, silky, rose-colored chemise that couldn't be said to do much for her modesty. It felt erotic, sliding between his hands and her skin, silk against satin, and its hem had finished up around her waist.

She'd laid a beatific smile on him when he asked her, ''Why the cover-up?''

''To save you from yourself,'' Maggie had laughed sleepily.

''Too late, sweetheart, it's a done deed.'' Just being in the same room as her brought temptation. Just breathing the same air she did worked like magic on him.

Darkness still obscured the room. There was no telling what time it was, not without moving his arm out from under Maggie and disturbing her. So he just lay there and let his hands wander in time with his mind.

The main issue troubling him was who had lain in wait for Maggie, tempting her to walk into danger. Whoever it was had trailed beams of light in front of her, like scattering bread crumbs to lead a bird into a trap.

Max still hadn't ruled out Maggie simply being in the wrong place at the wrong time and interrupting a burglary in progress. The crux of the problem was who would consider a life sentence a worthwhile price for a few bottles of wine? Spider, as Max had named him after the way he'd scurried across the heights, leaving only a shiver of metal in his wake, would have gotten away with next to nothing without transport nearby. Then again, perhaps his intention had been sheer bloody-minded vandalism. And maybe not. With the media attention focused on Maggie this week, they might be searching for a nutcase with a penchant for freak shows. Someone with the same disgust of psychics he used to have.

Used to have?

When had his head turned around?

When he'd first met Maggie he'd thought he could get away with leaving her dream sequences out of the equation. By ignoring that part of her, he could save himself the trouble of getting down and dirty with his own prejudices. Boy, did he have a lot to learn.

Maggie had said she'd called for him. Maybe he hadn't heard the words, but he'd felt the urgency, the need. And he'd come at a run! He'd give a thousand bucks to know the whys and wherefores of that little scenario. For instance, it was a given that cops thrived on instinct, a fact blurred by the huge amount of paper they pushed. Nine times out of ten it was the little voice at the back of his mind that said, "This is it, here's the link." Instinct pure and simple.

But what if there was more?

What if Maggie's innate intuition focused inward?

Get a grip, Max. Next you'll be believing the dreams drop straight out of the ether into her mind.

Nah, intuition was a better name for it.

So, who could fear Maggie enough to want to kill her?

Maggie resurfaced to the feel of Max drawing patterns on her breasts with his fingertips. The soft silky swirls of his thumbs across her nipples tugged at the invisible cord connecting them to her womb, making it tighten and her hips flex.

"You awake, Maggie?" he whispered in a low voice, sounding early-morning husky and sexy as hell.

"Um-hmm," she murmured, as if speaking might sharpen the edges of the beautiful haze she was floating in. Letting herself sink back into Max, rubbing her hips against him said so much more than a sigh.

"Oh yeah, you're awake," Max groaned, tightening his hold on her breasts as her hips gyrated once more.

Maggie quivered as he slid one hand across her belly, taking a quick dip at her navel before venturing between her thighs. "Oh, Max!" she groaned as his fingertip found the center of her sexuality. It took the circular route, round and round, winding her up, increasing the tension wave by wave. She was definitely awake now. Her blood sang in her veins, raced through them in the wake of Max's touch. No one could sleep through this cycle of pleasure, which stopped just short of torture. "Oh, Max," had become her mantra. She repeated it over and over, letting the last of his name whistle through her teeth like a steam kettle coming to the boil.

"I want you, sweetheart. I want to be inside you, but I don't want to hurt you. So tell me how you feel."

"Right at this moment I'm feeling no pain. I want you, too, Max." The way she felt right now the ceiling could fall in on her and she wouldn't turn a hair.

"Touch me again, Max. Touch me the way I want to touch you and can't because my hands are a mess." She'd almost managed to erase the events of last night from her mind and didn't want them intruding on this special moment, when she and Max were about to make love for the first time.

"Don't move a muscle, sweetheart, leave it all to me." His hands swiftly dispensed with her chemise, leaving her naked and trembling in his arms.

She'd give anything to wake up in his arms every morning—an impossible dream—but she had this beautiful, fantastic chance, and she would make the most of it.

Max slid his hand under the pillows they shared. Foil crackled in her ear as he bit into the packet, and his knuckles skimmed her back as he sheathed himself. Then he was over her, taking his weight on one elbow as he removed the second pillow. "How does that feel—comfortable?"

"I'm fine." His lips feathered across hers. "Good," she murmured. The kiss deepened and she could taste the hunger in his mouth. He was all around her—taste, touch, smell, his voice in her ear.

He was everywhere, inside her head, her heart…her body. She heard a guttural moan, her own, and her muscles wrapped themselves around him as if never wanting to let go.

This sensation was like nothing she'd felt before, this filling of her senses, her being, with pure unadulterated Max. She whimpered as he drew back, and sighed as he thrust again, opening her wider, deeper, stretching her till she thought she could take no more. He proved her wrong each time.

His hand slid between her thighs, adding an extra delight, Max whispered erotic, yet loving suggestions into her shoulders, her hair, her ears, punctuating each phrase with loving bites and tender kisses. Even his muted growls as he skipped her bruised neck aroused her.

With each thrust, Max took her to another level of sensuality, driving them both toward their ultimate goal in a frenzy of hot, damp skin sliding on skin and the rhythmic stroke of hard, pounding flesh. Her heart thudded madly against his and tremors raked him as they hit the peak and plunged, exhausted, from the heights. The way down was long and slow, neither willing to relinquish the exquisite pangs of completion. Max held her tightly all the way, groaning his release as her muscle contractions took all he had.

By the time she touched down, Maggie felt more loved, more treasured and cared for, than she ever had before.

The sun had been up all of twenty minutes when Max left the house. He carried a thermos full of coffee and had a plastic-wrapped sandwich in his pocket, to feed the kid on watch.

Max cracked a grin as he drove away from the house and through the vineyard to the bottling plant. Maggie was all-woman and then some. She hadn't spent the night crying and bemoaning her fate. Instead, she'd showed him her sense of humor. Not only did she set his libido on fire, he'd discovered he liked her, too.

It was a great morning, with the air clear and crisp. As he drove, a thin, transparent layer of clouds moved between him and the washed-out, blue-gray sky. There hadn't been a frost, just a heavy dew, and where the sun hit the trellises, condensation dripped off the wires in huge diamond drops pierced with sunlight. It was the sort of sight you never found in the city. And he'd much rather be sharing the beauty of it with Maggie, instead of spending it searching for clues to her assailant.

Max's fists clenched on the steering wheel. It still made his stomach churn to think of what might have happened if he hadn't arrived in time. And now that he and Maggie had made love, now that he'd tasted her sweetness, the urge to protect her, to keep her out of harm's way, was powerful. His private life and his job were tearing him in two. He wanted to keep them separate—one box marked Work, the other marked Maggie. But the stronger their involvement, the tighter were the ties connecting her and her gift to his case.

The coffee went down a treat as Max shared a cup with the kid, P.C. Bowden, talking inanities till they'd both warmed up. The scene looked different in daylight. The eerie effects of watery moonlight and scudding clouds reflected off steel tanks dissolved in the sun's rays, and the huge wine containers looked almost commonplace. Sure, and the Spider might be a figment of his imagination, gobbled up by the sun as it ate the dark, but Max didn't think so.

"What time do you expect the team from Warkworth?"

"The other three should be here by seven."

Max laughed. "You guys don't do things by halves, do you? I'll look around, then give Auckland a call to suss out the situation with the fingerprint team. Sunday morning in Auckland city, they might be run off their feet."

"You mean with stuff like the Khyber Pass Killer?" Bowden asked, all big eyes and eager face.

Heaven help me if I was ever that young, Max thought with a grin. He remembered the excitement of his first chases, though, and forgave the kid. How long would it be till he discovered the job was more about boredom and repetition? He'd like to see the lad's face when he told him they had the KPK under ice, ready to be chipped out.

"Yeah, something like that," he replied, tossing his coffee dregs on the gravel. "I'm going to sniff around. When your sergeant gets here, tell him where I've gone. I don't suppose anyone at the winery will turn up for work this morning, but if they do, you know the routine. Keep the scene secure."

Max grabbed some equipment from the trunk of his car, a pair of latex gloves and some plastic bags, just in case. His pistol lay hidden in its holster, the way he liked it. He'd never had a good result after taking it out.

Knowing nothing about wine making, he couldn't even guess at the amount of foot traffic this area might get, or assess their chances of finding anything pertinent to the Spider lying around. Not that they needed much—something small, but big enough for a latent print, like the one that had landed the KPK. That's all it would take to catch the Spider.

He looked at the network of walkways and thought about

the way the guy had scuttled across them in the dark. It wasn't something he'd care to attempt—not enough room. So it stood to reason they were looking for someone lightly built and agile, yet strong, depending on whether Maggie had saved herself or the jerk ran off after the horn sounded.

God must have been on Maggie's side, giving her a winepress to hide under. It was the only cover in sight. Max walked around it, then hunkered down. Bending his head, he looked underneath. Nothing jumped out and grabbed him. Thank heavens the days were long gone when it was his job to sift through the gravel.

At the steps, Max let his gaze measure the distance to the top, and added it to the speed of the guy, making up a composite picture of the suspect in his mind.

The steps looked sturdy enough. Maybe he would chance it.

Overnight the cool air had contracted the metal frame. As soon as he put his weight on the steps, they started to crack and ping, and protested with even more gusto when he reached the walkway. Max wasn't afraid of heights, only of falling from them. As he inched his way across, he felt a grudging admiration for the man who had run over them in the dark.

The system consisted of a central strip, with smaller bridges leading to each tank. Max examined the rails, slatted floors and any joints that might have picked up a thread or scrap of fabric. He kept his gaze focused, never lifting it to look ahead.

The unexpected find took his breath away. His head reared up and he clutched at the rail as the walkway rocked under him. The object hung limply just inches from his hand, beads of dew turned to rubies on its surface without a smidgen of breeze to dry them. Even without picking it up he recognized powder marks in the shade Maggie wore. He swallowed hard, forcing back bile. A leaden weight lodged itself in his gut. What a way to start the day, with all his theories crashing down around him and his heart telling him he should have known it was all too good to be true.

Carefully he unhooked his prize from a loose nut meant to hold the rails together, and with the red scarf tucked safely inside one of the clip-tight bags, made his way back down.

If she held the utensils just right she could manage to stir the eggs without her hand stinging the way it had in the shower. All in all, the way she'd coped so far pleased her. Maggie hummed along with the radio and looked out the window as she worked. She felt wonderful and had a good reason to.

"What the hell do you think you're doing?"

Maggie turned around at the sound of Max's voice. It rasped over her skin, setting off tiny sparks of tension. Hardly the greeting she'd expected, no stroking her senses with honeyed words like he had this morning.

She decided to ignore it, and asked brightly, "I'm cooking breakfast. There's enough for two. Would you like some?"

"You should have stayed in bed and let someone else do that."

"Who? You might have noticed there's a dearth of servants around this place and you were otherwise occupied." She turned her back on him, catching the eggs just before they burned. "It's only scrambled eggs and toast, nothing fancy, but you're welcome to share."

"No, thanks. Jo will be here any time now. But I'll take a cup of coffee."

"Jo?" Maggie felt her happiness slip a notch or two.

"I called her an hour ago, her and the forensic team, though they'll probably take longer to get here." He poured coffee from the pot.

"Why does that preclude you eating breakfast with me?"

Max sat down at the table and didn't quite meet her eyes.

"Don't tell me. You're embarrassed Jo might catch us eating breakfast, in case she thinks we spent the night together." Maggie scraped the eggs onto a plate, letting the fork scratch the bottom of the pan for an unnecessarily long time, before dumping it in the sink and turning to catch the toast just as it popped. Surely a man of his experience could deal with a morning after?

When he still didn't reply, her stomach knotted. Why didn't he deny it? What was the saying—Laughter before dawn, tears before dark?

"Max. Jo's a big girl, she could tell our attraction was mutual."

"Considering we haven't known each other that long, I just thought…" He looked over the top of his coffee cup, then took another long swallow. His eyes gave away nothing.

"Long enough." Why did she feel so angry, so aggressive? Whose reputation was he trying to protect? His or hers, and why? It just didn't gel. There had to be more. Something he wasn't telling her.

She sat down opposite Max. "Why'd you ring Jo, anyway? Surely the local cops can handle it?" She forked some eggs into her mouth and chewed, waiting. Max just kept drinking coffee.

"And the forensic team. Isn't that over the top? I mean, the guy probably only intended breaking in, and I interrupted him."

Max's cup clattered to the table. "Dammit, woman! He tried to strangle you!"

Maggie forced down a piece of toast as if it were made of cardboard. His eyes blazed, the only positive sign of emotion he'd displayed since returning from the bottling plant. "I've been thinking. Maybe this was all my fault. I should have run away and waited for you when the lights went out instead of stumbling around in the dark."

Max said nothing, just studied the dregs of his coffee. She could almost hear the wheels ticking, and something told her she wasn't going to like it when he eventually spoke.

"How come you didn't dream about last night? Or did you, and never mentioned it?"

Maggie squinted at him, puzzled. "No…no dream." His

eyes bored into hers, as pale and cold as the skies outside the window. She fidgeted in her chair. He was making her uncomfortable, and she didn't know why. She had done nothing wrong. Why the sudden interest in dreams he hadn't wanted a hint of before?

"They don't exactly happen on demand. If they did, I'd be able to take it on the road as a sideshow!" she blurted out, then took a long, calming breath. "If I knew any way to stop dreaming, I would. It tarnished my relationship with my father, and now it's doing the same with you. What happens to me is not by choice," she finished with a quiet finality.

Max leaned back in his chair, his hands lying loosely on the table in front of him. "And what about your friend Gordon, the one who had the accident? Did you dream about him?"

Dear heavens, what she'd just said hadn't even touched him, wasn't going to stop him from interrogating her.

Maggie drew herself together and squared her shoulders. Next step, the rubber hoses, she jibed silently. Well, bring 'em on, buster. If you think you can do better than Sister Marie Therese, you're welcome to try. It looked like her father had been right. A Catholic school upbringing did prepare you for anything.

"No, I didn't dream about Gordon's accident, either. Now why do you suppose that is? Maybe the dream fairy thought I'd had my quota for the month." She pushed her plate away from her. The eggs were cold, anyway.

Suddenly it dawned on her that she didn't have to sit here and accept what he dished out. This was her home; she could do as she liked. As she scraped her breakfast into the plastic-lined bin, it came to her. "Actually, there is a reason I didn't dream about Gordon or myself. It's quite simple when you think about it. Neither of us died."

She wished Max would go now; she had enough problems already. Gordon being one of them. Another, finding someone to replace him. If she failed, bang went the wine fest and all her plans. October and November were the best time for flowers, before the weather got too hot, and she'd really wanted to make an impression. And not only on the general public. She'd planned on inviting buyers to come and taste the wines on the two days preceding the weekend.

Maggie rubbed salve on her hands. The stuff had done a remarkable job. Her hands still looked ugly, but not the mess they'd been last night. To keep them clean, she slipped on a pair of white cotton gloves, relics from her schooldays she'd found stashed away in a drawer.

As she pulled on the cuffs, Max asked, "Going somewhere?"

"I have to work. Sunday's one of our busiest days in the wine shop. I called up a local woman who helps when we're busy, as I won't be able to lift wine cases, but I can take money and zap credit cards."

"Before you take off, I need someplace I can leave things, set up a few whiteboards to keep track of things."

Maggie raised her brows, questioning the lengths he was going to over an incident she'd determined to dismiss, wanted to forget. "I thought this area was out of your jurisdiction."

"Not anymore. Not since I called Mike Henare and told him about the scarf," he said casually. Too casually.

Her eyes got caught in his gaze, blinded by a field of blue, unable to turn away. She didn't like the feeling. It frightened her. "What scarf?"

Max's hand went to his pocket. "This one right here." A plastic bag emerged. "D'you recognize it?"

Behind the plastic, Maggie saw a soft fold of red. "Why would I?"

"Maybe from your dreams."

He held the bag high, by a corner, letting it twist back and forth as though in flight.

The light from the window glanced off the plastic and hurt her eyes. Tension clawed at the nape of her neck. She was going to have a headache, she just knew it. "You said the guy was locked up. Arnolds, you called him. Is he still locked up or did he escape?''

"He's still locked up."

She exhaled slowly. "This is a joke, isn't it? Just a joke." She raised her eyes looking for the answer in Max's face, but found no humor. Just a grim mask, like the one he'd worn the day he'd sent her away with Jo. After finding the last victim.

Was she to be the next?

There'd been no dream. No warning. Hadn't she read somewhere that you couldn't predict your own death? But she wasn't dead. She was alive, and last night was as close up and personal as she wanted to get to the Grim Reaper for a while, give or take a century or two. She'd hardly begun to live.

The memories began to unfold, and no matter how hard she tried, they wouldn't stay where she'd hidden them.

She remembered the hand on her shoulder, strong unrelenting fingers pulling her out of her hiding place. Scream! God, how she screamed. It didn't help. Max, where are you? Something soft round her neck. The silence, deadly silence. No curses to send her on her way. Choking…no air. She couldn't breathe! Her hands hurt like the devil as she clawed. Fought the soft, silent harbinger of death. She lashed out with her feet…kicking…fighting. Air, she needed air, and heard it leave like a rushing in her ears.

"Are you all right?" Max put his arm around her and pushed her into a chair. "You've gone white as a sheet— d'you feel faint?"

Maggie's chest heaved. "I can't breathe. I need air. He's choking me. He wants to kill me!" She gasped, in the grip of a panic attack. It had crept up on her silently, like the man had last night. And it was killing her.

It was Max.

He had done this. Max was killing her. Making her remember. Making her feel. She didn't want to feel, just float away.

"Here, breathe into this. You're hyperventilating." Max held a paper bag to her mouth. "Breathe slowly, in and out.

That's it. The carbon dioxide will help regulate your breathing. Yeah. Keep it up, it will soon be over.''

Surprisingly, it worked. Her breathing slowed and the attack gradually lessened. Max was holding her, and the hard man who'd been pretending to be him had disappeared.

"Thanks, Max," she sniffed, feeling childish about letting the fear get to her. "I feel better now. I don't know what came over me. That's never happened to me before."

"You've never nearly been killed before. At least, not that I know of. I should have known something like this would happen. You were too stoic last night, shutting it all away."

Maggie let a deep sigh pour from her throat. At last she could empty her lungs, and the light tingling in her hands and face had melted away. She breathed in. "No, I never nearly died before last night. I guess there has to be a first time for everything, even that.

"Max." She spoke quietly, framing her words carefully, sure he wouldn't like them. "What if that man you've got in jail—Arnolds—is the wrong man? What if the real one, the killer, read the newspaper reports? What if he thinks I can pick him out? They told him where to find me. And what if he was the one...the one who—"

"Stop!" Max held her shoulders tightly and put his face close to hers. "Don't keep doing this, panicking. It's over. It didn't happen and I won't let it happen again. I'll be here for you, at the vineyard, in Auckland, wherever. I won't let you be alone."

She could feel his breath on her face. He was so close she could pick out the tiny flecks of intense dark blue in his eyes. She could tell from the expression in them he meant every word he said. Impossible. No one could be with someone else twenty-four hours a day. He had his life to lead and she had hers. And all the wonderful what-ifs she'd let herself indulge in this morning evaporated like morning mist on a hot summer's day.

"Don't make promises you won't be able to keep."

"I'm not," he protested.

Maggie laid her finger across his lips. They were such beautiful lips for a man, full and yet firm. And the things he could do with them... But she wouldn't think of that right now, for it would probably never happen again. "Hush, Max. It won't work and, if you're truthful, you'll admit it."

"We could give it a go."

"No, I can't live that way. Just find whoever it was and let's get on with our lives. I know yours is always busy. Well, so is mine," she said with a ring of finality.

"Don't be so quick to count me out, lady," Max said, and leaned forward till their lips touched. He kissed her softly, sweetly.

Bittersweet.

A memory to keep and store away with the others.

"I'd been thinking, maybe we had a copycat on our hands. Someone who knew bits and pieces, but not all. For starters, we had a scarf but no doll."

"And the others took place inside." Hope stirred once more.

"Right," agreed Max. "And none of the victims were strangled. He broke their necks..."

"Because he wanted them to look beautiful," Maggie interjected. "He couldn't bear for them to look ugly, even after death."

"And if he'd choked them..." Max stood up and squeezed Maggie's shoulder. "Let's not take anything for granted. Arnolds hasn't been charged with anything more than an assault on a police officer. He went crazy when we picked him up, and landed one of Rowan McQuaid's young cops a good one. His mental stability is being assessed even as we speak."

"I hate to burst your bubble, but he doesn't sound anything like the man in my dreams. Although I never saw his face, he went about everything in such a calm, deliberate manner. Not like someone who would go off half-cocked and hit a policeman, more like someone who planned ahead and took pride in his work.'' Maggie rose from her chair and stood beside him. "Not that I think he's sane. He couldn't be and do what he does. He was cold and unemotional, yet a perfectionist."

Max shook his head. "We're going round in circles. A perfectionist wouldn't have wanted to leave you sprawling in the dirt, so that brings us back to a copycat. Did you ever discuss the contents of your dreams with anyone? Whoever was out there last night could have known you, might have known the place, the way he ran around those walkways in the dark."

Maggie tossed her head and dared him to dispute her. "No! Why would I? Talking to Jo was hard enough. And only the thought we might beat him forced me to go to you. I didn't want to know you."

"Until my gentle persuasion changed your mind."

"You can call it that if you like. I prefer to think of it as a momentary madness that I've recovered from."

"The hell you say," he drawled as his hands framed her face, holding her as if she were the most precious object he'd ever laid hands on. Then he proceeded to kiss her, and sent her conclusions flying out the window.

His mouth covered hers, lips met and clung and tongues danced and mated, reenacting the loving thrusts and withdrawals performed in the dark moments before dawn. Maggie's toes curled and she forced them to relax so she could stand up and get closer to the mouth at the center of her universe.

How could she ever have thought she could give this up? This pleasure. This love. This man.

Max.

Maybe there could be a happy ever after for them, or at least an ever after.

Reality intruded in the form of the doorbell. "I'd better get that," she said after the third ring.

"Let me."

Maggie looked at the lipstick on his mouth and passed him her handkerchief. "I'll answer the door. It is my home. You stay here and hide the evidence." She walked away with a satisfied smirk on her face, which disappeared when something she'd meant to tell Max popped into her mind.

"By the way, I told you I didn't have a dream about Gordon, but I did have a feeling about him. He was leaving my office when I had this urge to tell him to go carefully. If you want that confirmed, you can ask Steven, our wine maker. He was there at the time."

"I believe you."

What had he just said? *I believe you.*

Help, she'd just caught herself in a lie. Steven!

Her mind went into overdrive. She'd told Max that she hadn't discussed the killings with anyone but him and Jo. But there was Steven. A tiny slip, that's true, but a slip nonetheless.

No. Why would Steven want to hurt her? He was her friend. Maggie reached out to open the door.

With her gone he'd be out of a job.

"Morning, Maggie," said Jo.

Her eyes were on Maggie's lips. Damn. She'd told Max to get rid of the evidence and forgotten about herself. Her lips felt soft, full and just-been-kissed.

Jaw clenched, Jo said, "I hear you've been in the wars."

A residue of their conversation, as Jo had driven her away from the murder scene, seemed to have crept back into her friend's tone. The very thing Maggie had dreaded, had warned Max would happen, had come to fruition. Max was coming between her and her friendship with Jo. And after last night, the hours she'd spent in his arms, the fulfillment she'd found there, she couldn't find it in her heart to blame her.

"Yes, I guess you could say that," Maggie replied as she watched her friend's expression war with her emotions.

"You need to take better care, Maggie, now that I'm not around to look after you. Lucky Max was here, huh?"

"More than lucky. Don't stand on the doorstep all day. Come on in. Max is in the kitchen." She turned to call him, but he was already there.

"Got everything?" he asked Jo.

"It's in the car."

"Maggie, where did you say we could set up an operations room?"

He was all-business again. Maggie wished she could switch on and off as easily. "There's a games room at the back of the house that's never used," she said, indicating the direction with her hand. "You know where it is, Jo. Why don't you show Max while I fetch you some coffee? I'm sure you can do with some after driving all this way."

She left them to it, went back to the kitchen and filled two mugs with coffee. When she'd handed them over, she would leave them to it and go down to the wine shop. No need to drive. It was a wonderful morning for the time of year. The walk would help clear her head. She had thoughts hidden inside that she never wanted to revisit.

The door to the games room was open, and from the hall, Maggie could hear them both talking—a murmur at first, then clearer as she neared the door.

"Have you thought she could have set this whole thing up? We have Arnolds under lock and key. Who else knew?"

"Yeah, she could have, quite easily," Max replied.

Maggie didn't wait to hear more. She rushed down the hall, leaving a trail of coffee in her wake. Her white gloves were stained brown. She didn't care. The mugs clattered in the sink where she dropped them. "Damn them!" she sobbed. "Let them get their own coffee." And she hurried out the side door and down the slope through the vines.

Chapter 9

Jo's eyelids flickered then widened in surprise at Max's agreement, and she backed away as he stepped forward, intent on disillusioning her. "I mean, we both know she's bloody amazing...this *friend* of yours. Best friends since you were kids, wasn't that what you told me? If anyone knows what she's capable of it would be you."

The distance between them increased and it wasn't his doing. "All she had to do was half throttle herself, run up forty-foot-high steps, dash across a flimsy walkway, drop the scarf, run back and wait for me to find her. Easy. A real dawdle. She could do it in her sleep, and, like I said, if anyone knows that, it would be you."

Jo's face was almost as white as Maggie's had been earlier. She skimmed her forehead with the heel of palm, and as her color came back she said, "*Damn!* I can't believe I just said that."

Max couldn't bring himself to excuse her. "I can...Jo. If this little performance was to turn me off Maggie, you're too late."

She blinked, repeatedly. "T-too late?"

"Way too late."

"You mean, you and Maggie are..."

"Spit it out, Jo. Yeah, we're lovers. I've told you before, you and I are colleagues and that's as far as it goes. With Maggie...suffice it to say, she's what I want. And if you're wise, you'll never let me hear you put her down again."

"There's nothing left to say then, is there?" She looked down as if her feet had suddenly become much more interesting than the conversation. As she found the courage to face him again, her breasts lifted in a long sigh. "I hope that it works for you, this time."

A door banged somewhere in the house and Max stepped around Jo and out into the hall.

"Maggie!" he called. "Where the hell is she?" He turned back to Jo. "There's coffee all over the floor out here."

"You don't think she heard, do you?"

Max strode ahead of her toward the kitchen. "For your sake you'd better hope not." He looked down at the mess of pottery and coffee in the sink, then at Jo. The glare he fixed on her had the desired effect.

"I'll just go get the gear from the car."

"You do that, and while you're working you'd better think of some explanation for Maggie."

Muttering, "And so had I, so had I," Max cleared the debris. He caught a reflection of Maggie's distress in the broken shards of pottery as he dumped them in the bin, and his stomach turned over. Two minutes after resolving Maggie's anxieties, he'd slapped her down again. However inadvertently. He was in two minds about whether to get Jo that sideways transfer. Out of his hair. Out of his personal affairs. She was a disaster waiting to happen. Not only had she put their friendship on the skids, she'd practically decimated any chance of Maggie ever speaking to her again.

If only he could wind back time to the moment he'd wakened with Maggie in his arms. If only everything could be that simple. Man plus woman equals sex. No, more than sex. It had been every cliché ever written. Two sides of a coin…like two halves of a whole…like coming home. It had been all that and more. The earth had definitely moved for him, and if he had his way, before they were done they'd have the planet spinning off its axis.

And if it didn't?

He'd have only himself to blame.

There was no doubt in his mind Maggie was the woman for him. And if he could move the peripherals out of the way, like murderers and red scarves…

He'd been acting like a grade A imbecile from the moment he'd laid eyes on the scarf. It had thrown him for a loop to see it hanging there.

Suddenly, all bets were off!

No wonder Maggie had hightailed it out of here after catching Jo slinging off at her, and he was no better. Poor Maggie, being on the receiving end of the parcel of mixed signals he'd been sending, like bad cop, good cop all rolled up in one nasty little package. There was no denying the panic attack was due to him.

She'd fooled him with her stoic attitude, blinded him with her smiles. It turned out his well-armored little armadillo had an inside of gooey marshmallow. What he had to do now was find the weak spot in her armor, heat things up and start melting her.

Easier said than done. But nothing worth having ever came easy.

A big fat worm of remorse squirmed inside him, eating at his gut. He left the house with Maggie's words from the night before ringing in his ears. *We've known each other such a short while, but long enough to know you wouldn't deliberately let me down. I trust you. No matter what.*

The police had been hanging around the place for the last two days, turning over every blade of grass and sifting every speck of gravel. At last they were packing up. Did that mean Max would leave, too?

She'd hardly spoken to either Jo or Max since she'd overheard them talking about her. They were two of a kind, cops through and through, and she wished she could say Jo was welcome to him.

Her own ambivalence was tearing her apart. She was in two minds over what to do about Max. One of them said wipe the slate clean and forget him. The other couldn't bear to part with memories that could never be repeated with anyone but him. Bittersweet memories. Hers nonetheless.

She'd worked on it, worked on building a wall around her feelings, but it would take only a whisper, not a trumpet blast, to send her defenses tumbling.

Someone knocked at her office door, and she turned. "Come in."

Rowan McQuaid's head and shoulders peeked around the door followed by the rest of him. "Morning, Ms. Kovacs." He took his cap off, tucked it under his arm and strode across to her.

"Maggie," she corrected, and smiled. "What can I do for you, Sergeant?"

"I've just come to say goodbye. All the donkey work's done and the door-to-door canvassing is finished. Make that farm-to-farm. Man, it's lonely out here."

"You get used to it."

"Anyhow, I'm taking my team back to Auckland. The local police will finish off. I'd like to thank you for the use of your facilities. You've been very kind, considering."

Maggie didn't know how to answer that. She should have realized the tense atmosphere between her and Max would start rumors flying. "I only hope your work pays off."

"No more than Max does. He's been putting in more time than any of us and hassling anyone he thinks is loafing. In fact, he's been spitting fire from the moment we arrived." He held out his hand to shake hers.

"Thanks for the warning. I'll keep out of his way."

"If you don't mind my saying so, Maggie, I think that's part of his problem." He let go of her hand and put his cap back on.

Rowan reached the door, then turned, and spoke again. "One other thing. About you and Jo. I don't know what went on between you two, but I do know that she's hurting, and sorry. If you could see your way clear to giving her a break, I'd be grateful."

My God, he's in love with her, she thought, seeing the pain in his eyes. Why didn't he just tell Jo and save them all a lot of trouble?

"Don't take it to heart, Rowan. Jo and I have been through enough to know that this situation will be resolved eventually."

"Thanks, Maggie, and goodbye. I only wish we'd met under better circumstances."

The office expanded to its normal size after he left it. Like Max, he took up a lot of space. Mulling over what Rowan had told her, Maggie knew she'd been avoiding Max. Even in passing, when meeting was inescapable, their exchanges had been brief, to the point of nonexistence. Their eye contact had been the most telling. Each time, there'd been a plea for understanding in his gaze, but she'd refused to meet it, letting hers slide past him to focus on the horizon. No, next time he came asking for forgiveness he'd better be doing it from his knees. She used to be a quick learner. How many knockdowns did it take? How many chances did he want?

She could be strong. All she had to do was keep Max at a distance.

Her phone rang and she picked it up and listened. "Thanks, Gwen, send him through." This might be just the thing to brighten her day. Someone had applied for the gardener's job.

She pulled out the folder containing the details she'd taken over the phone, not lifting her eyes until she heard the door open.

The first thing she noticed was his shoes, in particular the gleam on them. This was a gardener? she mused. About six foot tall and medium build, he wore jeans, and a denim shirt with a tie. "Well, Mr. Armstrong, I see here you're ex-army."

Standing at attention until she gestured for him to sit in the chair before her desk. "Yes, Special Air Service," he replied.

Trying to keep the smile out of her voice, Maggie said, "I didn't know there was much call for gardeners in the SAS."

"That's correct. I was a gardener before I signed up and I've been doing odd jobs since I came out, but nothing I could get my teeth into. Not like this place. An old aunt died and left me her house in Warkworth, and then I heard you were looking for a gardener, and since I grew up in the area, I knew it was meant for me."

A mustache wriggled like a caterpillar on his top lip, and she found she had to fix her gaze on something else to keep from staring. Instead, she focused on the way his scalp shone through the short bristles of gray hair. Compared to Gordon, he looked well out of his milieu.

A frown furrowed Maggie's brow. "Did the agency show you the plans I've had drawn up and do you feel you could cope with a job of that magnitude within the time frame?"

"Positive, provided I can call in contractors to do the heavy work, like earth moving and building the structures." Stretching his arms in front of him, he laced his fingers together and cracked his knuckles.

The noise made her shudder, but she let the action slide past her and latched on to a new subject. "Thank goodness you won't have to travel far. Gordon, the man you're replacing, lived nearby, and the only other house we have on the property is already occupied by the wine maker. You have use of facilities for growing plants, though. Both glass and shade houses."

"Things have certainly changed. I remember the old house being the family's."

Maggie sighed, trying not to let her impatience show. She

wasn't in the mood for reminiscing. She had too many other things on her mind, with Max topping the list.

"You must have been out of the district for a while. My father built this house quite some years ago. Now, is there anything else you want to ask me?"

"You're certain these plans are what you want? Some of these plantings can grow into an untidy sprawl."

"The plans have received my full approval. I want the ambience to remain relaxed, with nothing regimented. Think Italy instead of army," she said firmly.

His narrow nose flared. "You're the boss, Ms. Kovacs. Everything will be exactly as laid out in the plans."

"Thank you, Mr. Armstrong... That seems a bit formal. Do you mind if I call you Edward? We're all friends around here," she said, believing it to be true, though she sensed a pall of loneliness cloaking this man.

"Make it Ed."

"Well, Ed. When do you think you can start?"

"Would tomorrow be okay?"

"Perfect. I'll expect you around seven." She held out her hand, willing him to leave as he got up. But he didn't seem to notice, just let his gaze wander around her office.

"Yes, things have certainly changed from the old days. I used to work here, you know. I didn't say so before, didn't want to influence your decision in any way."

What decision? thought Maggie. It wasn't as if she'd been overwhelmed by applicants. "I'm afraid I don't remember you."

"No, you wouldn't. You were just a toddler running around, and your brother would have been about six."

"You knew my brother?" Maggie's business demeanor dropped away and excitement took its place.

"Yes, and your mother and father."

"My mother, too? Oh, please..." she squeaked, as her throat tightened up with emotion. Suddenly, she felt less eager to see him leave. "When you have some time will you tell me about them? I don't remember them, you see, I was so young when they died. Only about sixteen months.'' What a bonus, she thought. Her father had never wanted to talk about either of them, he'd grieved for such a long time.

His eyes flickered slightly in surprise. ''They're dead? I never heard that. I did wonder why you had taken over the winery instead of your brother. He was a precocious kid. Even at that age he would strut around saying how this would all be his one day. Used to tell his mother on you if he thought you'd done something wrong. Well, well, well, dead eh?'' Something in his expression said he didn't mind speaking ill of the dead.

''It was a car crash in Australia. I guess I was lucky being left with my father. I might have been killed as well. If you don't mind me—''

A knock sounded and interrupted her line of thought. She couldn't remember when she'd last had so much traffic through her office. She looked up, and Steven had already entered. Her eyebrows raised, questioning his abrupt appearance. For a change he didn't look like a happy camper—in fact, ballistic might be more apt. She cut him off before he turned her spiel about them all being friends at the winery into a lie.

''Steven, this is Ed Armstrong. He's going to take over from Gordon.''

The wine maker stopped in his tracks. ''Thank heavens something's going right around here.'' He held out his hand and said, ''Steven Dexter, wine maker.''

She knew he'd been chagrined at having to stay out of the bottling plant, as his lab was at the far end. She watched the men shake hands, and as Ed's cuff slid up his arm she noticed a tattoo of a knife with wings inside his wrist. It struck her as odd that such a fastidious man would disfigure his skin, though it was probably a battalion or corps insignia.

''You're the one who lives in the old homestead?'' Ed asked.

Maggie could see Steven wondering why he'd been under discussion. So she explained, "Ed used to work here when I was a child. He knew my mother and brother when we all lived in the original house."

"Did he now," Steven said quietly. "That's interesting. Look, Maggie, I have to get on. The police have packed up and I can get back into my lab. It may take days to catch up. The shiraz will have to be checked as well to see if it has been adulterated." He turned to Ed. "Maggie got in the way of someone tampering with the wine the other night. The place has been swarming with police ever since and I haven't been able to do any work."

"It's been tough on us all, Steven, but they've gone now and things will get back to normal." She turned a smile on both men and watched the younger one leave.

"Steven is as passionate about his wine making as if this place belonged to him. However, what's good for the wine is good for the winery. I'll catch up with you tomorrow, Ed."

She had two hours to herself before Max appeared.

He didn't knock, just marched straight in and said, "You and I have got to talk." Then he collapsed into the chair Ed Armstrong had occupied, as if he had every intention of becoming a permanent fixture.

Maggie stood up and looked him up and down, starting from the silver streak of hair falling on his brow, touching on the breadth of his shoulders and sliding down the long, lean length of his thighs. He'd crossed his ankles and his elbows rested on the wooden arms of the chair. "Would talking serve any purpose?" she asked, even as she noticed how tired he looked. How the shadowed creases under his eyes did nothing to dull his sex appeal. Drat it! Staying away from Max was like one of those New Year's resolutions she never kept.

The last thing she wanted was to be a fool for this man, but the tension crackled whenever he came near.

She was only human.

And vulnerable, in the heat from those true blue eyes.

The reflection of the dark mauve sweater she wore turned her eyes purple, like pansies. The kind his grandma used to grow in pots on her veranda. Man, he was beat. So beat, all he could think of when he looked in her eyes was going to bed and taking Maggie with him.

"I think talking would help. It's certainly a big advance on not talking. You've avoided me long enough. I'm tired of it, and I'm tired of you turning your back on me as soon as I get within spitting distance. Hell, I know I don't come out of this smelling of roses, but I'm prepared to take my licks. Although admitting that doesn't turn you into a shining angel.

"I don't know how much you heard, but it couldn't have been all, otherwise you wouldn't have gone running off like you'd just been whipped. Why didn't you wait around to hear me take your side? If you'd shown some of the spirit I know you've got, you'd have come right in and stuck up for yourself." He didn't remember standing up, yet he was facing her over the desk. He only knew he could smell her, breathe her in till she filled his head and everything else disappeared. But it wasn't enough. Leaping over the desk would look plain foolish. So he took the easy way out and started to walk around it even if it took longer than he wanted to reach his goal.

Maggie.

"So you wanted to see us fighting over you." she said. "Sorry, I don't do cat fights." Her statement stopped him in his tracks.

"You have a wicked edge to your tongue, sweetheart. I could put it to much better use. As for Jo, the woman is getting to be a thorn in my side. She's a good cop, but that's where it ends." He moved closer, rounding the desk till they were both on the same side. He sat on the edge with Maggie trapped between him and her chair.

"I don't want you fighting over me—fighting *for* me is another story." In a rough voice, like whiskey over gravel, he forced out, "I'd fight for you." His fingers rounded the curve of her cheek. "I'd fight for you—I *am* fighting for you." His voice lowered another couple of notches. His heart pounded in his throat from touching her. Everything inside him, all that he was, threatened to spill over and un-man him. "I want you back in my life, Maggie. Back in my arms. Back in my bed. The last two days have been one big long pain in the gut without you."

Maggie made a small sound, almost a sob at the back of her throat, and her chest rose and fell sharply. Her eyes were huge in her face, softening and blurring like pansies in the rain.

He could see his reflection in them. A fierce, possessive wave ripped through him and tore at his heart. The thought of some other man's reflection in her eyes grounded him in the present. In what he had to do: win her back.

His hand shook as it left her face and touched the bruises showing at the neckline of her blouse. He wanted to hold her close and kiss them better.

He moved closer, whispered in her ear, "If you'd have stayed, you would have heard me tell Jo how wrong her assumptions were. She knew it herself. All she needed was to be shown how ridiculous she sounded. Jo has to learn to keep her emotions and her job separate. So do I. And every time I succeed at it, I do more harm than good. To you and me, that is." He could feel Maggie quivering like a deer mesmerized by headlights, wondering whether to run or stay.

"I missed you last night, and the one before." He tilted her chin, holding it with one finger, slowly moving her lips closer to his.

Maggie blinked, fluttered her eyelashes, but her gaze kept darting away from his. "You had Jo. She stayed at the same motel the last two nights."

"I don't want Jo. I didn't stay at the motel. I slept on the couch in the games room. Damned uncomfortable it was, too."

That made her look at him.

"I even used the shower. I hope you don't mind." Her lips were only a breath away. He caught the clean, minty flavor of toothpaste. "It wasn't as nice as the one off your room—that shower's my favorite. Lots of room for two. In fact, I think I feel a shower coming on. I need one. I'm getting hot and sweaty."

He brushed his lips over her soft velvet mouth as he pulled her into his arms and deepened the kiss. It was everything he remembered. He'd become addicted to her taste, the feel of her in his arms and the sweet, sexy sounds emitting from her throat as she let go of her inhibitions.

She stepped into the space between his legs and he drew her closer, splaying one hand over the lush roundness of her hip, cupping it. "And I'm getting hard, Maggie, so hard, and being inside you is the only cure." He thrust the almighty ache in his groin toward her and her hips flexed in welcome. The softness of her belly felt good, damn good, but it wasn't enough. He needed to be inside her, to feel her muscles circle him and soothe away the pain. "I've been hurting real bad for two days now. D'you wanna play doctor and nurse with me?"

Maggie rubbed her cheek against the new growth of stubble in the curve of his neck and chin. She was falling again, hook, line and sinker. Gullibility or love, it didn't make much difference. Being near this man showed her she was alive. One touch and her heart raced. One kiss and her blood sang "It had to be you" in her veins. She planted kisses under his chin and felt his carotid pulse leap and dance to the same tune.

"Do you want me to kiss you better?" she asked as her hand slid between them and rubbed his hard male length. Only a zipper lay between her and what they both wanted.

His answer erupted in her ear as a long, low growl. "I don't just want you to kiss me better, I want you to love me better."

Her fingers clenched around him and she felt his reaction ripple through his chest as he crushed her against it.

Max pulled at the tail of her silk blouse until he'd released it from her waistband. "I have to touch you," he whispered against her face, his mouth racing over her skin, eating her up like wildfire as if he couldn't get enough of her, couldn't taste enough of her. "Let me touch you—touch me. Please, Maggie, touch me."

She felt the brush of cool air against her skin, then his hands left a trail of fire as they sped over her back and up to her breasts. He cupped and massaged their fullness till she could swear every flower and leaf of her lacey bra had left its imprint on them as they swelled and peaked under his ministrations.

Her fingers slid under the placket of his zipper and reached for the tab, fumbling once, then latching on the second time as she slid it down over his quickening male flesh. She could feel the heat of him through the thin cotton covering as she searched for the second opening.

"My belt. Get my belt," he panted as her bra parted.

She found his buckle stiff to undo, and her haste didn't help.

"Here, let me get it," he said, when she wasn't fast enough.

Someone knocked on the door.

They looked at each other, startled.

"Who is it?" called Maggie, while Max let go of his buckle and fastened his zipper, moving back toward the chair. "This place has been like Grand Central this morning," she hissed under her breath, trying to tuck in her shirt. As it was, she only caught the tail in her waistband, and pulled her sweater over the lot. Her bra would have to wait.

"It's Carla, dear. Can I come in?"

Maggie got out of her chair and hurried to the door, flashing a glance at Max as she went to make sure he was decent. He'd feigned being relaxed, with one leg over his knee and a finger hooking his pocket to keep his jacket in place. She nodded to confirm that he looked respectable, and opened the door.

"Carla, this is an unexpected pleasure. I don't see you for almost a year and now twice in one week. Come in, come in. I'll get you a seat." Maggie pulled another chair over. "You remember Max, don't you?"

"I certainly do. You never told me he was a detective,

though. I had to read that in the paper.'' The look she gave
Max was telling. ''I didn't expect to find you here, Sergeant.
Isn't this out of your area?''

''What brings you all this way?'' Maggie asked, without
giving Max a chance to answer. ''I didn't think you liked
driving outside the city limits.''

''Needs must, my dear. I read that piece in the paper about
you helping Sergeant Strachan. I was surprised, as though you
hadn't suffered enough…'' she cast a scathing glance Max's
way, her dark eyes flashing from Maggie to him and back
again, ''…at the hands of the police.''

Maggie watched Max sit up in his chair, his brow furrowed.
''Oh, Max is more than a policeman, Carla. We're friends,
aren't we, Max?'' she asked, demanding his agreement.

''Sure,'' he drawled, ''if that's what you want to call it.''

Trust him to get in a snit now when she wanted a little
cooperation. So what if he was frustrated—he wasn't on his
own there!

''Is that why you agreed to help him?''

''Actually, I went to Max and offered my help, not the other
way around.''

His eyebrows lifted, but there was no rancor in his eyes.
''That's exactly how it went down,'' he said in a good imi-
tation of a tough TV cop.

Maggie felt exasperated. The brute was being no help at all.
''We met through my friend, Jo Jellic. Do you remember her?
We were at school together and she works in Auckland now.''
Talk about running off at the mouth. ''With Max,'' she fin-
ished.

Max just threw them both a bland smile.

That was it! She'd had enough of his nonsense. See how
he liked her really setting Carla onto him? ''Anyway, you
should know, Carla, being practically the only family I have,
Max and I are lovers.''

Max's eyes narrowed slightly, glinting a warning flash of

blue-steel, tempered by the roughness of his voice as he said, ''More than just lovers.''

It just went to show, some days a girl couldn't win. Max was on to her game, and he had decided he wanted to play, as well. His gaze softened as he continued to look at her. Suddenly the stakes had changed, and she saw something in his eyes that made her chest expand as if something wonderful had blossomed inside it.

''Well,'' he said on a sigh, ''I'm glad you finally made it official.'' He glanced at Carla, still grinning. ''You're only the second person to know.''

''The second?'' Maggie inquired, puzzled.

''Jo. I told Jo.''

Maggie felt a feeling of peace wash over her and let her happiness show. ''You did? You told Jo? I'm *really* delighted about that.''

Carla was forgotten as they stared at each other. ''If it has this effect on you, maybe I should take out a full page ad?''

Maggie just giggled, ''But not in the *Tribune*.''

''No, definitely not the *Tribune*.''

''Oh, you two remind me of when I first met Maggie's father. Did you ever meet him, Max?'' said Carla, twisting around in her chair to face him.

''No, I'm sorry to say I never did.'' He glanced over at Maggie and his eyes showed he meant every word.

''Frank Kovacs was a wonderful man. So handsome. Maggie looks just like him, only more feminine and dainty.''

Maggie smiled to herself at that. At five-ten she was never referred to as dainty. But then, her father had been a big strong man, not quite as large as Max, though. She let her gaze trail over him, mesmerized. All sound of Carla's describing her father faded. She could still hear Max's rumbled reply, because she was focused in on him. She'd never felt this indescribably joyous bliss before, like her feet didn't touch the ground. Until she'd met Max, she hadn't known what she'd been missing.

The conversation floated around her without her picking up on anything, until Max said, "I wish I had met him, Carla. He sounds like a good man. I'm glad Maggie had a father like him to make up for not having a mother." His gaze snagged Maggie's, then he turned back to Carla and asked, "Do you think he would have approved of Maggie and me?" he said seriously.

Yet there was something else in his voice. Something that made her feel as if she'd fallen through a hole in the ozone layer. Maggie felt hot and cold at the same time. A slash of heat burned her cheeks, yet her hands were freezing. Never once had she imagined her relationship with Max being anything more than lovers.

The timbre of his voice still echoed through her. *Maggie and me…and me…and me.* What were these feelings tumbling around inside her? It wasn't what she wanted. Her future was all mapped out. Kereru Hill Winery would be the best in the Southern Hemisphere and everyone would know her father hadn't been cheated by having a daughter in charge, instead of a son.

Maggie's nails stabbed into her palms and grounded her in reality. It was just a joke, after all. The only one not in on it was Carla.

Overcome by embarrassment at her original take on his words, the bubble of hope she hadn't even known existed burst. Her gaze sought refuge in looking at the floor. Her eyes felt fluid, ready to spill over with the agony of what might have been, had he not been teasing her, and leading Carla on.

Presumably Carla was happy to be led. She had immediately pounced on the subtext in Max's statement that had caused Maggie such bittersweet angst.

"Oh, Maggie! You never let on. Fancy not telling me." Carla jumped up and kissed her. "I'm delighted for you, my dear." Then, before Max could duck, she took his face in her hands and planted a kiss on him.

Carla sat down in her seat again, happily smiling about a

situation that was rapidly getting out of hand. "I'm so glad I made the effort to drive up here today, with news like this waiting for me. When will you announce it?"

Maggie felt stunned. Had Max thought that far ahead when he'd made his rash announcement?

Too dazed to answer, Maggie glanced at Max, panic written all over her face. Had he thought this far ahead when he'd rashly made what was almost a statement of intent?

Obviously meaning to reassure Maggie, Max answered for her. "Not until I've closed this case, but I've a feeling that won't be long now."

But Carla wasn't to be put off. Practically jumping up and down in her chair, she demanded, "You must let me arrange everything. Please. Maggie, may I act as mother of the bride? Let me give you this wedding. It would make me so happy to do this for Frank's daughter."

She started to weep openly, and let the tears run down her face, oblivious of her perennially immaculate makeup. "I loved your father so much, and there is nothing more I can do for him now, except make sure his daughter gets married in the style she deserves. The manner he would have wanted." She looked from one to the other. "Please, it would give me such great pleasure."

Max looked at Maggie, who, though her stomach churned, forced a smile, nodded, and left the decision up to him.

"What more can we say but thank you, Carla? I'll be delighted to have you as a mother-in-law. I don't understand, though. If you and Frank loved each other so much, why did you never marry?"

Carla's tears dried up and her face became serious. "I see I was wrong. There is one more thing I can do for Frank." She sat back in her chair, cloaked in a stillness that conveyed the import of what she was about to say.

Maggie reached for her pen, but before she could begin

twisting it in her fingers, she felt Max stand behind her and place his hand on her shoulder; the pen fell onto the desk.

"Your father and I never married because, being the good Catholic he was, he never divorced your mother."

Chapter 10

"Divorced!" Maggie came back to earth with a thump as the meaning of Carla's words sunk in. If her father needed a divorce to remarry, then her mother must still be alive. She felt herself shake. Her lips trembled as she hovered on the verge of tears. In less than a moment Max had her out of her chair and into his arms, holding her close.

She let his strength steal over her, and used it as a shield against the bombshell Carla had dropped, and the firestorm to come. She could face the world unafraid as long as she and Max were together.

As if he'd read her mind, he whispered, "Take it easy, sweetheart. I'm here. I've got you. Let's just listen to what Carla has to say. Maybe it won't be so bad." To Carla he said, "You'll have to understand, Maggie's been through a lot lately."

"I know. Gwen told me when I called yesterday. That's the reason I drove up here today. I wanted to help if I could."

From the shelter of Max's arms, Maggie found it easy to

say, "Go on, Carla, let's get it over with. Maybe it won't be as bad as it sounds."

"Maggie, I begged Frank to tell you this himself, but he kept putting it off. Too chicken, I guess. You'd never think it to look at him—he was a big man—but he'd backed himself into a corner and didn't know how to get out of it without spoiling your relationship. The last thing he wanted, baby, was to hurt you. Did you know he still used to call you that some-times? You were still his baby, his only child."

"But my brother. I had a brother." She clutched at the jacket beneath her hands, ignoring the roughness of the wool against her tender skin.

"Yes, you did. But your father never had a son." Her gaze sized both of them up from the other side of the desk. "I'd feel easier with you two sitting down while I...what is it they say on TV? Spill my guts?"

Carla's words added to the unreal atmosphere. For her to say such a thing was unheard of, this woman who'd always been as fastidious in speech as appearance.

"C'mon, sweetheart," Max said, hooking Maggie's chair and pulling it closer. "Sit on my lap, there's plenty of room."

She sank onto his knee. Wrapped in his warmth, she felt like the baby her father had still thought her. Only she wasn't. She was a woman fully grown and about to hear news of a family she'd thought lost to her forever.

This had to be the most important day of her life, and the most bizarre. Twice today she'd learned something of her mother and brother, and then Max's teasing had led her thoughts down paths she hadn't really wanted to tread. Now he was holding her, letting her know he was there for her. He was an unlikely angel, but surely, when you most needed help, God sent the one best suited to the job.

"Sometimes sticking to your principles is harder than giv-ing in and taking what you most want. Frank loved me and wanted to marry me, but he couldn't do it without revealing his deception. You were about twelve when your father and I met, a difficult enough age for a girl without a mother. And a long time for a man to go without a wife. Over ten years.

"It seems like a hundred of them since Frank first told me his story. I never knew your mother, so you'll have to excuse me if what I say seems biased in his favor.

"When your brother was six and you eighteen months, the boy had an accident, gashed an artery up here at the vineyard and lost a lot of blood. You remember what it was like then, with no motorway to Auckland the way there is now. The local G.P. patched him up, then raced him to Auckland Hospital.

"It turned out your brother had a rare blood type, AB negative or some such thing, and the hospital was short of that group. Frank demanded they take his. In fact, both your parents offered to donate blood, only as it turned out neither your mother nor father had a matching blood type. That's how your father discovered Ivan wasn't his son."

Maggie's brain fizzed as if some feral bees had followed their queen there. She couldn't take any of it in, nor string enough words together to form a question.

Max could. The cop in him could. "I can see that breaking up his marriage. The shock of it on top of the accident." He hugged Maggie closer, showing he knew it was no easier on her. "What I don't understand is why Maggie was told they had both died."

"When Frank discovered Stella had only chosen him as the father of her child because he owned the vineyard, and the other man in her life had nothing, Frank was devastated. Their marriage wasn't in the best shape, and I wish I could say having you helped them, Maggie, but your mother hadn't wanted any more children."

So that, too, was taken from her. Pain sliced through Maggie and shattered the picture she'd formed of a mother grieving for her child. Great chunks of her life crumbled away in front of her eyes, leaving her nothing to fill the gaps.

Carla rose from her chair and reached for Maggie's hand.

Squeezing her fingers, she said, "Remember, this isn't my story. I take no pleasure from putting Stella down. Not if it hurts you."

"It's okay, Carla. I know. You and I were simply bystanders in this debacle." None of them had found anything to applaud in the story, least of all Carla. Maggie felt sorry for her.

What was Max's take on this woman who'd cheated her husband and hadn't wanted her child? Did it make him see *her* differently? Most of the anger Maggie had felt against her father when he'd died needlessly came racing back. He'd done right by neither of them.

Once the older woman returned to her seat, the telling began again. Carla smiled, remembering. "It was love at first sight when I met your father. Later I learned about the baggage that came with him. Too late. I couldn't give him up. And it hurt him, too, that we couldn't marry. I wanted a family, you see, Frank's children. And I would have shunned convention and had a baby anyway, but Frank said no. It would raise too many questions.

"You came first, you see."

Maggie found it hard to see the truth in her statement. Were the years at boarding school "coming first"? Was him ignoring her gift?

"He worried that Stella might try to get you back just to spite him. She moved to Australia with your brother, and Frank made out they'd been killed in an accident over there and that's where they were buried. He supported her and told her it would stop if she tried to contact you, and he made her sign a waiver, stating that if anything should happen to him, she couldn't contest the will. As far as I know, she never tried. If she had, you would have known all this. Frank's lawyer would have contacted you by now.

"Eighteen months ago, something happened that upset Frank. That's why he went to Australia, not for a holiday."

"I thought it strange he hadn't taken you with him," Maggie stated. "But of course he wouldn't, if he was seeing my mother." She listened to herself speak, talking naturally about her mother as if she'd never thought she had died.

"He told Stella he'd start divorce proceedings as soon as he returned to New Zealand. The separation was official, so the divorce would have gone through quickly. I don't know if he'd informed his lawyer, though he said he wanted to break it to you before you found out from some other source."

"I never knew—he never even hinted. I remember saying his holiday hadn't done him much good. I wonder what happened to change his mind after all those years?"

She remembered how tired he'd looked. All the expansions at the winery had worn him out. When he'd mentioned taking a holiday, she'd urged him to go, saying she would pick up the slack.

"Frank could be pretty taciturn when he wanted, and he gave me only the bare details when he returned. It was just before he died. So he never had time to make his last confession, did he?" Carla began crying again. "You'll never know how often I've wanted to drive up here and tell you. I just never knew how to broach the subject, and ended up deciding it wasn't my place. But with you getting married I had to tell you. You had a right to know."

"Yes, I had a right, but it was my father who should have fulfilled it, Carla, not you, so don't blame yourself. I loved my father, but he could be bloody stubborn at times. Most of the time. Always thinking he knew best, especially when it came to my dreams."

"That was because of your great-grandmother, Frank's mother's mother. That's who you get your psychic gift from, though Frank never called it that. To him and his mother it was a curse that led to the death of his grandmother, in the old country before his mother came to New Zealand."

"It seems there was a lot my father didn't tell me."

"He wanted to protect you, but being a father doesn't make

one perfect. He was only a man and men have faults.'' She looked from Max to Maggie.

"Now you're going to be married, maybe you'll realize there are some things you can share with only one person. The person you love.''

Maggie felt Max's arms tighten their hold, but he didn't speak. "You're right, Carla. Sometimes there is only one.''

"At least I knew I was loved. At least I had that.'' Carla let out a long sigh. "All this emotion has taken it out of me. What I could really use now is a nap. Would you mind if I drove up to the house and put my feet up?''

A kind of stunned silence filled the office once Carla left. Neither of them moved from Maggie's chair. Her head was on Max's shoulder, but her mind was elsewhere. Both of them were preoccupied by their thoughts for different reasons. Hell, he'd just put them both in an untenable situation.

He'd all but proposed to Maggie, albeit a sideways gesture through Carla. Thank heavens Maggie wasn't the type to press home her advantage. He ought to be explaining his actions, making sure Maggie understood. Instead, the words were locked up tight inside him and wouldn't come out.

As he examined his motives, his fingers kneaded the knots in the nape of Maggie's neck above the bruising. Now they slid into her hair where it grew longer and silkier on top, and began massaging her scalp.

"Mmm, that feels good. A scalp massage is so relaxing.''

"I don't think Carla's the only one feeling tired. Maybe you should take a nap, too. It's been one drama after another. Your emotions must feel trampled.'' He kissed the spot between her eyebrows as she gave a tiny shrug. "D'you want to go home?''

"I don't want to move. How much weight do you reckon these chairs can take and for how long?'' she asked, then squirmed in his lap as his fingers hit the spot that ached. "You should take this up as a profession, Max. You have brilliant hands.'' She expelled air in a low whistle of release. ''Then again, maybe not. I wouldn't want to share.''

''If I took you home, I could demonstrate how good I can be. How about a head-to-toe massage?'' Just picturing Maggie lying naked on her bed made him hard again. ''Then again, maybe not. I'd forget about the massage and start making love to you.''

''I'd enjoy that—we both would—and you know the reason why? I'm glad we're on speaking terms again. I've missed you.'' Her fingers splayed over his chest and a couple poked through an opening in his shirt and stroked the hair. ''Max? We can't go on sidestepping this issue forever. You know we need to talk.''

Max dropped his hand to her nape again and circled his finger and thumb in the hollows where her neck met her skull. ''Where do you want to start?'' The circles got smaller and slower as he waited for her reply.

''What are we going to tell Carla—about us not getting married?'' she asked. ''How long should we wait, before telling her we've changed our minds?''

The words were still there, inside him, tangled up in a heap of junk he was carrying, like murder and mayhem. He ran his other hand though his own hair, exasperated with his own shortcomings. ''Don't worry. When the time comes, I'll tell her the truth, but not yet. Right now, I've got Arnolds being held for possession and assault with enough physical evidence to prove he's the Khyber Pass creep and he's got no alibi, yet I'm not happy. Don't ask me why.''

''Okay.''

''Okay what?''

''I won't ask you why.''

Suddenly he wanted to look at her straight on. Swiveling in the chair, he stood up, sat her down on the desk and took a step back.

Maggie appeared unfazed by the sudden about-face. ''You've changed your mind. You do want me to ask you?''

"Yeah, do you mind being used as a sounding board?" He examined her features minutely. Was she upset at how quickly he'd changed gears from discussing how to tell Clara there wasn't going to be any marriage into the mystery that bugged him? He was a selfish oaf to do this with her mind full of family business. Dark smudges lined her eyes, smudging that hadn't been there earlier, when they'd almost made love.

Maggie wryly laughed. "Why should I mind? At least you asked. People have been popping into my head for years and using me as a sounding board without so much as a by-your-leave." She dismissed his equivocation with an elegant wave of her hand.

He could see her palm had begun to heal, yet there were patches that still looked raw and sore. The memory of how they'd happened would never leave him. Which brought him back to his uneasy feelings. "Tell me why I'm unhappy about the whole deal."

"Well, for starters—what happened to me. Arnolds couldn't have been the man who attacked me. He was locked up. Secondly, who knew about the red scarf?" She stared at him, her eyebrows arched question marks, but when he said nothing, Maggie continued to speculate. "What about an accomplice? One who could have attacked me to put you off the scent and give Arnolds an out?"

"Good point. We can do another search into his particular friends, find out where they were on Saturday night."

"Then there's the point that the women I dreamed about died from having their necks broken, not strangulation."

"Which leads us to think it was either an accomplice who couldn't reach you under the winepress and decided to make use of the scarf, or it really was our killer and he had the same problem." Max checked Maggie's face for any signs of the panic she'd experienced two days ago, but she appeared comfortable, more interested in helping solve the mystery than reliving being attacked.

"The second scenario leaving Arnolds as an innocent party?"

"That's what worries me, Maggie, though we can't rule out the coincidence factor. But *two* guys using red scarves? It's a bizarre thought."

"There's also a possibility the killer set your resident suspect up by leaving that button in the shoe. He could have cut it off Arnolds's jacket. You'd reckon after all the trouble he's taken to leave no tracks, dropping something so obvious seems out of character."

"You're right, it *was* obvious."

"And you're unhappy because, in the end, it all came too easily."

Maggie stopped for a moment. She had the heels of her hands on the desk and gripped it as she leaned toward him. Her hair spun out in a gleaming, black silk circle when she shook her head, as if clearing her thoughts. The scent of her hair came straight at him and he wanted her.

Right here. Right now.

He wanted to be inside her instead of using her concise mind to help clarify his own thoughts. It took him a minute to refocus.

"The other thing nagging you is the *Tribune*. Did the killer come after me because of all the garbage Babcox wrote? All his inane hype about you consulting me to get to the killer could have him scared that I will identify him."

"Are you reading my mind?" He softened the question with a grin, not giving away the knowledge that his own reconciliation with her psychic talents wasn't a given. Oh, he'd stopped denying it existed, he just hadn't gotten real comfortable with it yet. You might say it had him spooked, but he wouldn't tell Maggie that.

"No, I'm not. Don't worry. I've left all my parlor tricks in my other suit. Speaking of which—" Maggie wrinkled her nose and fidgeted uncomfortably "—do you remember me saying all my other dreams were of people I know?"

''I remember. You also said you didn't know any of the victims. That leaves only the killer. You want me to check out *all* your acquaintances?''

''No, I don't. I just think you might not have a choice. Do you think you can float the idea past the powers that be? D.I. Henare is going to want you back in Auckland soon.''

''For starters, we could look into people around here. Easier access to the property. It would look like part of our ongoing investigation into your attacker. But we could probe deeper. Any of your friends collect dolls?''

Maggie shook her head. ''Who do you mean by 'we'? You and Jo?''

''No, I'm talking about you and me. You're the obvious choice, Maggie. You know the area. Besides, the budget won't stretch to keeping Jo up here. She can start checking out Arnolds's friends.''

''It all boils down to money, doesn't it?''

''Every time,'' he drawled, but his thoughts suddenly darted in another direction. ''Tell me, Maggie, did your father leave a will naming you as his heir?'' He'd just found something else to worry about, but he wouldn't tell Maggie yet. She had enough on her plate.

''Yes, he did.'' Her eyes widened in surprise when he changed tack. ''Why, do you think I owe my mother and brother something?''

''No, I just wondered whether he'd left a will or died intestate. As for your mother and brother, from what Carla says, they did all right out of your father. But if you like, I can make some inquiries. I know a cop in Sydney who owes me a favor. It would be no problem and they'd never know they'd been checked out.''

Maggie shut her eyes for a long, drawn-out second.

If she didn't agree, then he would go ahead on his own, Max decided. He had a sudden urge to know more about Ivan Kovacs. ''What do you say—will I go ahead with it? It can't hurt.''

"Okay. I ought to do something now I know they're alive. They probably don't want to know me, though. I mean, my father's been dead fifteen months, and neither of them has tried to contact me."

"Yeah, they have to know he's dead. Otherwise the money would have dried up. Maybe your father left her an annuity. You should check with a lawyer." Though somehow Max doubted that was true. If he could rid himself of these qualms that Arnolds might not be the KPK, then he could concentrate on Frank Kovacs's accident, for Maggie's take on her father's death was starting to make perfect sense. He stepped closer to her and put his hands on her shoulders. "Let's go on up to the house and see how Carla's doing. After all that thinking I need some brain food," he teased, giving her a quick kiss on her open mouth as she started to speak.

"Why you—"

"Gotcha!" Max kissed her again, slanting his mouth across hers to give him better access to the taste he couldn't get enough of. Her eyes looked soft and dreamy, maybe it was only his imagination, but the bruised circles underneath them seemed to have faded. "Let's get out of here before we get carried away again. There are too many people around, and if Carla is still asleep, I might find time to make love to you." Max planted another kiss on her mouth. "But not until we've eaten."

"Oh, Max I—I " Maggie's dark, pansy eyes were huge in her face. He'd confounded her again.

Hell! He'd confounded himself. It was becoming a habit, but she was so easy to tease, and so easy to…

He placed a finger across her lips. "We've been serious long enough. I want you someplace where we can make love without interruption. First we'll go home, see to Carla and send Jo back to Auckland," he said, punctuating his words with yet another kiss. "Although I think you should make time to hear her apology before she goes."

"She might not want to apologize. She might think she was right."

Believe me, he thought, if she knows what's good for her, she'll want to apologize. "She knows she was wrong, but we won't let it ruin what's left of today. There's only so much a person can take," he told her, fitting his arm around her shoulders as they walked to the door.

"Yeah. Carla already did a job on it."

"Only a part of it, not all. Just wait. You'll see." There was one more question he needed to ask before he called his friend in Sydney. "Tell me, Maggie, have *you* made a will?"

The bed yielded comfortably to her weight, and she'd drawn the curtains to shut out the light, leaving a shady green haze.

She still couldn't sleep.

Max had insisted she rest while he dispatched Jo and most of the equipment from the games room. A lot of the notes he wanted to hang on to.

To think that all the time she'd imagined him at the motel with Jo, he'd been sleeping downstairs.

Soon he'd come upstairs to her bedroom.

Maybe that's why sleep evaded her.

Anticipation.

To be able to feel him under her hands at last, to discover how the planes and angles of shoulder and chest fit together, to stroke the long, lean strength of his arms and feel the play of muscle under his skin... She had a need to explore his intriguing wedge of chest hair and test the crispness of the curls. She wanted to discover everything her damaged hands had so far denied her. She wanted to savor all his contrasting textures, the smooth and the rough, and she wanted it at the first opportunity.

Max would show her how much he wanted her and she would return the favor. It would be enough.

For now.

They'd set all talk of marriage aside and she was happy

with that. For one moment, before she'd realized her error, she'd felt Max had handed her the moon. But now…now she'd found she had a mother and a brother, and was glad she'd been mistaken.

Which part of her makeup came from her mother?

And what of the old saying "blood will out"?

Maggie hoped not.

In her heart, she'd found no empathy with a woman who could foist another man's child onto her husband. Her mother couldn't have been certain who'd fathered her brother, but neither had she cared to find out. Her father had owned the vineyard and therein lay the difference.

The winery hadn't been as expansive back then. Frank Kovacs had taken over from his own father, who'd stuck mainly to the fortified varieties of wine. Selling them mostly in half-gallon jars.

Frank Kovacs had changed all that by dumping the old vines along with their family name, the one they'd brought from Dalmatia. Kovaleski had been anglicized for the sake of the business.

Her grandmother hadn't lived to see it; she'd never liked New Zealand and pined for the old country till the day she died. And without Nadia, his wife, her grandfather hadn't cared to live.

It had always puzzled Maggie where her father's ambition had come from, but on reflection, her grandfather, Matte, had risen from a deprived childhood, where his father grafted in the gum fields, to growing grapes. An upward leap that he'd topped by wedding Nadia, a woman he'd never met, in a marriage arranged by their parents.

He'd loved her just the same.

And she'd loved her homeland.

What terrible thing had happened to the great-grandmother Maggie had inherited her gift from? Had *she* seen her own death?

Questions, questions, questions.

And no answers.

At last Maggie fell asleep, but without the aid of pleasant thoughts to cushion her way.

Asleep. At least one of them would be rested. There was a kink in his back from lying on too short a couch. A small price to pay for making sure Maggie didn't sleep in the house alone.

He loosened the knot in his tie, slipped it over his neck and tossed it on the chair where he'd already dropped his jacket. His shoes came next, and as he pushed them under the bed on his side and unfastened his belt, he laughed softly at the thought that he was the guy who could leave his shoes under her bed. Anytime.

Maggie was lying on top of the spread, covered with an old patchwork quilt. He liked it. Among all the sleek designer perfection of this elegant bedroom, it looked homey.

Lifting the quilt gently so as not to waken Maggie, he slid in behind her.

As soon as his arm went around her she rolled to face him. "Max?"

"Were you expecting someone else?" he teased.

She frowned, her face crumpling like a baby who doesn't want to be woken.

"Joke," he said. "Just a joke."

"Sorry, I'd been thinking about my mother before I fell asleep. I can't understand how she could have done that to Dad."

"Unfortunately, she's not the first and she won't be the last. You'd be amazed how much of it there is around. There's this one guy I knew... No. I'm not here to talk of other people, just us."

He pulled her closer, saying, "There's something I have to tell you." He tilted her chin, "Look at me." Max brushed his lips across hers, once, twice, three times.

"Maggie Kovacs, I find you a wonder. An absolute wonder. So don't lie here, stewing over your mother. There is no comparison." He punctuated his words with soft kisses, and on the last one her mouth opened and met his as a great outpouring of yearning and desire passed from her to him in a torrent of passionate avowal. There was a honeyed sweetness to the kiss as her mouth flowered and her tongue chased his, urging him to respond.

His chest swelled and his muscles tensed. He felt as though he could go fight giants, slay dragons. Whatever Maggie needed to set her life to rights, it was hers from that moment on. He felt a sudden spike of sympathy for the courtly knights of old, burning with ardor under all that armor plating.

Her lips moved against his. She was speaking without breaking the kiss.

He pulled away. "Sorry, sweetheart, I can't hear you." Even the dim lighting in the room couldn't conceal her heightened color.

"I said thank you. Thank you for knowing how I felt." Her hands moved to his face and her fingers began to explore his features as if committing them to memory. They traced his lips, his cheekbones, his brow, and stopped to linger tenderly on the scar scoring his forehead.

Max loved the feel of her hands on him, but as she touched his scar a wave of déjà vu flooded over him. Was Maggie strong enough to live with a relationship that included his job? Did she even need to?

"Now that my hands are healing, I mean to touch as much of you as I can, and make up for lost time." She ran her lips over his scar and curled a twist of the silver hair above it around her finger. "How did you do this?"

"Just lucky, I guess," he replied, and shrugged. Damn, he was sidestepping important issues. If this relationship was going to last, he needed to be honest. "Nah, it's a long story, but I'll cut it short since I don't come out of it too well. I thought I could handle things on my own, before the Armed Offenders Squad arrived, and talk some guy into giving himself up. It didn't work. On the upside, I managed to throw myself back as I saw the curtains move.''

Maggie's hands clenched around his face. "He shot you!"

"Hey, hey. I'm here. The bullet only creased me."

Maggie's fingers went back to smoothing instead of clinging. He'd never been petted before. It felt great. Yeah, he could put up with this on a regular basis. Like every night.

"He might have killed you."

"What, with my hard head? Not a chance," he answered, brushing it off.

Maggie didn't get the joke. Her bottom lip trembled and her eyes shone like dark, liquid stars in the dim light.

"Seriously, sweetheart, you don't have to worry." Max turned his head, placed a kiss in the center of her palm and did a little soothing of his own.

"It could happen again."

"No way! I've got too much to lose, and the longer I work on this case, the more benefit I see in walking away." He could do it, too. Hand in his resignation and flick the job off, maybe go into security. He could definitely see himself as his own boss, especially after this KPK business.

"Have you ever thought of being a part-time vintner and looking at the winery as an investment?" he asked, changing the subject.

"I could never do that—live in the city and depend on a bank statement to tell me how things were going. My family has too much sweat and blood invested in this piece of land to let go of it lightly."

Her words were the clincher. She had a history here. Would he fit in? The place had already gotten to him. Even in the dead of winter it had a stark beauty that appealed to him, a sense of the earth's rhythms. There was a sameness to life in the city, where the most he saw of nature was the changing flowers in the florist next door to the pub he frequented. And most of them were forced, with daffodils already nodding their heads over the side of a pail in June, instead of September.

Max pushed her hair back from her forehead, the better to see her eyes. The anxiety in them had faded. "There are certainly more delights to be found in nurturing grapes than in my line of work. I only get to see the downside of nature. How 'bout we do a little natural nurturing right now?" he asked, kissing each eyelid in turn and working his way toward her mouth.

Her hands slid to his waistband and unfastened the front hook. "I've just been waiting for a window of opportunity."

"Well, sweetheart, wait no more. We have an opening."

When they were both naked, Maggie straddled his hips.

Touching Max was more gratifying than she'd imagined. He'd given the power into her hands and she took advantage of it. Who'd have known how electrifying it would be to control this giant of a man's reactions with a fingertip? Or two to be precise. The wet ones that circled his flat brown nipples and made him moan at the lightest pressure.

Tongue followed fingers as she lathed them. Leaning forward, she pressed her belly down on his hard flesh, sliding her hands up and down his shoulders and arms.

Max trapped her wrists, holding them against his sides. "Maggie, if I don't get inside you soon, I'm gonna die from overstimulation," he groaned, then released her.

Maggie straightened. Sitting as tall as possible, she rolled her shoulders back and flicked him a sultry look from under her lashes. Her gaze skimmed the proud thrust of her breasts with their dark peaks.

She blew him a kiss. "Let's see if I can solve your problem."

With his heat clasped in her palm, she lifted her hips and guided him between her thighs. Shuddering, she came down onto his tip and slowly filled her damp cavern with Max. In the hazy green light it felt like sliding into a sea of warm, green waves. Floating in their undulations, she rocked to their rhythm of the winds and tides.

The creature under her thrust and bucked, and her body flexed to keep up with it. Arms outstretched, she rode the sea monster down to the very depths of the ocean. Blood pounded in her ears and her lungs strained, fighting her held breath. One of them must give soon. And as the creature twisted and plunged beneath her she knew she had conquered him and let go, to breast the surface in a rush of life-giving oxygen.

Drenched with sweat, they clung together, drifting into sleep. Until the baby's cries wakened Maggie.

Such pretty little faces on the shelves.

Which one looked most like Maggie Kovacs? His hand hovered, then changed direction. So many to choose from, all his wife's little babies.

His fingers curved around the head of one and lifted it down. The French bisque had the same glow as Maggie's skin. On the bench by his right hand lay the scalpel. He picked it up and made an incision in the back of the skull.

The leather-hard porcelain, no match for the sharpness of his blade, parted as he circled the scalp and slid it off to lie in his palm.

Each eye he pierced in turn, exchanging blank stares for dark sockets.

Two firings would change all that.

He should wait—there was much to do before it was time— yet he couldn't resist removing the box from its cupboard. The box was very old. There were flowers on the lid, pansies and marigolds crazed by the passage of time.

The dark brown eyes he'd chosen for her stared up at him as he lifted his other prize from the box. Carefully he un-

wrapped the wig from the tissue paper. Short, black, silky hair, straight as a dye, just like Maggie's.

Holding the clip joining the eyes between finger and thumb, he fitted them through the hole in the head and held them in position.

The dark brown irises stared at him blankly.

"Ah, pretty baby. Your mama is waiting."

Chapter 11

They were planning a wedding.

Last night she and Max had told Carla the truth. And although their plans seemed to contradict everything that had gone on before, the moment that squalling baby had invaded Maggie's dreams, all options were off.

Luckily, Carla had seen the funny side. It was the gleam in Carla's eye that bothered Maggie now. The impression that her old friend wasn't above doing a little matchmaking. Carla had certainly thrown herself into the planning of the pretend wedding. Maggie just hoped she saw it as a lure to catch a killer, and not as a dress rehearsal for the real thing.

"How long do you think we've got?"

Maggie put down her fork and knife and stopped eating. Carla had cooked breakfast this morning, as well as dinner the night before. But Maggie hadn't been able to do justice to the food, then or now. Max, of course, was shoveling it in like there was no tomorrow. In fact, going by the plans he'd cooked up, that was at the back of his mind—no tomorrows!

Maggie shivered involuntarily.

A goose walking over her grave.

"I wish I knew, Max. Probably a week, maybe less. How long does it take to make a doll?" She looked up at Carla, who stood alongside her refilling the bright yellow mug with blue fish swimming around it. Round and round, the way their conversation had gone since last night. But in the end Max had had his way.

"Thanks," Maggie said, and took a long slurp of coffee. It was black, boiling hot, and darn near took the roof off her mouth, but she needed it to stay awake.

"So you reckon he makes the doll himself and it isn't until he starts work on it that you hear this baby crying in your head?"

"I think I start hearing the baby crying as soon as it becomes alive in his mind. And that's while he's making them. I mean, he isn't plucking his victims out of thin air, the dolls resemble them too much. Even to the mole above the lip, the same as,…which one was it? Oh, the little waitress."

"So you noticed that?"

"Who could miss it?" She didn't think there was anything about the last few weeks she'd ever forget. This one in particular. Since the first cries had woken her yesterday, Max had been organizing her and Carla. He was a continual source of amazement. When he'd finally coaxed her to tell him what was wrong, he hadn't turned a hair, and she'd thought, was this the same Max she'd met a week ago, with all his beliefs buttoned down tight?

Then he'd further confused her by making her pull out all her father's old papers and go through them to see if she could find any mention of Stella or Ivan Kovacs.

Max being with her made all the difference. Having someone to share this task she'd put off for want of a little courage meant the difference between reading the papers accurately and missing stuff while she bawled her head off each time she found a quirky notation in the margin. The essential Frank Kovacs.

That's when she'd found the magazine article mentioning Ivan's name. Her father had marked the page with the itinerary for his trip to Australia. Written on an annual award, given to the top student attending a well-known college of viticulture. The sought-after prize, a year's work at one of the most prestigious wineries in Australia, had gone to the second-highest-placed student, Ivan Kovacs. The top student having died in a freak auto accident. Whatever her father had read into the announcement was hidden from her. She saw nothing that could have startled him into traveling to Australia at such short notice.

But Max pounced on it. "This will give Strinati somewhere to start looking," he said, referring to the cop who owed him a favor. "I'll put through a call straightaway."

Maggie couldn't see the rush, but Max had his own agenda and he wasn't telling her everything. She'd had to settle for, "I'm just feeling my way here, sweetheart. And if it gets results, then we'll both know. But don't hold your breath. I'm goin' on a fishing expedition, but I could be using the wrong bait." After that he'd put a call through to Sydney, and when he'd finished collecting on his favor from the Australian cop, he'd conned Carla into doing some business for him in Auckland.

Max ate the last piece of toast, eased his chair back from the table and cradled his coffee mug in his large hands. "In that case I think we ought to allow ourselves five days max. Are you sure you can manage that, Carla?"

"Positive. I'll get the ball rolling as soon I reach Auckland. Five days is more than enough time for my part of your scheme. I'll have you know you're dealing with an expert. The tighter the deadline, the better I like it!"

Deadline.

Five days.

Deadline said it all. Whose death this time? Hers? Some other unsuspecting woman? And even when she'd dreamed her dream Maggie knew they could be too late...again.

The minutes had begun to tick down from the moment the baby cried. Maggie heard each one in the back of her mind. Tick…tick… She listened to it with a part of herself that stood back and waited, while what was left hid her feelings in this mixture of commonplace and bizarre, pretending everything was normal.

And normal it was, if your name was Maggie Kovacs.

Maggie blinked and brought herself back to the present. A girl could get depressed or scare herself spitless if she concentrated on what might happen instead of getting on with life.

"You've surprised me, Carla, the way you've fallen in with all of Max's plans, without a murmur."

"You were expecting a wringing of hands, perhaps? Your father and I were together long enough for me to learn men get these hunches. Sometimes they're right, sometimes they're wrong, but in the long run I always found it easier to go with the flow. Besides, what can it hurt?" Carla's benign smile encompassed both of them.

"Gut instincts—that's what it's called, Carla." He winked at Maggie, then turned back to the older woman. "One day she'll realize we're right."

"You mean a premonition, huh? And this from the guy who wanted nothing to do with my psychic mumbo jumbo!" Maggie smiled, robbing her words of any sarcasm, as he came toward her.

"You've been talking to Jo," he said, but without rancor.

"Yeah, but not after we agreed on our non-aggression pact yesterday, a long, long time ago. At least a week."

"It feels that way doesn't it, as if I've known you forever." He bent and brushed his lips over hers. The touch sparked enough heat to start a flash fire. Unfazed by Carla's presence, he deepened the kiss, letting their tongues meet and mate, the way their bodies had done most of the night.

Two seconds and Maggie's mind emptied of everything but Max. His feel, his touch, his smell. She wanted him. Wanted him right here, right now! There was a world of meaning in the blue gaze that broke over her when he ended the kiss. Without turning his head, Max said, ''C'mon, Carla, let's get this show on the road.''

The doorbell gave a peremptory ring as he and Carla reached the entrance hall, and another as they got to the door. Steven waited on the other side.

Max didn't know what it was about the guy. Maggie liked Steven, but his own hackles rose each time he saw him. Now, as Steven eyed him, the vintner's eyebrows lifted quickly in surprise.

''You looking for me, Dexter?'' The challenge Max threw at him didn't go unrewarded as the guy stepped back a pace.

''No, I thought you'd gone. I'm looking for Maggie.''

''She's getting ready for work,'' Max said. ''I'll call her.'' Then he remembered his social responsibilities and introduced the woman by his side.

He could tell Carla found the interaction between him and Dexter amusing. They'd met head-on like stags staking their claim, clashing antlers and blowing out testosterone. ''Carla, this is Steven Dexter, the wine maker who's taken over from Frank.''

''Oh, but we've met.''

Steven frowned at Carla. ''I don't think so—I'm sure I would have remembered. Must have been someone else. I haven't been here very long.''

''No, well, I recognize you from somewhere else. Do you like opera, Steven?''

Steven smiled. ''Sorry, I don't have time for anything but wine. And before I came here I worked in Australia.''

''Never mind, it'll come back to me. I never forget a face.''

The wine maker's smile flickered, but righted itself after a moment. His gaze shifted as Max heard Maggie arrive.

Max felt a snarl form in his throat, and clamped his teeth down on it. He had no desire to leave Maggie in this man's company. ''Looks like your problem's been taken care of,

Dexter.'' He breathed easier as he took Carla by the elbow and they left the others behind. ''C'mon,'' he said softly and winked. ''Let me walk you to your car.''

Gravel crunched under their feet as they headed toward her vehicle. They'd gone only a few yards when he felt compelled to look back. Great move, wine man! Steven had not made Maggie's day, and over the sound of footsteps, Max caught the words, ''Lost five thousand gallons of shiraz.''

''Maggie!'' he called. Their gazes tangled and he dipped his head slightly, sending her a small, silent message to remind her she wasn't alone. ''Don't forget, page me when the courier brings the papers from Carla.'' Anytime, anywhere, whenever Maggie called he'd get there, come hell or high water. She was his. His woman.

He wished he could feel as positive about the steps he'd taken since last night. Maggie had asked for an explanation, but he couldn't give one. And she'd be a helluva lot easier to convince than Mike Henare would, when he called him from the mobile phone in his car. By tomorrow Max would know if his boss had gone along with the idea.

Somewhere along the line, all the happenings of the last few days had gotten intertwined, and he still had to work out which thread led where. But he was positive one strand would have a killer dangling from the end.

And he'd come to the conclusion that it wouldn't be Arnolds.

The one given in the whole business was that Maggie needed protection. Max just hadn't figured out from whom or what yet, but he intended doing his damnedest to keep her safe.

Any way. Anyhow.

Gwen knocked on Maggie's office door, opened it slightly and peeped in. ''Sorry to disturb you, Maggie.''

''No problem. Come on in.'' Maggie was glad of the interruption. Her mind couldn't settle on work. The moment she loosened her grip on her thoughts they wandered away on their own, veering out of her comfort zone onto side roads where darkness and terror lived. Even Gwen's knock on the door had sent anticipatory tingles of fear rippling under her skin.

Maggie noticed something in Gwen's hand, waited a moment, then inquired, "Is that for me, Gwen?"

"Oh…yes, this came by courier. He's waiting. Is there any reply?" she asked, passing the envelope over.

"Give me a moment and I'll take a look." Maggie picked up a letter opener and slit the red-and-white plastic courier pack. It was from Carla.

Maggie took out a form and read it, checking the details to make sure they were correct. At last she had something to smile about—Max's birth date. A Scorpio. The little critter with a sting in its tail. Well, she'd been on the receiving end of that more than once since meeting him. She looked up at Gwen. "Ask him to wait for the reply."

"You look happy. Get some good news?" Gwen asked, her gaze glued to the paper in Maggie's hand.

It was going to be simpler than she'd imagined to carry out Max's instructions. "Here, see for yourself," she said, and passed the form to Gwen.

"A marriage license!"

"Just the application."

"But for you and Detective Sergeant Strachan. I never suspected a thing."

"Well, now you know."

Gwen's eyes lit up. The news would be all around the neighborhood by nightfall.

"I forgot to say Steven wants to see you," said Gwen, still scanning the paper in her hand as she laid it down. "He's waiting outside with the gardener who's replaced Gordon. I think there's some sort of dispute over the glass house."

Rolling her eyes heavenward, Maggie said, "Ah, I knew things were too quiet around here. Time for a lesson in humility to keep me anchored before I let getting married go to my head.''

Secretly pleased at the distraction, she looked at Gwen and sighed as if irked. ''You can't win them all. Send them in. And give Max a beep on his pager, so he can sign his half of this. Tell the courier we'll pay for his time. Feed him if you have to, give him a free bottle of wine, just keep him here till Max arrives. It's urgent that this gets back to Auckland today.''

''Why? When are you getting married?''

''Sunday.'' This was the point where she should blush, but that particular talent was beyond her acting abilities. Instead she smiled coyly and played with the form, centering it on her desk where it could be read easily.

Gwen, for once, appeared struck dumb.

The moment Steven and Edward entered her office, Maggie knew the news had been passed on from the way their gazes slid toward her left hand, then locked on to the paper in front of her.

Steven stood to one side of the desk and Ed went to the other, like opposing teams ready to do battle. She quirked an eyebrow at Steven, asking, ''Did we forget something this morning?'' then nodded to the other man. ''Afternoon, Ed.''

She couldn't remember Steven ever being so testy. He'd been acting strangely since the night the wine spilled and the police invaded the vineyard. Maybe all he needed was to get back into his routine. Some people found that soothing.

''Okay, guys, what's the problem?''

The courier had departed with a big tip from Max, and the rest of her life signed, sealed and on its way to be delivered.

Maggie's part of the plan had gone well. Too well.

Max's elation rang in her ears like a death knell.

Something was bound to go wrong.

Maggie took her time walking down to the bottling plant. Steven had taken it personally when she'd come down on Ed's side, and had left the office before she could get around to inviting him to the mock wedding on Sunday. She expected to find him in the lab and was intent on doing a little feather smoothing. Truth be told, they both knew he was good at his job, so why did he have to pick now of all times to act insecure? He shouldn't need her confirmation of his worth. He'd had a pile of glowing reports in his CV.

"Steven, we have to talk."

He stood at the bench with a beaker of red wine near his right hand and a meter in his other, conducting a test. Stubbornly, he didn't turn around, so Maggie had to join him. No point in both of them acting like children.

"Is this some of the shiraz?"

Steven looked at her sideways.

He really wasn't much taller than her, yet when it came to wine he always gave the impression he'd grown an inch or two, and she was lagging behind when it came to knowing her wines. It wasn't as much height as attitude.

"No, it's the cabernet merlot from the cellar. The lot your father put down in the American oak barrels. He was very good, your father. A pity the industry had to lose him." He smiled, but it didn't reach his eyes. "Of course, if he hadn't died I wouldn't be here, and we wouldn't be having this conversation."

Maggie picked up the beaker of wine and swirled it around, bending over the rich red liquid to catch its bouquet. "Mmm, it is good, isn't it? Yours could be just as good—"

"Mine could be better."

"That remains to be seen." She gritted her teeth and pressed on. "Steven, what's bugging you? You haven't been yourself for the last few days. It's not like you to quibble over a bit of space in the greenhouse. I told Ed he could use it. It's important that Ed can get on with the landscaping. I should have thought you'd feel the same. It's your wine we're launching."

Steven set the meter he was using down on the bench. "I realize that. I just don't like his manner. Hell, the guy's so full of starch he'd crack if he had to unbend a little."

"He's not long out of the army. Give him a little time, Steven, he'll settle down. Ed remembers how it used to be here, years ago when my father was alive and my mother and brother were here." She realized at once that had been the wrong thing to say.

"Ahh, the good old days."

Maggie didn't want an argument, but the man was acting impossible today. Thank heavens this wasn't his usual demeanor. "All I'm trying to say is to let these little things slide past you, don't let them grow into issues. The loss of the wine upset me, too, remember? I was the one who nearly died through it. I know you don't want to be reminded of Frank all the time, but if he'd let the death of my mother and brother get to him, the winery wouldn't be what it is today."

The words spilled out before she remembered them to be a lie. For years she'd mourned the loss of people whose images had faded, long before she'd learned the need to hold on to them. It would take more than a story from Carla to bring them back to life. She needed to meet them in the flesh.

Instead of answering, Steven held the meter up to the light from the window. His hand shook, and after studying it for a few seconds, he asked, "Was there anything else you wanted, Maggie?"

"Steven, I wondered if you had too much on your plate. Maybe I should hire a vineyard manager. Just because Dad did everything doesn't mean you have to do the same."

His eyes turned opaque as if he'd dropped a shutter over his feelings. "Yes, it's hard trying to walk in a dead man's shoes. Thinking of bringing your new husband in as vineyard manager, are you?"

"Good grief, no! Max doesn't know the first thing about vineyards. I simply thought you needed a break. Is that what's bothering you? Don't worry, Steven, your job is secure."

But the idea had taken root—her and Max living and working alongside one another every day to bring out the best in the vineyard. If they could put in one tenth of what had gone into their relationship so far, they had the potential for greatness just waiting to be released.

Now there was one dream she wouldn't mind coming true.

"Thanks, Maggie." He sounded happier. "You can be sure I'll do everything in my power to make certain it stays that way. A break would be good, though how am I supposed to do that with you on *honeymoon?* We both can't be away at the same time."

Maggie found herself coloring up with heat at the mention of a honeymoon. "Oh, we aren't going away," she told him quickly. "So there's no problem."

She could honestly say it hadn't even crossed her mind. With all the talk about putting on a wedding at the weekend, she'd forgotten some things might not look quite normal to people on the outside. "We will go away, when the weather's better. Spring, probably."

"And is Max giving up his *stag* night, too?" Steve laughed for the first time in days. "What do cops do when they get rambunctious? Arrest one another?"

Max had already clued her in on her reply, should anyone ask. "Yes, he's going out with some cops from Auckland Central. I'm sure you'd be welcome to join them. He's driving into Auckland on Saturday afternoon and coming back with his friends on Sunday," she informed him, knowing Steven would refuse. Whenever the two of them met, the air was electric with challenge. It hadn't occurred to her before that Steven was worried about his job. That explained a lot of things.

No way could she issue an invitation on Max's behalf that anyone might accept. Only she and Max knew he wouldn't go anywhere that meant leaving her alone. In fact, she'd had to promise never to be alone with anyone but him.

Max had the idea that the killer might try to get rid of her again. She couldn't quite see how pretending to marry would help, or leaking the news to the media, but then, she wasn't a cop.

"Actually," said Steven, "I was thinking of going down to the Gisborne acreage to check on the contractor down there."

Maggie wanted to leap at the opportunity, but caution tempered her enthusiasm. "Oh, I was hoping you'd come to the house Sunday evening for the wedding. It'll be a small, informal affair with only a few of our friends." Actually, Steven was the first person she'd asked. She ought to invite a few more. Not too many. That way there'd be fewer to inform of the cancellation if someone ended up dead— No! She wouldn't go down that road again.

Stop anticipating the dream.

"Well, if you'd like, I could leave early tomorrow and return late Saturday? With a stop overnight at Tauranga, I'd get home by Sunday afternoon," Steven said, smiling affably.

"Great, we'll see you there." She'd turned to leave, thinking how pleasant Steven could be when he tried, when his next question floored her.

"Why the sudden rush? You're not pregnant, are you?"

"Steven!" She whirled on him. "No, I'm not! Not that it is any of—" Without realizing he'd moved to pick up the beaker, Maggie's arm caught his, emptying the container of wine over his sleeve. The glass smashed on the bench. "Oh, dear. I'm sorry...look at your shirt!" Grabbing a fistful of paper towels from a dispenser on the wall, she began to dab at his arm.

"Don't bother. Leave it!" he snapped.

"But it'll stain your shirt. You didn't get any glass on you, did you? Maybe if I unbuttoned your cuff and you—"

He pulled his sleeve out of her grasp. "I said leave it," he snarled through clenched teeth.

"Okay, okay. I've said I was sorry, but you'd no right to say what you did. I'll go now. And since you're so insistent on it, you can clean up the mess.'' Maggie turned on her heel and left.

''Bad-tempered jerk,'' she muttered as she stepped outside. He wasn't the only one who'd gotten splattered. She brushed at her trousers, but it was too late, they'd have to be dry-cleaned.

''Been in the wars again?''

She hadn't realized Max was there. ''An accident,'' she said. ''Though this time I didn't bathe in it. Just splashed around.''

''I hope they'll clean up. Shame if you couldn't wear them again. They do things for your butt that sets my libido on fire.'' He slid his arm down her back and gave her a little squeeze.

''Feeling horny, are you?''

''Around you? All the time.''

When she was near Max, all her reservations about what they were attempting flew out the window. Even after such a short time she knew she trusted him—with her life.

It was enough. Enough for her to let herself be used as bait.

Max worked by the light of a table lamp. He had papers scattered all over the side table and on the floor next to the large sofa facing the fire. Maggie curled up in the corner a one end while he occupied the other. Neither spoke much, bu he could feel her watching him and it ruined his concentration The names on the list he was collating wouldn't stay still. O rather his eyes wouldn't. They kept checking out Maggie.

Being in a half-aroused state all evening was no help. N help at all. But if he let his mind dwell on the pleasurabl measures Maggie could take to help him out, he'd never ge finished. The one thought that never left him was the way tim had of sucking up every day, every hour, every minute, an the moment it started dragging in the seconds, he'd know i had run out.

He let his restlessness flow to his feet, and got up to pu

another log on the red heart of the fire. The bark was tinder dry and flared into blue and yellow flames the instant it contacted the embers.

He saw their frenetic dance reflected in Maggie's eyes as soon as he turned to go back to his work. The intensity of her gaze burned hot and strong, consuming the air between them till he found it hard to breathe. It hit him low, it hit him hard, coming at him like wind-borne sparks leaping a firebreak. He went from putty to rock hard in the space of a heartbeat.

Maggie stood up and glided toward him. "Forget the fire, I'll keep you warm." She held up her hand, palm facing him.

The lines on it stood out strong and clear, her heart line, her life line. Max laid his against hers, let their hearts, their lives, their futures mingle in a soft shiver of skin against skin as each palm circled the other.

Her fingers speared his and drew his hand down to her breast. "Come to bed," she murmured, stretching up to reach his lips in a kiss that would make a statue get up and walk.

Max was hard as stone, but he was no statue, so it was easy for him.

He'd always known his mother hadn't raised a fool.

Chapter 12

The next morning, Maggie stood in front of the vanity wearing another of those silky robes that knocked his equilibrium sideways. Deep melon this time, it molded her body like a caress, and from Max's vantage point, the back view was all he could ask for. The tie belt drew his eye to her narrow waist, then his gaze followed the flared curve of her hips. The feel of her soft lushness had imprinted itself on his senses from the first touch, and his palms tingled at the recollection.

He was glad they were past the stage where walking around naked would embarrass Maggie. He stood behind her wearing nothing but the suit he'd been born in, and wrapped his arms around her. The tiredness in her eyes tore at him as their reflections filled the mirror. He intended to take away some of her weariness with a hug to show he understood what she was going through, but his body had other ideas. Unashamedly, it reveled in the feel of her against him, quickening as she leaned back and let him support her weight.

"Not feeling too hot this morning?" He dropped a kiss behind her ear and let his hands slide up to cup her breasts.

All that stood between them was a thin scrap of fabric, about as much barrier as nothing. Her body heat penetrated the weave, searing his skin, which protected itself with a fine film of sweat as the blood rushed to his groin. "You should have stayed in bed this morning and caught up on your sleep."

"Sorry, Max, I know I kept waking you."

"No problem, just doing my bit to chase the crying baby out of your head. Don't be sorry, though—it was my pleasure, believe me."

"It was mine, too. Even if it didn't shut the little devil out, at least it distracted me from the noise in my head."

"Anytime you feel the need to be distracted, just let me know."

Maggie laughed softly and undulated her hips against him. "Does the way you're always ready for action have something to do with being a cop?" Her eyes spoke to him through the mirror. Sparkle added highlights to their dark depths, accompanied by red-hot flashes of need that told him everything he wanted to know.

Max twisted her in his arms until she faced him, then pulled her up higher, till her bare toes balanced on top of his feet. "The kind of action you're talking about isn't listed in the police training manual. The headings Love and Lust, got left out of the *L* section and are only known to a privileged few. Their main cause is being turned on by a beautiful woman." He rubbed his mouth across her lips and felt hers go soft and pliant under them. He sucked in oxygen. "It's a result of breathing the same air she breathes."

Maggie's mouth opened on a sigh, giving him access to a very sensitive part of it. Lips, tongue and teeth shifted position, slanting first this way, then that—anything to give him deeper penetration of her honeyed sweetness. He couldn't get enough.

Their chests heaved and the tight nubs of her breasts marked him for life as they brushed against him. He eased away. Not so far, though, for Maggie's leg was hooked behind his, clamping him to the apex of her thighs. He burned with need, ached to be inside her. Pleasurable as this might be, it wasn't enough.

His hand fitted around her face and tilted her chin with the pressure of his thumb. He kissed her with a butterfly caress for the space of a heartbeat, yet it held a mountain of loving tenderness. "Tasting you is another trigger that turns me on," he whispered in the shell of her ear, then nipped her lobe in a love bite.

His friends would think he'd run mad, plunging headlong into this wonderful, mind-blowing relationship. Even he found it hard to believe how serious it had become in such a short time, but this woman had only to crook her little finger and he'd come running. He wanted to carry her off to a place where no one could find them, and slake himself in the wonder of her.

And not only for the sex, though it was the best he'd ever had. Last night had shown him her gift—her curse—brought no pleasure, only pain. It sure wasn't an experience he'd wish upon a friend. He had a whole new respect for Maggie, and when he thought of her coping alone with this mental torture, his heart squeezed like a giant fist had it in its grip. The more he knew of her courage, her determination to see this through—damn!

How could he do this to her?

The cost could be too high. For them both.

A lump swelled in his throat, almost choking him, making his eyes water. God, if he should lose her... It didn't bear thinking about. His arms tightened reflexively.

"Max, you're squashing me."

Fear had manifested into a ferocious hug, a need to hold her close and never let her go. Unsteadily, he released her, saying roughly, "Let's go have a shower. I'll give you a back massage to make you feel better."

"And that's all?" Maggie looked up at him and laughed.

Max sent up thanks. None of his fear had transferred itself to her. "That's all," he said. "I promise."

She looked down smugly and gave his body a brief scan. "Tell me why I should believe you on the evidence put before me?"

Max threw up his arms in surrender.

She shouldn't be feeling this way. Why should a strong, liberated woman who was CEO of a winery—one that had increased its market share by fifteen percent since she took over—feel as if she'd lost her anchor as Max drove away? It just didn't make sense.

Maggie stood on the top step and waved as his car went through the gate and turned onto the road.

Part of Max's apprehension must have gotten through to her. She could tell he hadn't wanted to leave her, but his chief, D.I. Henare, had been insistent. She would have gone with him, but Max said no, she'd done her share. It was Arnolds's day in court this morning and Max had evidence to give on two charges— resisting arrest and assaulting a police officer. Enough to hold him till the other business was resolved.

One way or another.

Instinctively, she felt Max had concluded Arnolds wasn't the KPK. The reports Jo had sent him, since she'd rejoined the team heading the investigation, had been inconclusive. So far, the button and the fingerprint were their only hard pieces of evidence. Everything else was circumstantial.

Maggie stopped with her key in the door of the wine shop. A truck carrying a small digger lumbered into the drive. She was pleased Ed hadn't wasted much time. It looked like one of her problems was well on course to being solved. The truck pulled up with a hiss of air brakes just as Ed appeared from the side of the building. Maggie grinned; she couldn't get over him. He was a dandy among gardeners, and him swapping his spit-and-polish shoes for high-topped gum boots didn't change her opinion one iota.

Maybe he had a little woman in the background who pressed his shirts and polished his shoes. Maggie hadn't got round to asking him if he was married, and he hadn't volunteered.

The two men shook hands, then the driver clanged runners into place, clipped on ear protection and started the engine with a screech and a roar. Heavens! There wouldn't be much work done today with that racket going on. And the smell! Phew!

At ten o'clock she took a coffee break and wandered outside, carrying her mug. The engine had ground to silence while the driver wolfed down sandwiches in the cab of his truck. Ed Armstrong hadn't stopped, though. His hands were full of plans, which he studied as Maggie strolled over.

"It looks as if you've made a good start. How long do think he'll take?"

Armstrong rolled up the plans, stopping to measure the long scar of dark earth with his eyes. "Two days if he keeps this up. Don't worry, I'll have it looking reasonable before your wedding."

"Oh, someone told you the date then?" She'd almost forgotten about the wedding plans. It was the tire tracks on the lawns that worried her.

"Yes, Gwen did. Congratulations," he said, rubbing his hand on his jeans, as if it were too dirty to offer her. "I hadn't realized you and the sergeant were an item. The papers said you were helping the police with your psychic powers. I didn't know Strachan had a better reason for hanging around."

"It just shows you shouldn't believe everything you read in the papers. I'm sure you've heard Steven moaning about how much wine we lost."

"When I'm around, Dexter turns complaining into an art form," he said grimly.

Nodding in sympathy, she said, "Max has been looking into the loss." She took a drink of coffee to wash down her white lie. "He'd just arrived for dinner when it happened."

"They say the vandal had a go at you. They also say you predicted your father's death." He let the statement hang in the air between them, challenging her assertion.

"That's right. I did, but don't get the wrong idea. I don't keep a crystal ball in the house, it was simply a dream." She began to walk away, then remembered she wanted to ask him about Stella and Ivan. "I've been wondering what you remembered about my family. How well did you know them?"

His lids narrowed. It didn't lessen the chill in his light gray eyes, but he did give her an answer. "I worked here on and off for about three years after I finished school. Until I got fired, that is."

"They fired you?" Maggie gasped, suddenly sorry she'd started this conversation.

"Yes. I didn't say anything before, in case you held it against me and wouldn't give me the job." His hand clenched and the landscape plans began to crumple.

Maggie quickly reassured him before he ruined Gordon's good work. "That was a long time ago. I wouldn't have let it influence me." *Besides, I was desperate.* What was it about her that brought out everyone's hang-ups? First Steven, now Ed. "Why don't you tell me what happened?"

"It was your brother's fault. That kid could never take no for an answer. Spoiled, he was. Your mother let him have his way every time, treated him like a little prince."

Maggie let out a sigh as Ed seemed to let go of his ire and began to relax, smoothing out the plans he held. Feeling like she'd opened a can of worms, she said, "Go on."

"You know that bank down to the pond on the other side of Steven's place, the one that's too steep to mow?"

"I know the one you mean. Gordon always used a weed eater to clear it. The slope could knock you off a riding mower."

"Yeah, well, they hadn't been invented then, and I had to clear the long grass with a scythe. It was the summer holidays. You were only a toddler, about two-years-old, and Ivan would have been six. School wasn't due to start for a couple of weeks and the kid was bored, kept following me around. Proper little toad he was.'' Ed glanced at Maggie as if expecting her to bite. ''Sorry for speaking ill of the dead, but it's the truth.''

''That's okay, Ed. Tell me straight, warts and all.''

''I told him to stay away, it was dangerous on the bank, too easy to slip and fall into the pond. Little devil told me it was his property and he could do as he liked. He kept rolling down the bank, daring me to let him reach the water. The last time really was an accident—he tripped and lost his balance. Not being close enough, I just threw myself at him and reached out for his arm. I'd forgotten about the hook.''

Maggie moaned as it played in her mind like an old movie she'd forgotten she'd watched. And from the way Ed's face twisted, the retelling was just as hard on him.

''In less than a second his feet were dangling in the water, the hook keeping him from sliding farther and me on the other end of it. I was only nineteen then. It gave me a helluva turn. But if I'd let go, he'd have landed in the water and might have drowned with all the weed in the pond.''

A shudder racked his neat frame. ''Ever since then, for twenty-six years, I've hated the sight of blood.''

Maggie frowned. ''But you were in the army! The SAS.''

Ed's laughter was dry and humorless. ''They teach you to kill without making a bloody mess of it.''

Maggie shivered; that goose was back stomping on her grave again. She'd let herself in for this by asking about Ivan. It was just too close to home after the recent happenings.

Strangulation and broken necks...ugh.

''Anyway, I missed Vietnam, and the Gulf was more long-distance stuff,'' he rationalized. ''When your brother got hurt it was up close. There was blood all over me, blood on the grass, blood in the water. I'd hit the artery in his wrist and it spurted out in huge bursts. I didn't blame the kid for screaming—I wanted to scream myself.''

Oh, poor little boy, thought Maggie. To go through all that

and then be rejected by your father. Her heart went out to him. Ed's story suddenly made her brother seem real. So what if he'd been precocious? He'd only been a child. The blame wasn't his but their mother's for acting so selfishly.

"What happened then? How did you save him?"

"I managed to find the pressure point and slowed the bleeding, then I picked him up and ran for the house like my heels were on fire. Stella arrived before I reached it. She'd heard the screams and came running out to meet us. Her screeching didn't help. It was one helluva sight. A real nightmare. She grabbed Ivan and he started bleeding again. The three of us were covered in blood by the time your father arrived and took care of everything. I have to admit he was cool in an emergency."

Maggie nodded. Her father had always handled things calmly. Too calmly. Like the way he'd climbed into his plane and flown off to his death as if he hadn't a care in the world.

"And where was I while all this was happening?"

"You were in the house. Ivan didn't want to go home because you were bawling your head off. 'Crybaby,' he called you."

Maggie felt nauseous; she needed out of there. The deep breath she dragged in didn't calm her. Ed's gaze caught hers. Could he see the panic there, see the need to run even as she held her ground? He probably already suspected she was weird from all the stories doing the rounds, and she didn't want to confirm his suspicions. Gathering her willpower, she said, "I'm sorry to make you relive that experience, Ed. It must have been harrowing for you."

"There's nothing about that day I'll ever forget. It changed my life. Next day, when I turned up to ask how the kid was, I thought Stella would skin me alive. I'd never seen her that way before. She was *so* angry. She threatened to tell everyone I'd attacked her son. Then she fired me. I never got a chance to speak to your father, and the day after that I signed up with the army. Best thing I ever did."

Maggie smiled weakly, holding the smile in place every time she felt it waver. It had been a week of discoveries, most of which she could have done without. Except for coming to know Max. He would always be the exception.

"I'm glad you came to terms with it, Ed. I hope we can make up for my mother's lack of compassion now that you're back here."

"I'm sure you can, Maggie. In fact, I'm positive. There's a lot to be done and I love my work."

The light blinked on her answering machine. As soon as she sat down at the desk, she pressed Play, then sat back and listened.

"Hi, Maggie, this is Steven. I should reach Gisborne this afternoon. If you need to contact me use my mobile phone number, as I'll be moving around and don't know where I'll be staying."

Well, that was one problem out of her hair. She felt some of her tension fall away like leaves off the vines, and sighed. That made one less person to worry about. She hadn't *really* suspected Steven of being the man in her dreams. Until Max had appeared on the scene they'd been good friends. She knew now he'd let insecurity get the better of him. Still, with Steven gone for a few days, she could leave off tormenting herself about the faux pas she'd made over the scarf. Her mistake was understandable. People did those things when they were distraught.

They don't all lie by omission, though.

I would have told him if it were absolutely necessary. I still can!

You're agonizing over nothing, girl!

Then there was this wedding that was supposedly taking place on Sunday. Gwen kept asking questions about her dress and the caterers. She must think her a very indifferent sort of bride for leaving all the arrangements to Carla.

Heavens, what if nothing happened and they had to go through with it?

There had been the moment in her office, with Max and Carla, when the look in his eyes had made her think he was serious. How would she feel, if the arrangements Carla was making for Sunday were for real? But they weren't. They were simply another of Max's bright ideas. He was an inveterate planner. She watched him at night while he went over his notes, his brain ticking as he scribbled down his thoughts in his own peculiar shorthand. From her own observations she'd say Max was the kind of man who inevitably betted against the odds.

If Arnolds's arraignment kept to schedule, Max should be home around 2:00 p.m. It shouldn't take him too long to pack. He'd had a few extra clothes in his car, but for the last couple of days he'd been reduced to borrowing some of her father's clothes she'd had stored.

Perhaps that's how she could fill her day until Max came home. *Max came home.* She liked the sound of that. By the time he got back she'd have all her father's gear packed to send to the city mission, and a start made on closing that part of her life.

"Hey, anybody around?" Maggie hadn't been in her office, and Gwen had said she'd gone home.

Home.

Max had been thinking about coming back here from the moment he'd turned out of the driveway. Realization had hit him as he'd packed a bag with necessities: shirts, underwear, extra pants and a suit—mustn't forget the suit. He couldn't get married without one.

It had been a long time since he'd had a place he could call home. Until now. Until he'd found Maggie. Until he'd found a woman he could live with, bring up a family with and never want to walk away from. He didn't know if this was love, but it was what he wanted.

Maggie. She would be his home.

He couldn't wait to see her eyes light up when she saw him. Maggie had a special look just for him. He'd never seen her look at anyone else that way. When he handed her the box resting in his pocket, how would she look then? How would she feel then? Would she think he was jumping the gun? It had barely been two weeks. Or would she think it was simply part of the pretense, the way it had started out?

Buy a cheap ring, Carla had said. But the moment he'd started looking, he wanted something better. The perfect ring.

The lounge was empty, so Max checked the kitchen, thinking she might be cooking dinner. Maggie had completed one of those *cordon bleu* courses and could turn anything into a five-star meal.

As he walked down the hall he patted his pocket. The box was still there. Not that he would give it to her in the kitchen. Maybe after dinner, while they finished off a bottle of wine.

She wasn't there, either. "Maggie!" he called out as he checked all the other rooms on the ground floor. The rooms were as empty as he felt when he couldn't find her. "Maggie!" He leaped up the stairs three at a time, hoping for the best but fearing the worst.

He thrust her bedroom door aside and stood with his fingers clenching the door frame in a grip intensified by a rush of adrenaline. With very little effort he could have ripped the frame straight off the wall. His body shook and he couldn't tell if it was from relief that she hadn't been laid out on her bed, sporting a red bow at her throat, or fear because he still hadn't checked the other rooms.

His fist crashed into the wall. This was his fault. He should never have left her on her own. It was tempting fate, dream or no dream. The moment she'd started hearing that crying baby he should have stuck to her like glue. *"Maggieeee!"* her name ripped out of him in an agony that came from way down in his gut.

One after the other, he threw back the doors and left them

shuddering in his wake. Each empty room flung a message of loss and loneliness back in his face.

He found her in the smallest room at the end of the hall, kneeling on a pile of clothes and crying her heart out. Black mascara stained the backs of her hands where she'd wiped her eyes, but her face was hidden from him.

He knelt down on a pile of men's suits he guessed were her father's. "Maggie, sweetheart, what's wrong? What happened?" Cradling her in one arm, he cupped her shoulder and rubbed gently, while his heart pounded from an excess of fear. What he really wanted was to pull her into his arms and never let her go. But first he needed to discover what had brought on this storm of weeping.

Maggie shrugged his hand away. "Don't touch me!"

His hand jerked as if he'd been burned. What had happened to get her in this state? "Maggie," he said firmly but evenly, concealing his anxiety. "Tell me what's wrong, sweetheart. Let me help. I can't if I don't know what's gotten into you."

From red-rimmed eyes she flicked him a look she might give a stranger who was accosting her. The makeup she'd worn that morning was long gone, except for the black streaks smudging her cheeks. "I'm good and mad, that's what's wrong."

Her words had a childish ring and almost made him laugh, but he refrained. "Who are you mad at, sweetheart?"

"I'm mad at me! I'm mad at the whole damn police force and especially mad at you!" She scrabbled in her lap, coming up with an envelope, and shoved it at him. "Here, take a look!"

The crumpled envelope was slightly the worse for wear, and a sharp crease scarred the center, showing the paper had been folded a long time. The other marks were cleaner, fresher. Maggie's handiwork.

The letter had been posted from Melbourne two years earlier, with *Frank Kovacs, Kereru Hill Winery,* printed on the front. Max turned it over and checked for a return address, but found none.

He held the envelope upside down, squeezing the sides till the paper inside fell into his palm. "I take it you think this is some sort of evidence?"

Maggie didn't reply, just nodded and watched him.

Taking hold of the corners, Max pulled the letter open. One edge was ragged, indicating the sheet had been torn from a larger page. A paper now crisscrossed with paper folds, someone had written, "YOU'LL BE SORRY," in bold black strokes of a felt-tip pen.

His stomach churned as he saw his hopes slip out of reach. He didn't let it show. "Give me your reasons for being mad at the world," he said gently.

Maggie took a deep breath, letting it out slowly till her shoulders sagged and her breasts were concealed by the folds of her sweater. "I'm mad at myself for not having the guts to make someone listen to me, and for hiding away when the police laughed at me. They forced me into a loop with no beginning and no end, and I should have broken out of it and made them listen. I knew there was something wrong with the way my father died. They shouldn't have done that to me."

"You've always been angry with the cops. So what's new?"

"*That's* new," she said, pointing at the envelope. "I couldn't bear to give my father's clothes away before. Once I did, he'd be gone forever. I wasn't ready for closure because I felt I had let him down. Then this afternoon I began sorting through his things and found the envelope." Her eyes pleaded with Max to understand, her hands reaching out, but not quite touching.

His heart squeezed knowing she wouldn't go the extra distance. Maggie hated cops, but he'd thought he might be the exception.

"Don't you see? If I'd found this earlier, maybe they would

have listened, but now it's too late." Her hands dropped into her lap and she looked away. Resigned, no longer begging.

Surely Maggie knew she would never have to beg him for anything, that all she had to do was ask. It seemed he was wrong.

It didn't change anything. He still loved her.

"Tell me why you're especially mad at me?"

She concealed her thoughts, guarding them beneath her lashes as she looked at him. "You and me...both of us. I let you use me as bait to catch this killer. It's not enough that my father died needlessly, I have to go and make the same mistake. And you because you're the one who's using me."

Max felt his hopes fade at her accusation. Partly because it was true. Oh, he'd always wanted her, even before he'd had an inkling that it might be more than just wanting. And he had decided to use her to catch a killer, once he realized her dreams were for real. What Maggie hadn't cottoned on to was that he wasn't only looking for the Khyber Pass Killer, he wanted to find her father's, as well. But it still didn't excuse him.

"I can't argue with that."

"Not only have I lied to all my friends about a wedding, *you* tried to announce it in the newspapers for everyone to read."

She was getting her dander up again, he could tell. So he wouldn't mention just yet the fact that he'd succeeded.

"What had you planned to do if I didn't have another dream? We could have people coming to a wedding that's nothing but a ploy to help you get your man. What will you do then?"

"Marry you."

"I can't believe even *you* would stoop that low, just to catch a killer!"

Chapter 13

Maggie's stubborn streak appeared to be the only thing working this morning. Everything else, energy, enthusiasm, and excitement at the prospect of maybe catching the killer, had burned up with the emotions she'd expended yesterday.

All she wanted to do was stay in bed and sleep, but Max had had other ideas. First off, he'd chased her out of bed. No way could she stay there with him threatening to pull her out from under the covers and dress her himself.

Next, he'd forced her out of the house. This time she was digging in her heels. Her black high heels. The ones Max had laid out for her along with most of the other clothes she had on. He'd gone through her wardrobe and picked out everything she'd worn the night they'd first met, and if she hadn't been so mad at him she would have found it endearing.

"I don't give a damn how much work you've got. I'm not leaving you here. So get in the car."

Max stood by the passenger door, holding it open, waiting for Maggie with an I'm-not-putting-up-with-any-more-non-sense expression on his face.

Maggie didn't budge. "In that case I can take *my* car," she said stubbornly. She'd been crossing him all morning. So far, the score stood at Max two, Maggie nil, and she was determined to win this round.

"How can I protect you if we're in separate cars? Be reasonable, Maggie. I have to go to Auckland, and so do you. Have you forgotten you have an appointment with your lawyer?"

Some excuse, she thought. Visiting her lawyer had been his idea.

Max let the handle go and strode over to the entrance, his sports jacket flying open in the breeze. He'd worn a gray-blue tweed jacket this morning, and the blue cotton shirt underneath it flattened against his chest with the force of the wind. She remembered that chest and touching its sculpted muscles as if it were yesterday—and it had been. It only seemed like years.

The color of his shirt matched his eyes. True blue eyes. The ones that set her thinking she must be insane to chuck all this away.

She'd missed him last night. There'd been no warm body to snuggle up to. No one to massage her shoulders and neck when the baby cried its loudest. No sweet, magical lovemaking to take her out of herself and distract her.

That confirmed it. She was certifiable!

From the moment she'd found that note with its stark message, her emotions had been in turmoil. In her heart of hearts she blamed herself, but she'd taken her hurt out on Max.

Trust, or the lack of it, was at the root of her problem.

Her own feelings were carved in granite. Solid. Indestructible.

But Max's?

What were the odds that such an indescribably sexy hunk of a man could love her that way after only twelve days?

So she'd let the good times they'd shared be crowded out by her doubts and insecurities, by the memory of his ruthless determination to find the Khyber Pass Killer.

He stopped a mere step away, restlessly shoving his hair back from his forehead with his long fingers.

Wind-tousled? Maybe.

Exasperated? More likely.

Drop-dead gorgeous? Definitely.

Needing a distraction, Maggie let her eyes shift to the miniature tornadoes dancing across the paving stones at their feet, sucking up dust and dry leaves and dumping them yards away from where they'd started. Maggie drew in a needy breath of cold, fresh, air and tasted Max. Warm, sweet, spicy, the kind of guy you could eat.

She looked up into his eyes and time stood still. Nothing existed but her and Max. A man and woman who had shared— no, given themselves each to the other, and in so doing had found some sort of meaning in their lives.

Maggie blinked and the moment passed.

Oh, God, what had she done?

A residue of emotion threaded her voice as she asked, "Are you trying to tell me you wouldn't flick on the siren and chase through a red light after me?"

"Damn straight!"

Maggie relented. What was to be done with a man whose bearing had all the impassive resolve of a monolith? What would it take to move him? Whatever the answer, she wasn't willing to put it to the test just yet. She'd accused him of using her, and no matter how often she ran the scene through her head, he still hadn't denied it.

At the crux of the matter was the magnetic sway he had over her every time he came near. She loved him. But was she strong enough to stand being reduced to an object of desire, when she'd just discovered she wanted more?

"I suppose if I don't get in the car you'll carry me."

"Got it in one."

"You leave me no choice." She marched past him, sat down in the passenger seat and closed the door before he could do it for her. She looked around. This was the same car Jo had driven when she'd taken her back to the city.

Maggie studied the dash. She hadn't paid much heed last time as her thoughts had been elsewhere—on the man now sitting in the driver's seat. High-tech equipment took up most of the space—a laptop, a printer, a mobile phone. When Max reached over to switch the radio on Maggie turned her attention to the view out of her window, avoiding his eyes.

"Fasten your seat belt," he said, ramming his into the clip.

Maggie had no problem with that command. She'd seen Max drive, and he didn't hang around. She pulled down the strap, clicked it into place and jerked upright as a folded newspaper landed on her lap.

"Take a look at that," Max said, spinning around the paved area in front of the house and down the drive. "You're looking for page three."

"What a comedown. Detective Sergeant Max Strachan usually makes the front page," she said, revealing her interest in his progress with the case. The first time she'd seen his picture in print she'd been hooked. Maybe that was why he'd been the last person she wanted to talk to about her dreams.

"Been keeping an eye on my publicity, have you?" he asked, flashing her the first grin of the day.

Maggie loved the way the corners of his eyes creased, making them twinkle, as if he were happy again. It took a major effort to wipe the serious lines from his face. Max had reaped a full harvest of creases from working in a grim job most people couldn't handle.

Rape!

Murder!

Violence!

She didn't know the half of it. Little enough there, though, to bring a smile to Max's handsome face.

While they were in bed the other night, Max had said the longer he worked on this case the more benefit he saw in walking away. Just pillow talk, she'd decided. Could he handle leaving the police for the real world?

A stronger, more vivid memory danced in front of her.

Marry you…

He'd stunned her with those words last night, and in her pent-up state she'd flung them back at him. *I can't believe even you would stoop that low just to catch a killer!*

What if she'd gotten it wrong, and he saw more in her than a useful tool to catch a killer, with a great line in sex on the side? Well, if that was true, she'd blown it!

"Finished reading yet?"

Maggie came out of her daze. "No, I was thinking of something else." She folded the paper into a more manageable size and looked at the picture of Max and her. "This is a different shot from the last one."

"Yeah, we look cozier, which suits his purpose. I hope you like the picture, because it's the icing on a particularly sleazy cake."

Maggie read the article, breaking her silence with an occasional indrawn breath as she scanned the newsprint. "I'll sue him!"

"Much as I dislike Babcox and would love to see him in court, you wouldn't have a leg to stand on. He hasn't written anything that couldn't be true. Read it again and you'll see I'm right."

She read the article through once more and her opinion didn't improve any from a second reading. "It's what he's implied! Making out we were checking out maternity homes because I'm pregnant and that's why we're getting married. Well, he'd better not show his face when we reach Auckland."

"He set us up good, didn't he? It couldn't have gone better if I'd planned it myself. Which I did." He laughed out loud. "Little does he know we've turned the tables on him for once and gotten the result we wanted. Now the killer will surely know where to find you, and then we'll catch him."

"You'll excuse me if I don't share your happiness," she

said tartly, and pouted with righteous indignation. Maggie flung the paper over her shoulder onto the back seat in disgust. It made a mockery of their relationship.

But it did make her realize nothing had changed.

She still had feelings for him.

He laughed. "I love it when the plot thickens."

"Sickens is what you mean," she countered, but couldn't keep her eyes off him as he drew up at the turn into Warkworth and looked for a gap in the traffic.

"Is this where you came through doing a hundred and twenty?" he asked.

"Yes, I wish I'd never told you about the incident. It was stupid. The guy was probably in a rush to get home. Why do you ask? Are you thinking of giving me a ticket?" she jibed, still letting Babcox's article color her mood.

"At least acquit me of that, Maggie. I know things aren't too hot between us, but have I really sunk so low in your estimation?" Max gunned the engine, shot out to merge with the flowing traffic and stared fixedly ahead as if he could no longer bear to look at her.

Maggie reached over, laid her hand on his thigh and gently squeezed, which made him jump as though she'd branded him. Quickly, she took her hand away. "Sorry."

"No, it's not your fault. I guess I'm a bit twitchy this morning. I didn't sleep so good," he said, and as if to confirm it he covered his mouth with his hand and yawned.

"Neither did I."

"Yeah, but you had a good excuse. I bet that baby was hollering all night. Was that your old room I slept in?" Max asked, glancing across at her as she nodded. "I haven't slept in a single bed since I was a kid. My feet hung over the end." He reached out and took her hand in his. "It would have been better if you were in it with me. I missed you."

Her heart jolted at his words and raced at his touch, going out of control as his thumb caressed the center of her palm. "I missed you, too."

"Don't think I'm trying to worm my way back into your bed. I can handle cold feet. It's the cold shoulder that hurts. I've a feeling all of this has knocked you for six and you're still spinning. Just remember, I'm going to be there to catch you when you stop."

He took her hand and put it on his thigh. "Leave it there," he said, overtaking the car in front.

Maggie looked at his hands on the wheel, large, strong and magnificently competent at everything they did. She could vouch for that. Running her fingers over the long, lean lines of his leg was too much temptation to resist. His muscles tensed. She'd learned the strengths and weaknesses of his body already. Knowing the spots where a touch of her hands would turn his bones to water. But the last thing she had on her mind right now was causing an accident.

"Whoa, sweetheart! If you wanted hard, you've got it, but this isn't the place or the time." His hand came over hers and held it clamped to his thigh. "We have a problem that needs settling before we go down that road again. First off, I want you to know you were right. I guess I *am* using you. No, no doubt about it—I'm using you. But I promise, it's for your own protection."

That's the same thing he'd said when he'd insisted she go to her lawyer and have him write up an ironclad will. But, Max still hadn't come right out and said who he thought he was protecting her from.

Maggie's hand tightened on his thigh and he let out a groan. What did he expect? That she'd keep on stroking him when he'd just confessed to her worst nightmare? Where did he get off saying it was for her own protection?

"I gave you my word to help, and I will. But heaven help me, I can't work out how protecting me from that Khyber Pass lunatic has anything to do with getting married."

"Maggie, I didn't suggest this scheme to protect you from some jerk haunting your dreams. It's to protect you from your family!"

* * *

Max stopped the car outside the vehicle entrance to Auckland Central. Maggie had been silent most of the way since he'd explained his reasoning. Hell, he hadn't wanted to take the edge off her hopes of finding her family before she'd even made an attempt. There was a fifty-fifty chance he might be wrong. Yet he felt certain this scenario was going to fly, especially after reading that note.

"You're sure you don't want me to drop you off at the lawyer's door?"

"No, I can walk from here. Nothing's likely to happen to me in the middle of Queen Street." Maggie undid her seat belt and gathered up her bag from the floor. "How long will you be?"

"Give me at least three hours."

"Three hours? What am I supposed to do while you're catching up with your good buddies?"

"I'll be working, not cracking my jaws. I'm gonna take the note in to the boffins and see if they can lift any prints off it, then check to see if Strinati has sent anything here from Sydney. Nothing's come through on my machine. Also, I have to keep Henare sweet for a little while longer, so he doesn't insist on dragging me back to Auckland before I'm ready."

Max let his gaze linger on Maggie. He hadn't been able to resist pulling out the clothes she'd worn the night they'd met, the camel coat with the sexy slit at the back that turned him on. Twelve days. It felt like a lifetime. He'd grown up a lot since then. Learned to open his mind and shed his fixed ideas. There were more things in heaven and earth, etc....

"Why don't you act like a bride? The vineyard staff will expect to see you with a few carrier bags. Go buy something for a wedding. Something green," he said, reminiscing about that green silky robe she'd worn, reminding him of a wood sprite. Or maybe she should just wear that. "I like you in green."

"Green is unlucky for weddings. Nobody would believe I'd wear green to be married in," she said, dashing that fantasy.

"Then cream. When you wear cream your skin looks like honey."

"Cream? I've never worn anything cream."

"The sheets… Remember that time you wrapped one around you?" He enjoyed being able to make Maggie blush. There was something very intimate about sharing memories that could bring color to her cheeks.

"If I buy a dress, I'll have to find one I can return or one that can be worn for other occasions," she stated with a contrary gleam in her eye.

"Try not to be so negative, Maggie. I'll bet Carla's bought something classy for the great day," he teased, but his insides churned. When would Maggie ever bring herself to trust him? There wasn't a thing about her he didn't want to embrace. Including her gift.

She'd been out of circulation for too long. Ever since her father died she'd been hiding up at the vineyard because of the notoriety the media had landed her with. He needed to find a way to make her believe in herself as a woman, not only as the CEO of a wine business.

"Carla looks great no matter what she wears," she murmured.

"And you look great wearing nothing," he growled, and gave her an eloquent wink, looking for another blush.

"Get serious, Max," she said, revealing her confusion in a slow flutter of her eyelids and a slash of red on her cheekbones. "You're certain I'll be doing the right thing, making Carla my beneficiary in the will?" Mentioning Carla had set her thoughts off on a tangent.

"We agreed that would be best. Speak to your lawyer, see what he says, and if there's anyone else you trust, leave the estate to them. Just make sure whatever you do is ironclad and can't be overset." He leaned over and took her hand. It felt fine and narrow boned compared to his own huge mitts. Easily crushed. "It's only a precaution—in fact, I'll give you my word you can go back and change it or throw it away once this is over. Your last will and testament won't be needed until you're an old lady of a hundred, guaranteed." And God willing he'd be with her. "I swear, on my life, I won't take chances or let anything go wrong."

"If the lawyer's read in the newspapers that we're getting married, won't he think it's funny that I haven't named you?" Maggie leaned forward as well. Her eyes were clear and bright without a particle of doubt showing. "I could name you, Max. I don't have a problem with that."

"Well, I do. Maggie, I'm here to protect you, and the fact that you'd trust me that much blows me away." He swallowed a couple of times, but he couldn't budge the lump in his throat. "God, I feel choked. You've cut me off at the knees this time, darlin'."

Max traced the wing of her brow with his thumb and cupped her cheek. "Let me give you some free advice, sweetheart. Your lawyer would charge you for it. Never make the person responsible for guarding your life the one who has the most to gain from your death. Hell, if anything happened to you I'd have to shoot myself. They'd be sure to blame me, and that wouldn't get any grapes crushed." And I'm starting to believe my life would be unbearable without you.

He cuffed her gently under the chin and smiled at her, although it was the last thing he wanted to do. He wanted to take her in his arms and love her. Right here, right now. Whether she knew it or not, Maggie had just given him the finest gift he'd ever received—her trust—and he wanted to thank her for it.

Maggie. His Maggie.

"You wouldn't want people to get the wrong idea, would you?"

"Seems like I've been full of wrong ideas lately. I'll have to rely on you, Max, to set me straight," she said huskily, edging closer until her taste was on his lips.

What could he do but kiss her?

He'd been through a drought and he couldn't wait to drink from her lips. Max slanted his mouth over hers and drank deeply, filling all those places in him that had dried up for want of a taste of Maggie. His hand slipped the button on her coat and found its way to her breast. "Ahh..." He let his moan fill her mouth.

The steering wheel dug him in the ribs so he leaned forward to avoid it, forcing Maggie back against her door as a tap sounded on the window.

Maggie's eyes widened and she pulled her mouth away despite his protest. "Max, there's a cop outside watching us."

Max looked over his shoulder and saw Rowan McQuaid. "Let him get his own woman," he grumbled, and turned back to Maggie.

Although they'd said goodbye with a kiss, the drive home was mainly conducted in silence, both of them lost in their own thoughts. Maggie had arrived loaded with bags, complaining that the whole of Auckland had been shopping in Queen Street. She'd told him the lawyer had refused to discuss her mother, but the rest had gone well, and the official papers that elected Carla her heir had been signed on her way to the car.

What worried Max most, though, was the chance of the will being needed, because then his plan would have failed and Maggie would be dead.

He'd gone into the situation like gangbusters, full of his own ability to make things happen, and it hadn't taken Mike Henare's, *If this fails your ass is mine,* to make him realize what he had to lose. Maggie.

Everything had to go according to plan. It was the only way he could be sure of Maggie's safety.

Rowan and Jo had volunteered to act as back up, and once Max had parked his car at the far side of the house, he would slip inside the back way. Then if the balloon went up, Jo would use his car.

In part, his conscience wished nothing would happen, but logic argued that if the plan was a fizzer, he'd be back in limbo again. Both with his job, and his relationship with Maggie.

The ring he'd bought was burning a hole in his inside breast pocket. And the closer they got to zero-hour, the time Maggie would have her next dream, the more it seemed to sear into him, like his pocket held a ruby laser instead of a ring.

Max turned the corner where the Kereru Winery sign appeared. "Nearly home, Maggie."

"I used to love this part of the drive when I returned home from boarding school. Somehow, it doesn't have the same appeal today."

God, help him, he'd never wanted to make her feel like that about going home. "Well, don't forget, I'll be in the next room if you need me tonight."

She smiled her thanks, but her expression was bleak. For almost two seconds he pondered swinging the car around and whisking her out of there. But that would only be postponing matters. Sooner or later the situation would reach the crisis point, and he'd much rather be prepared.

A few minutes later he turned into the vineyard and drove them up to the house to wait for whatever the night might bring.

Maggie stretched across the bed, reaching out, needing the comfort of another human being. Not just anyone, though. She wanted Max. The sheets were cool to touch. No warm body had consumed their chill. She was alone, because Max had stuck to his guns and lay sleeping in her old bed, his scent on the pillow the only part of him left to her.

Frustrated, she kicked the covers off and rolled back to her side of the bed, taking the pillow with her. Burying her nose in its yielding softness, she inhaled his essence into her lungs, into her heart. It wasn't enough. She wanted more. His scent was merely a memory, like his presence in her bed. It turned her on, but it couldn't distract her. Couldn't drive this screaming child out of her head. It wanted its mama, and it wasn't going to stop howling till it found her.

She knew it was driving her crazy. Had to be. Why else would she have tried singing a lullaby to shut it up?

Now that *was* crazy!

Singing to a baby who didn't exist outside her head.

Anyway, it hadn't worked. She needed Max. Needed him to act as a painkiller till they discovered a cure for what ailed her. Maggie pushed the cotton-covered substitute down farther and rubbed her breasts against it till they generated tight buds. A useless effort; the pillow yielded too much. She missed the hardness, the rough hairiness of Max's chest.

Using the pillow as a placebo, she brought her legs up and wrapped them around the lower half of it, squeezing it with her knees. An ache the size of a fist filled the emptiness inside her—a space only Max could fill and make her whole again.

She could almost touch the silent darkness surrounding her. What if she reached out and grabbed a handful? Would it deaden the noise if she stuffed it in her ears? If only! Her head seemed like an island of clamor floating in this sea of silence. Tears she'd been holding back for hours spilled over and wet her cheeks.

Bravery was easier to hold on to when you weren't alone.

Maggie fell asleep clutching the pillow to her breast....

The knight wore armor, shiny and black, the sun glancing off its visor blinding to the eye. On his lance, a plain white banner flew.

Defiant.

All wanted a piece of this snowy, virginal symbol.

Too small to share.

Hands everywhere, so many hands—scarred, tattooed, lily pale.

All reaching, grabbing, rending the delicate fabric till it ripped apart and floated in milky streamers over the fallen black knight.

Frayed streamers coiled around his neck, white on black. Hands, heedless of razor-sharp armor, seized, twisted, yanked tighter...tighter...tighter...while bloody scratches seeped into the fabric, dying the fabric crimson. Bloodred...

Maggie woke up screaming.

Max's feet hit the floor running before he knew what had woken him. Every hair on his body stood at attention as his muscles prepared for action. Like a ghost he raced barefoot to Maggie's bedroom and eased the door open. Her screams had ceased, fading to heartrending sobs.

Weapon held tight against the curve of his shoulder, with boxer shorts his only shield, he reached in and switched on the light. Apart from Maggie's shape outlining the covers he could see no one. No intruder. "You okay, Maggie?" he whispered, sliding into the room.

The covers moved and Maggie's head emerged. "Max? Sorry, did I wake you?" she asked groggily, blinking like a little owl in a spotlight as her top half appeared.

"You could say that," he replied, crossing the room.

"I guess I was screaming out loud. It's all right if you want to go back to bed. I..." She stopped speaking and her jaw dropped as she saw the gun. "Do you sleep with that thing?" she asked, nodding pointedly at the weapon.

Suddenly feeling overdressed for the occasion, Max laid the 9 mm Glock atop the nearest dresser. "For the moment I do. Didn't you believe me when I said I would protect you?"

"But, a gun?"

Max sat on the edge of the bed. "Whatever it takes," he said. "Wanna tell me about it?" Her eyelids were pink and her lashes thick with tears. It didn't matter. To him, Maggie always looked beautiful. Seeing her still breathing was all he needed. "Was it the dream?"

"I honestly don't know. It was pretty weird. Not like any of the others. Perhaps I just had a nightmare."

"Classify 'nightmare' for me," he said as he reached for her left hand. It looked pale and cold so he began rubbing it, paying particular attention to the finger he'd bought the ring for, then warming it with a kiss.

"All mixed up and kind of crazy. It scared me."

"Me, too."

She smiled at that and he basked in the warmth.

"The baby stopped crying, but I never saw it in my dream. Truth to tell, I never saw anyone, at least not their face." The strap of her mauve chemise slid off her shoulder and gave him a glimpse of satin-smooth breast.

Maggie's eyes fluttered as they followed the direction of his gaze.

He wished he'd asked her to buy a dress in that crushed lilac, even though the wedding was a pretence. It definitely made her eyes look like pansies, old-fashioned ones that had just been drenched from the spout of a watering can. His grandmother would have liked Maggie. She would have wanted him to tend this woman and keep her out of harm's way, the way she'd looked after her flowers. No frost had ever burned his grandmother's pansies.

"Do you want to come in beside me?" Maggie invited, lifting the bedcovers on the other side of her. "It's cold, and you haven't got much on." Slipping her hand from his hold, she drew a finger down the center of his chest.

His heart jolted and his pectoral muscles went into spasms.

"Come in beside me and I'll tell you about my dream."

Max didn't have to be asked a third time.

Chapter 14

"**I** think we're being thrown offtrack. Last night's dream didn't feel real. All the others have been like I was sitting up there behind his eyes. Not this time." Maggie lifted her eyebrows and waited for some comment from Max. It didn't happen.

"You've got no intention of helping me out here, have you?"

"I'm learning, Maggie. As far as brainstorming with you goes, the best thing to do is give you your head and let you run. All that's needed from me is an occasional nudge to keep you from jumping the rails."

"Great."

Maggie went back to making sandwiches for an early lunch. It helped her thinking process if her hands were busy.

Max leaned over a kitchen chair, watching. He was dressed for the city and wore a green shirt today. Although she preferred the blue, Maggie wouldn't tell him that. He was far too full of himself already after last night.

Maggie felt her womb clench and a ripple of sexual excite-ment raced through her as she thought of the night before.

Shortly, he would get in his car and leave for the city. Or pretend to. Maggie would wave him off like a good little wi-fey-to-be, and then they would wait. The problem was, she thought, they could be waiting in vain. "You'd think if he was going to come after me today I would have seen myself in the dream. What if it's someone else entirely?"

"Maybe that was you in the black armor."

"No, the body in it was too solid, like a man's... Now how did I know that?" She shook her head as if that would loosen the answer. "What if it was meant to be symbolic? The man in black, the bad guy, getting his comeuppance. That could be the reason for him being there, and it means you're going to catch him. Let me look at your hands."

Taking Max's hands in hers she turned them over and looked at the back. Large-knuckled and bony, they weren't the ones that had yanked on the scarf, but they were the ones she'd imagined on her body the first night they'd met.

She pushed up his sleeves and looked on his wrists. Ab-solutely clear of self-inflicted blemishes or scars. "No, you weren't in my dream, unless... Her hands landed on his shoul-ders and gripped tightly. "What if you were the black knight?"

Max just laughed, pulling her into his arms and nuzzling his head against her breast. "Hey, sweetheart, I'm the white knight, remember?"

Maggie took a deep breath to calm her thundering heart. Her nerves were on edge, that's all. They kept zapping her brain, then she jumped to the wrong conclusion.

Max's hair was thick and crisp beneath her hand as she ruffled it. "Of course. Who else could you be but my hero? It's just that I feel as if everything I've been through lately is part of a multiple-choice exam. They say no news is good news, and now I know why. A few days ago I was happily minding my own business. Nothing urgent to see to, unless you count dreaming of some unsolved murders. Then, wham! The family I thought was dead spring back to life, and I hire a gardener who turns out to have been the catalyst for my parents' marriage failing. You realize, if it hadn't been for Ed Armstrong, we could all have lived happily ever after with no one the wiser?''

Max reached up and cupped her face in his large palms. Pulling it down to his, he kissed her—not hard, but sweetly, softly. All of his feelings for her poured out, flooded her with sensation and heat. Bone-melting, mind-blowing heat.

Emotion burred his voice. ''Then we wouldn't have met.''

''Oh, I think we would. Don't you know that it's written in the stars?''

Max pushed her away from him. His gaze held no humor, only devastating candor. ''I believe it could be…fate, kismet. You've changed me, Maggie. I believe in you, in your gift. And *I* think your dream means we're going to get him. If not today, then soon.'' His bold statement brooked no argument.

''Well, well. I see there's none so fervent as the converted.'' Her lips curved in a smile. ''Thanks for your faith in me, Max. I only hope it's not simply a consequence of my tangled life. I'm sure one pair of hands were Ed Armstrong's—the ones with the tattoo. He has a knife with wings tattooed on the inside of his wrist.'' She turned her hand over and showed Max where.

''Yipes, that must have stung. But it'll be a bayonet, if he was SAS.''

''Whatever. As I said before, Ed was the catalyst. The other pair, which had a scar, had to be my brother. That leaves my mother. She was blond, so she'd be bound to have fair skin and pale hands.''

Maggie sighed. ''Maybe it was just a nightmare, without any meaning at all. Yesterday, on the way home, I'd been wondering what my life would have been like if it hadn't been for Ed slicing my brother's wrist with that hook. Wondering if my mother would have been any more tolerant of my gift than my father. Maybe what I dreamed was the residue of my thoughts and tonight, when I go to sleep, the baby will still be crying.''

Hoping she'd come to the right conclusion, Maggie went back to her sandwich making. But Max's words stopped her mid-step.

''I think you're wrong!''

Maggie turned, intrigued. He acted so unlike the Max she'd first met. The blinkers were off and he was taking a real interest in her dreams. He really had changed.

''Okay, tell me where I've gone wrong, in your expert opinion,'' she said impudently, stopping short when she saw Max's serious mien.

''I think *you* were the catalyst.''

''Me?''

''Think back. Do you remember telling me Armstrong said your brother didn't want to stay in the house because you were crying? He called you a 'crybaby.' That's the way you put it.''

''Oh, but, Max, you can't believe it's the baby I've been hearing. That's too far-fetched. I mean...so long ago.'' Maggie felt flustered. She couldn't dredge up a particle of enthusiasm for the two chief hassles in her life being connected.

''No, I can't stretch my reasoning that far, either. But you're psychic, Maggie. It's probably been something you've always had, whether you were old enough to realize it or not. What if you'd dreamed about your brother's accident. About him being hurt. That would be enough to make you cry,'' Max speculated. ''Don't you think?''

''You mean I dreamed he would have an accident and it made me cry. And my crying was what drove Ivan out of the house.'' Her breathing grew shallow, rapid, the way it had when she'd experienced that panic attack.

''Oh, God! You could be right, Max. I could have sent Ivan off to his death. He could easily have died if Ed hadn't known where to find the pressure point.'' She clutched at the back of

Max's chair, feeling sick. "It looks as though I've only myself to blame for the loss of my family."

Her head buzzed. Maggie sucked in a few deep breaths to combat oxygen starvation from the way her mind was racing. "Maybe I should just walk away and hand the winery over to my family! After all, it seems my brother's a wine maker. He'd probably do a better job of running the place than me."

"Don't you dare think that, Maggie. I wish I'd never brought up the idea. Dammit! Here's the rationale. You might have had this gift all your life. But you'd be too young to remember or know what was going on." He reached out and took both her hands in his, massaging the backs of them with his thumbs. "Don't ever be ashamed of who you are, Maggie. Your gift is part of you, and whatever happens, from now on, we'll deal with it, together."

Maggie was right when she said this old barn hadn't been used for a while. He only hoped it didn't fall down around his car. Max unlocked the padlock and pulled the heavy door open to a squeal of protesting hinges. What he should have done was check the place out yesterday.

Huge swaths of dusty gray cobwebs hung from the rafters, but apart from them and some timber in a corner, the place was empty. Picking up a piece of two-by-four, Max cleared some of the cobwebs. He shuddered as he walked to the car, and ran his fingers through his hair just in case any spiders had lodged there. He'd rather face the two-legged variety patroling the walkways than a tiny one crawling across his scalp. With a grin on his face he imagined telling Maggie about his run-in with the spiders. She could do with a good laugh.

Inside the car he picked up his mobile phone and dialed. "Hey, Jo, you and Rowan arriving anytime soon?"

"On our way now, Boss."

Max drummed his fingers on the steering wheel. "No word from Strinati yet?"

"Not a whisper. I sent him another message, stressing the

urgency, and Central will reroute anything that comes in to this car.''

"Okay. You know where you're going, don't you?''

"Yeah, the big old barn at the back of the vineyard, full of spiders.''

"That's the one. I hope you two brought something to eat— it could be a long wait. How far out are you?''

"Twenty, twenty-five minutes.''

Max calculated it would take him twenty minutes to walk back to the house. "You got the spare key to my car?''

"Yeah, no problem.''

"I'll ring you when I reach the house. Out.''

He drove into the barn, retrieved the clip of his semiautomatic Glock from under his seat, then secured the car. The barn doors made even more noise on being closed, enough to wake the dead. So much for playing least in sight.

Zipping his dull khaki jacket, Max circled the barn, though with the vines stripped of leaves it probably wouldn't make great camouflage. Clearing a load of brush out of his way, he jumped the fence and headed for the hill, toward Maggie and home.

Time to heat up the toasted-sandwich maker. Max should be back in about fifteen minutes or so. He'd be cold walking back through the vineyard, for the wind was brisk and none too warm. They should have eaten by now, but Max couldn't wait. He'd been simmering with impatience, forcing the action, instead of hanging around waiting for it to happen.

Maggie filled the pot and put on fresh coffee to brew. She'd just started toasting the first batch of sandwiches when the front doorbell rang.

Who could that be? It couldn't be Max; he intended sidling in the back way and hoped that no one would see him. She marched down the hall, determined to say "Hello and goodbye,'' then get rid of whoever it was before Max came home.

Carefully, she opened the door, using the only two digits not smeared with butter.

Ed Armstrong stood on the mat, his arms filled with a large box covered in silver-and-white paper etched with wedding bells and tied with an intricate silver bow.

Astounded, she felt her stomach lurch. She hadn't really thought of anyone spending money on presents for them. "Ed. What a surprise. I didn't think we'd see you today. I thought you'd be moving your stuff up from Auckland."

"I am, but I thought I'd drop this off first," he said, proffering the box.

"Oh, you shouldn't have, Ed," she murmured, feeling a hot wave of embarrassment. "We didn't even invite you—it's only a small affair."

"It doesn't matter, I won't be here, anyway," he answered, thrusting the box closer.

"Look." She held out her hands. "I'm covered in butter, making toasted sandwiches that will bake black any minute now." She checked her watch. "Can you bring it through to the kitchen while I rescue them?" She heard the door shut and Ed follow her along the hall. The kitchen was redolent with the smell of toasted cheese. Smartly, she retrieved the hot snacks, putting them on a plate beside the pile still to be toasted.

"That's a lot of sandwiches. Are you expecting someone?" asked Ed, laying the box on a table that was set for two.

"No, I mean, Max was here but he decided he couldn't wait. He had to meet some friends in the city." Off the top of her head she said, "Rugby first, then an evening out."

"I'd heard about it." He smiled knowingly, one hand guarding the box while Maggie washed her hands.

"That's better." She hung the hand towel back over the rail. "Now I can open this deliciously wrapped gift. You didn't do this by yourself, did you?"

"Yes, I did," he said with a sigh. "My wife loved beautiful things. I learned to be creative for her sake."

"Your wife? I didn't know you were married," Maggie said as she reached the table where he'd placed the gift.

"I was. She died."

His somber voice came from over her shoulder. She turned her head. "I'm sorry," she murmured sympathetically. Slipping the card from under the ribbon, she opened the envelope and read the standard printed message, plus a written one signed by Ed.

"May all your troubles be little ones."

Maggie shivered. That darn goose was doing a tap dance on her grave again. Why?

She looked over at the kitchen clock. Only four minutes had elapsed since Ed had arrived. Contrarily, the urge to rush through opening the box disappeared, even though Max would be home shortly.

The distance to the house was shorter than he'd imagined, with nothing but vines in sight until he crested the brow of the slope. Now he could see journey's end. His stomach grumbled in hungry anticipation. He should have taken Maggie's advice and eaten before he left. Just watching her sashay around the kitchen made him hungry. But not for food.

He'd felt the longer he took to leave, the longer before anything happened. Jo and Rowan should arrive soon. He owed them for this. Both his friends should have been off duty, but when he'd called, they hadn't hesitated.

On the downhill stretch the wind blew in his face and tugged at his jacket, making it balloon out behind him. Max shivered, suddenly cold, as though the wind had crept under more than his jacket—rather, beneath his skin to chill his soul. Automatically, he reached down and covered the weapon at his waist.

She'd been painfully careful, easing the bow off the box, but she couldn't procrastinate any longer. Maggie could hear Ed breathing behind her. Fear had magnified the sound. Even the tick of the clock seemed inordinately loud, ticking off the seconds as time ground to a halt.

Max, where are you? she repeated over and over in her mind.

Easing the lid off, she planned her next move, her brain working overtime. Ed wasn't that much taller than her. It was a question of leverage. He'd learn that she was no easy victim.... But first she had to make sure she wasn't imagining things.

What a fool. She should have realized.

Her dreams were starting to come true.

May all your troubles be little ones.

That's what gave it away. Did he think she was a complete idiot? What should she do to give Max more time? Surely he couldn't be too far away.

Max. Hurry please, I need you!

Maggie pushed aside the tissue paper and let out a sigh of recognition. The black-haired baby lay on its back, asleep, and as she picked it up its brown eyes opened, staring at her as it cried, "Ma-maaa!"

Max heard his name and turned, thinking Jo had come up behind him. Not a soul in sight. He shook his head and began running faster.

"Max."

The second time it put him off his stride as he jerked around, swearing, "Bloody hell! What's going on here?" There was panic in the rhythm of his feet pounding the turf as he took the bottom of the slope in a rush, then slowed as his steps thudded across the bridge spanning the creek.

"Max!"

The third time, fear shot through him. Memories of the night Maggie had been attacked came back loud and clear. What had she said? "I prayed for you to come."

Maggie was calling him now!

* * *

The moment she felt Ed move, Maggie stepped back. Luck was on her side—as was fate. Max had shown her just how to deal with this situation last night. Her foot slid between Ed's ankles, and in the fraction of time he took to raise his arms, reaching for her throat, she hooked her leg behind his and flung herself backward, knocking him off balance and down to the floor.

He'd forgotten she knew all his moves. Knew the way he'd killed those defenseless women, from behind.

And surprise had been on her side.

Miraculously, she managed to avoid falling on top of him by grabbing the back of a chair to steady herself while she untangled her feet from Ed's. The doll lay on the table in front of her. She didn't have much time. Soon Ed would recover and come after her. Clasping a leg in one hand, she swung the doll, aiming for his head as he started to rise. She knew it wasn't hard enough to knock him out, but it might make him see stars.

It shattered! Broken porcelain scattered, pattering onto the terra-cotta tiled floor as Ed went down again.

It was too much to hope he might have broken something. Maggie raced around the table, pushing the chair behind her to obstruct him. Time slowed like a sports replay on TV. Sounds magnified. Harsh curses came from Ed as he scrambled to his feet behind her. The breath ripping from her throat, the table screeching on the floor—all noise amplified like wind through a tunnel. Every millisecond took a second, each second lasted a minute.

The knife she'd used to cut the sandwiches glinted at her from the countertop. She took it as a sign and grabbed it on the way past.

Broken porcelain crunched under Ed's feet, and the chair crashed to the floor as he pushed it out of his way. Maggie didn't have to see him to know he was breathing down her neck; she could hear him. She didn't stand a chance in hell of reaching the door before he was on her!

"You won't get away," he jeered from behind her.

Maggie held the long knife in front of her as she turned and faced him. The edge being serrated didn't trouble her, for she knew how sharp the point was. "Maybe not, but I can make you bleed."

He took a step toward her and laughed. "Well, they say blood calls to blood."

Maggie threatened with a couple of jabs of the knife. It was enough to halt him, keep him back where he couldn't reach out and take it from her. "What do you mean?"

"I'm your uncle, girl. The one who killed his mother just by being born, so they threw me away."

Maggie was stunned. "They threw you away?" She had no time to figure it out, but if he'd told her the truth, then the puzzle was solved.

"As good as. The couple they gave me to were rubbish!" His eyes rolled wildly in their sockets.

Maggie shivered with fear and the knife shook in her hand.

Ed didn't notice; he had years of vitriol he wanted to let fly. "They treated me like a slave. I couldn't wait to escape. As soon as I could, I was off, and lady bountiful, your mother, took pity on me and gave me a job. You know how that turned out. She got rid of me as well, because of her precious son." Ed made a sudden movement with his hands, as if trying to catch Maggie off guard.

"Stay where you are. I can read your every move," she said, hoping he might wonder if she could get inside his head. People had the weirdest ideas about psychics. Her words might have had more authority if they hadn't squeaked out.

His eyes widened for a moment, then he obviously cast the possibility aside, sneering, "Good try, but if you could do that, why didn't you recognize me before? Those tricks might work with the police, but not me. I'm on to you."

"You have to be excited for me to read you. Like when

you make the dolls. Tuesday you started, wasn't it?'' she said, thinking fast. Thinking of something, anything, to delay the end he had in mind for her. She could see the uncertainty in his eyes as she hooked him with her lie. Her mind whirled, and tossed out a memory guaranteed to put him off-kilter. ''Got your camera in your pocket, have you?''

His hand moved as though drawn to touch it in his pocket.

She clenched her teeth on the sigh of satisfaction trying to escape. Don't give the game away, Maggie. ''Consider yourself an artist, don't you? Arranging their hair, using your little red scarf, making your pretty pictures.''

Out of nowhere, pure, primeval anger erupted within Maggie. Her jaw tightened and her nose flared as she breathed hard. He might kill her in the end, but the least she could do was hold him off long enough for Max to catch him. ''Well, get this, you pervert! Your fashion sense stinks! Save your bow for someone else, because I wouldn't be caught dead wearing it!''

''You bitch!'' His hands shook as he reached behind him. He pulled out a wallet.

This time she couldn't prevent the tense sigh escaping.

''See this?'' He thrust a photo of a woman in her face. She wore a pert red bow, tied under her collar, and though she smiled, Maggie could see sadness in her eyes. ''This is my wife. She was a saint. All she ever wanted was a child. We gave adoption a try, but the bastards said we were too old. She never gave up, though, and in the end it killed her. They killed her, with their rules and regulations.'' His face crumpled as though he might cry.

Maggie didn't trust him. And she couldn't let his sob story get to her. He was pulling out all the stops to play on her emotions. ''Well, you've a damn funny way of resurrecting her. What you're doing won't bring her back!'' she shouted, letting her anger take rein. Once more she waved the knife as he edged closer. ''I'm warning you! Keep away or—or I'll stick you.''

He laughed at her. "Do you really think you can damage me with that little thing? Compared to my SAS training in hand-to-hand combat, it's pitiful, less than nothing. I'm only keeping you alive because it amuses me to toy with you."

"Oh, yeah? We both know how that works, don't we? SAS BS. You couldn't face those other women when you killed them. No way. You had to come at them from behind. The coward's way."

Ed growled and clenched his fists. They looked hard, like lethal weapons. "Those women didn't deserve to live," he retorted. "They gave their babies away. Sent them into a life of purgatory." The veins at his temples began to bulge as if they might explode.

Maggie would have loved to step back, but she was already against the wall. No place to run. No place to hide. "You were playing God! No one deserves to die before their time. But don't worry. They won't kill you for all your misdeeds. They'll just lock you away for a long, long time."

"My wife died before her time. Why not them? She bled to death trying to have a baby. Why shouldn't they die for getting rid of theirs?"

He took another step.

One more and he'd be up against her knife. Maggie's eyes flickered from his face to the knife and back again. Nausea threatened to engulf her. Could she really do it? Could she take this knife, plunge it into his flesh and wound him if her life depended on it? She had no answer. Only the instinct to fight for survival.

Oh, Max, where are you?

"Right here, sweetheart."

She looked up, saw Max, and her heart lurched. Her white knight had arrived in time. Suddenly her mind did a double take. Max had answered the question she'd asked inside her head!

"Police! Freeze!" He aimed his pistol at Armstrong, holding it steady, arms outstretched. It would be so easy to shoot the jerk threatening Maggie's life. Too easy. He'd had enough of cleaning up after him these last few months. Lucky for Armstrong, Max didn't intend putting his life on hold for the next few months while an internal investigation decided it was a righteous kill.

He'd done the right thing yesterday when he'd handed his resignation to Henare. It was time to get out before he became as callous as the criminals he locked up.

"Maggie, sweetheart. Come over here to me. The long way around. Don't get between me and Armstrong." Max saw Armstrong's gaze slide to Maggie, gauging the distance between them. "I wouldn't if I were you. Know this—I have no compunction about shooting you. Just give me an excuse and you're dead."

He heard a commotion outside the kitchen just as Maggie reached him, and pushed her behind him without taking his eyes off Armstrong. "What took you so long?" he asked as he heard Jo and Rowan come through the door. "Keep him covered while I cuff him," he told Jo, and signaled for Rowan to follow him.

Jo trained her handgun on Armstrong while Max put the bracelets on him, and Rowan read him his rights. "You have a right to remain silent, but anything you do say may be taken down and used in evidence...."

"So, this is the Khyber Pass Killer," said Jo. "Been under our noses for more than a month and we didn't pick it up."

"What do you mean?" Rowan and Max asked together.

"He's shaved his hair off, but I'll swear it's the same guy I interviewed at the maternity home. Works there as a gardener."

The life force appeared to flow out of Armstrong while Max and Rowan held him, and he shrank visibly when Jo recognized him and pricked his bubble.

Rowan laughed, "Buddy, you're nicked," he said, and began pushing Armstrong in front of him. "Which car do you want him in?"

"Take Jo's. I'll collect mine later." Max could hear sirens in the distance. The local cops. "Called them, did you?"

"I promised young Bowden I'd let him in on the action if there was any," Rowan said. "Looks like he missed out again."

Maggie had been strangely quiet, breaking her silence only to say goodbye and to thank Jo and Rowan as they marched Armstrong out to the car. She was in shock, Max reckoned. He only wished he could stay and do something about it. Heaven knew when he could get back.

As the others cleared the room, Max pulled her into his arms and held her close, using the tightness of his hold to convey his feelings. "You gonna be okay? D'you want me to leave young Bowden here with you for a while? If you like, I could get him to stay and take your statement?" he murmured, his voice as rough as broken glass.

She shook her head. "Max, I've something to tell you. Armstrong was my uncle, my mother's brother. He just told me. That's why I dreamed about him."

In a defining moment of brilliant clarity, another piece of the puzzle slotted into place. "Don't you start fretting about that," Max said gruffly. "Everything will sort itself out, you'll see. We'll talk it over later."

"I know we will. Don't let me hold you up, I'll be fine. We can talk tonight," she said reassuringly, and returned his hug.

It was easy to see the day's events hadn't sunk in yet. Max wished he could be here for her when they did. But it could be days before he got back. He'd phone later and check up on her.

Maggie had her own inner strengths. She'd needed them over the years, but nobody could come a hairbreadth from death twice and not be changed by it. "Call Carla, sweetheart. Get her to stay with you."

"Honestly, Max, I'll be all right."

"I don't want to leave you here on your own, love." He pulled her head to his shoulder and kissed her brow, wishing it were her lips. But once his mouth touched hers he wouldn't stop. Not till he'd made her his own just one more time. Until then, he'd be toting a huge weight in his chest as his heart ached for her.

"I heard you, you know. As I was coming down through the vines I heard you calling me." He pressed another kiss on her brow. "I guess we might be what they call soul mates. What do you reckon?"

"I reckon you could be right."

Reaching into his pocket, Max brought out the box he'd been carrying around since Thursday. "I want you to take this, but don't open it till I'm gone."

He tilted her chin to look into her eyes. There were no doubts reflected in them. Still, he had to be sure. "No more playacting. This is for real. If you're wearing it when I come back, then I'll know."

Maggie made a fist around the small, red velvet box, clasping it tightly. "It's all right, Max. I love you."

His resolve fled as she said the words. He looked at her mouth and pressed a hard, fervent kiss on it to keep him going till he came back. A kiss so hot they both erupted in flames. Their hands were everywhere, as if they couldn't get enough of touching each other. Then someone called Max's name, shouting, "What's the holdup?" and they broke apart.

"I love you," he whispered, for her ears only. For a second, he held her hand where his heart beat like a giant eagle's wings in his chest, then he rushed out of the kitchen before he changed his mind.

Maggie looked around the disaster area that used to be her kitchen. Chairs were everywhere—one on its back—and the table stood at an odd angle. When Jo came in, Maggie wished it was Max, though deep inside she knew why he hadn't returned. A mixture of gladness and sorrow penetrated her heart at knowing he couldn't bear to leave her again. How could she blame him when she felt the same? Holding the ring box tightly in her fist like a talisman, she asked, "Forget something, Jo?"

Jo grinned and said, "Max forgot his doll." Her humor didn't last, though. "I really am glad you're all right." She moved closer and gave Maggie a quick hug. "The other day? It wasn't much of an apology. You know how it bugs me having to say I'm sorry."

"Yeah, I know. It was all the penance Sister Marie Therese made you do. I did my fair share, too."

"She never labeled you the ringleader, though."

"No, she never did. And most of the time you were sticking up for me. I don't forget that." Maggie held out her hand. "Friends?"

"Oh, definitely," Jo said, clasping Maggie's hand in a firm grip. "Always."

Jo started to move farther into the kitchen, then stopped. "You should have heard Max when he called us in. Or, maybe you shouldn't have. He wouldn't want you to know how vulnerable he is where you're concerned. He really loves you, Maggie."

Opening her palm, Maggie showed Jo the box resting there.

"I guess I didn't need to say anything," Jo whispered, her voice choked. "I hope you'll be happy, Maggie. Hell, listen to me, I'm getting maudlin. Time I was out of here! Nobody likes to see a cop cry. Invite me to the wedding." She picked up the doll and looked at the porcelain all over the floor.

"I'll sweep it up and put it aside for you."

"No. Officer Bowden will take care of it." Jo started to leave.

Maggie put out her hand to stop her. "Be my bridesmaid?"

"Yeah, okay. I guess I can hack it, as long as you remember no pink and no frills."

The kitchen was back to normal. The young cop had cleaned up and left. Maggie had poured herself a cup of coffee and sat down to drink it. The ring box lay on the table before her, still unopened. It wasn't that she didn't want to look at it. She did. More than anything.

What plagued her was the feeling of unfinished business. Her mind kept returning to the dream, making her mood a poor reflection of the happiness she ought to feel. It wasn't as if she didn't want to marry Max. She did, without reservation.

She studied the box while she drank her coffee, as if she could see inside without opening it. Max's romantic gesture hadn't escaped her—picking the ring out on his own. He had good taste, but she'd love the ring no matter what. Simply because it was his choice.

Maggie opened the box.

Nestled in a bed of white satin, a ruby glowed up at her. The setting was plain, the cut square, and the white gold set it off like a good red wine in a plain glass. A shiraz.

Maggie took it out of the box and slipped it on her finger, wishing Max could be here to do it for her. She wasn't surprised when the ring fit perfectly.

Chapter 15

Maggie was sick of moping around the house on her own. She was almost jumping out of her skin, she felt so restless and prickly. Every few moments she'd look down at the ruby ring glowing on her finger and think, what's Max doing now? Did she have a place in *his* thoughts? Though she knew her feelings were selfish, she couldn't help it. She missed him already.

Wandering to the lounge window, she looked out over the vineyard. In the valley below someone had left a wheelbarrow full of cuttings burning, and the smoke swirled around in the wind. Opening the window, she took a deep breath of air. Smoke, damp moldering leaves, winter. The dead season. But not for long, she thought. Out in the garden, the first spiky green tips of Erlicher bulbs pushed up through the dark earth. Gordon had planted those. "Early cheer," he called them.

Closing the window, she decided to stop moping around. The smoke from the barrow called to her. Pulling on an Aran sweater with a roll-neck against the wind, she exited the house through the garage, picking up a pair of secateurs as she went.

A pair of soft lambskin gardening gloves covered her hands and protected her ring. Nothing could force her to part with it, neither love nor money.

She felt herself relax as she worked. The secateurs were sharp, making her job easy. The job of pruning was the first task her father had taught her as a child. She would work the bottom; he'd cut the tops.

Gradually she worked down the trellised row, pushing the barrow as she went.

The surrounding silence enveloped her in a soothing blanket. The shop was closed now; everyone had gone home. She'd already completed the task of informing them the wedding had been postponed. No way would she let the word *cancelled* pass her lips.

Getting into her rhythm, she thought of Max as she pulled back a stem, clipped, tied, pulled and clipped. The sound of an engine made her lift her head, but didn't surprise her. It was as if she'd known...been waiting.

The rider was dressed all in black, including bike and helmet. His face was hidden behind the sheen of late sunlight glancing off his visor.

Maggie pushed the secateurs into her back pocket, pulled down her sweater and then stripped off her gloves.

The dark rider lifted his helmet with both hands.

At last she saw his face and greeted him. "Hello, Ivan."

One after the other, Jo, Rowan and Max filed out of Henare's office. Max closed the door behind him and turned to his friends, who were grinning, much like himself.

"I don't know about you two, but somebody just lifted a weight off my shoulders. I can't stop smiling."

Jo clicked her fingers. "Wowee! I'm in shock! Blindsided! I never believed it could end so quickly."

Max looked at his companions, whose smiles were as wide as the Harbour Bridge. Would they still feel as happy when he told them he'd already handed in his resignation, effective with the end of this case?

Rowan nudged Jo with his elbow. "Good spotting, Jo. I could see him start to cave in the moment you recognized him from the maternity hospital. Shaving off his hair and growing that caterpillar on his top lip didn't fool you."

Jo shrugged. "Well, I was the one who interviewed him," she said off-handedly, dismissing the importance of her police work. She eyed the other two slyly. "What'll you bet against the mustache being a phony?"

"I'll take ten," said Rowan.

"No thanks, Jo. I'm saving my pennies," Max stated. "I'm about to become a married man."

Rowan clapped Max on the shoulder and gasped, "You're not going ahead with it tomorrow!"

"No." He looked at Jo, pleased that nothing but happiness for him showed in her eyes. "When we decide, you'll be two of the first to know, after Maggie and me."

The door behind them opened. Max turned and caught Henare glowering at them. There was no pleasing some people. They'd just caught the most wanted criminal in New Zealand and he still wasn't happy.

"Have you people got nothing better to do than stand outside my office, laughing? Getting a confession out of Armstrong doesn't mean all the work's been done."

"Yes, sir. We're just going, sir," Max said, grinning at his D.I. and giving him a thumbs-up.

"Did I tell you guys you'd done a good job?"

"No, sir," all three chimed.

"Well, I have now." There was no mistaking the twinkle in Henare's eye.

Armstrong's lawyer had insisted on a psychiatric report. Not that he needed to; they would have done it anyway. But with a confession under their belts, things would go along smoother, provided his lawyer didn't try getting him off on diminished capacity. No, sir. Armstrong would go away for a long time, and not to any mental hospital.

Time to leave. Max wanted to go to Maggie's place. He had an urgent need building inside him to rush up there and hold her tight. The problem being he'd never want to leave. Unfortunately, confession or no, a load of work still had to be done. On second thought, he could make sure Armstrong's house in Warkworth had been properly sealed. Rowan had seen to his one in Auckland, and forensics would start on them both tomorrow, starting with the shed out back of his Auckland address, with all the doll parts in it.

Max got up from his desk just as someone knocked on the door and opened it. "Hi. Any luck?"

It was the boffin who'd taken the note to be fingerprinted. "As you said when you gave me the letter, Ms. Kovacs's prints are all over it, but I couldn't lift any others. Either they are too old, or were never there to begin with."

"Too bad. I had great hopes of getting what I needed and sending the information to a cop I know in Australia."

"Maybe this will do instead. I found a partial thumb print inside the envelope, pretty clear, too. The guy must have gotten careless with the felt tip pen, that's how I was able to identify it."

"Identify it?"

"Yes. It matches fingerprints we took from the vineyard workers."

Max almost snatched the results from his hand. "Let's take a look." His head bent over the report and he let out a groan of pain. "Hell and damnation! I've gotta go."

Rowan met him in the hall. "This fax arrived from Sydney. Guess what?"

"It's a photo of Maggie's brother."

"Yeah, but guess who he is?"

"Already know. Grab Jo. I want her and I want you with me. Did I hear Jamie land a few minutes ago?"

"You couldn't miss it."

"Look, don't ask questions, just tell him to be ready to take off. I've a terrible feeling in my bones. It's a matter of Maggie's life or death!"

"You don't seem surprised to see me, little sister."

All those months he had worked for her, making wine, trying to fill her father's shoes and she'd never realized that he was her brother. She still couldn't think of him as Ivan.

"I had a message you were coming, Steven," she said, amazed at the calm inevitability filling her. As if something had sent her out there to meet him.

"A message?" he barked, as he climbed off the bike.

"A dream. I dreamed about you last night." Everything made sense to her now. He'd come to make sure of his inheritance before she married Max.

"A nightmare was it? Why haven't you run away then?"

"Because I *know* you can't win," She crossed her fingers behind her back and prayed it was true. Just wishing for Max to rescue her wouldn't make it happen. Not this time, not with her at the winery and him eighty kilometers away, in Auckland.

She could try to delay the inevitable, though, and do her best to prevent it happening. "It was you, wasn't it, who..."

"The other night? Who else? If it hadn't been for Strachan, we'd all be out of our misery by now." Steven stripped off his gloves, unzipped a pocket in the black leather and pulled out a red scarf.

Maggie let out a bitter laugh. "Stupid me, I intended asking about my father's accident. I should have guessed. You meant the Khyber Pass Killer to take the blame. But it's too late this time. They've caught him now."

"Ridiculous name." He tucked the scarf in the open neck of his jacket, where it lay like a red wound. "You don't honestly expect me to believe he's been caught. It won't work."

Little by little he moved closer.

Stepping backward, Maggie kept the distance between them the same.

"They never found out I killed your father. It was so easy," he snorted, laughing at his own cleverness. "I worked there, you know, at the airport—that's where that old bitch remembered me from the other day. Not that she'll ever put two and two together. All I had to do was fix the fuel line and hold it with a sealant I knew would melt as soon as the engine heated. And to be doubly sure of giving him a good send-off, I drained the haslon gas from the fire extinguishers and replaced it with liquid oxygen. Boy, did it light up the sky."

Steven's boastful arrogance made her blood boil. "You bastard!" she raged, clenching fists she wished she could pound him with.

Maggie discovered she'd been too busy listening to notice how much closer he'd gotten. Hastily she took another two steps back, only to stop when she felt the heat from the fire in the wheelbarrow through her thick sweater.

"Yes, that's always been my problem, being a bastard. Though I never felt like one until your father sent us away. Until then, Mother always maintained this place would be mine. And she never failed to remind me of it, even during all the years we lived in Australia."

"We could share it. You are my brother," she coaxed desperately, all the while trying to decide if she'd left enough space between the wheelbarrow and the trellis to slip through. "There's more than enough to go around."

"Nice try, Sister, but it's too late. I want it all."

She had to chance it!

Before Steven reached her, Maggie swiveled on her toes and dived toward the small space between the wheelbarrow and a support post. She scraped the back of her hand on a twist of wire as she passed. No time to look, only to flee. Her brother was mad! First her uncle, now Steven!

What did that say for her?

She kicked out behind her and sent the barrow flying. Hot

ash spewed over the grass, but Steven had seen it coming and dodged the other way. Maggie put her head down and ran.

He caught her within fifteen meters.

His shoulder smacked into the back of her knees in a rugby tackle and Maggie's body hit the ground with a thud, curling and rolling as she fell. Kicking and screeching, she fought his hold, slapping at leather her nails couldn't penetrate.

Steven subdued her legs by weighing them down with his body. The scarf forgotten, he reached for her throat, but her thick roll-neck sweater hampered him.

Working her legs free, Maggie wrapped them around Steven's waist and rolled, taking his weight off her. All her fury poured into the elbow she struck at his face. The blow pushed his teeth through his lip and loosened his grip on her neck.

She held the scarf in her hands and, without thinking, wrapped it around his neck, yanking it tight, tighter. Maggie looked down at her hands. They were deathly white, with blood spilling from scrapes and scratches, bleeding onto the scarf as she strangled the black knight of her dreams.

She let out a cry and dropped the ends.

Sheer horror thrust her to her feet and sent her running. Every breath lanced her throat with cold air where he'd tried to crush it, this time with his hands. She heard his feet drumming on the ground as he drew closer and closer.

He had her again!

Steven cracked the back of his hand across her face. Her head rolled back limply as he gripped her sweater in his fist. Stunned, Maggie heard a terrible echoing in her ears. She saw stars before her eyes—and then, over the top of the shop and offices, a helicopter.

"Max..." The word slurred from her battered mouth, but Steven didn't stop. Instead, he dragged her, pulling her by the tail of her sweater.

Had Max seen her?

There was no place for the police helicopter to land except the lawn Ed had dug up, a fair bit away from where they were.

Her head might be groggy but she knew Max couldn't reach her immediately. But Steven would have to drive past that spot if he stuck to the road.

Steven stopped by his bike and tied her hands with the scarf. "Get on."

"Steven…Ivan…let me go…" She stumbled over the words. "You could easily get away without me."

"No way! You're my insurance policy." He threw her up in front of him and started the bike.

Maggie swayed dizzily. Her head ached and she had nothing to balance herself with. The bike tore up the grass between the vines. They weren't taking the road.

Dirt spattered behind them and wind bit her face. All she could see were endless strands of wire stretching ahead. At the speed they were traveling, surely they'd skid into the trellises.

Rowan counted four of them from Auckland—Max, Jamie, Jo and himself—with five cops from Warkworth. They'd closed up shop in the little township and arrived in two cars, a sergeant and four men. Young Bowden was practically wetting himself with excitement.

The team from Warkworth had arrived just in time to cut Steven Dexter's flight off at the gates. Now Dexter was holed up in the wine maker's house and Maggie was with him.

The problem was that no one knew if Steven had a firearm in there with him, though they would check with Auckland Central to see if he was licensed to own a gun.

Rowan only hoped Max kept his cool. Sure, they were all armed with 233 Remingtons and wore Kevlar vests, but if Max went off half-cocked trying to rescue Maggie from Steven Dexter's house, he might end up with more than a crease in his forehead this time.

Rowan could hear Max talking now, issuing instructions to the Warkworth mob over his radio. Max was in charge, but by rights, it should be him, Rowan; he was the senior sergeant, and Max was too emotionally involved. Not that he blamed him. If it were Jo being held hostage by that lunatic, he'd be exactly the same. But until the Armed Offenders Squad arrived from Auckland they'd have to make do with what they had. Eight men, and Jo.

Being the middle of winter it would be dark in less than an hour. Hindrance or help? He had still to make up his mind.

"Rowan, A-okay where you are?" Max's voice came over his radio.

"Yeah, I have a good view of the side of the house, and young Bowden's with me," Rowan answered. "Don't worry, I'll keep an eye on him. Out."

Suddenly a shot rang out from the house. That confirmed it; Dexter was armed. Bowden fidgeted. Rowan saw the muzzle of his rifle waving around. "Take it easy, Bowden, and unless you're aiming at something, point that weapon towards the ground."

"The next shot's for your lady friend, Strachan! Take your men and leave. I'll give you five minutes. Hear me, Strachan. Five minutes! I have nothing to lose but a little sister." Dexter laughed, and Rowan shuddered at the devilish sound.

Hell! Five minutes. Max must be spitting tacks.

Jo had taken up a position between him and Max, most of the shrubbery being on Max's side. "Is Max all right?" he whispered, pitching his voice toward her.

"Breathing fire, probably." She turned in Max's direction, stood up, startled, shouting, "He's gone!"

Rowan saw Jo stand. "Damn and blast!" Did the woman want to get herself killed? Three steps and he'd reach her and pull her down, out of the line of fire. He heard the shot as he took his third step and grabbed Jo, then his leg went out from under him as a hot, searing pain tore into his thigh. The bastard had shot him.

Maggie watched Steven fire the second shot, and wished she could cover her ears. Noise erupted outside where before there had been silence. She heard screams. It sounded like Jo. Had she been hit? Would Maggie be next? If Max had gone down, she would have nothing to live for.

Steven had her tied to a chair inside the house where they'd lived as children. She'd never thought they'd be here again. And never like this—her brother holding her hostage and Max maybe lying dead outside. Tears flowed freely down her face. She'd held them until now, but the thought of never seeing Max again produced a physical pain more terrible than anything Steven could do to her.

All this time he'd been living here and she hadn't suspected a thing. She knew now that her father must have kept an eye on Stella and Ivan, receiving regular reports. It was all a joke to Ivan, tampering with the engine to take the prize from his rival. Nothing had been proved. He'd simply done what was needed to get what he wanted. And now he wanted the vineyard.

He'd boasted of it and laughed at her father.

She wanted out of here.

Maggie wriggled in her chair, trying to free her hands. Something dug into her hip. The secateurs. If only she could open them. Sitting up straight, she eased her fingers through the bars and pressed the catch through the fabric of her hip pocket. They sprang open. She'd have to be careful not to cut herself as the blades were razor sharp.

Steven stood at the window, and the room gradually grew darker as the minutes passed. Soon he would find it hard to see anyone. But then he might turn his attentions back to her.

Pushing her hip against the bars of the chair, with a bit of effort she succeeded in lifting her sweater out of the way. Maggie slid her wrist up and down the bars and felt the silky fabric fray. Twice she jabbed herself in the hip and once she cut her wrist.

She didn't let that stop her.

Finally her hands were free. She kept them hidden behind

her in case Steven turned around. Only two options were open to her. She could try sneaking out the other way and get shot in the back. Or she could pick up the poker from the fireplace and hit him on the head as hard as she could.

The second option made her feel squeamish, but her life was in jeopardy. This time she'd have to save herself.

Softly she rose from her seat and crept over to the fireplace. Carefully she grasped the poker, almost dropping it as Steven began shouting at Max.

"Your five minutes are almost up, Strachan. If you want to see my sister alive again then you'd better get out of there fast."

Maggie gripped the poker tighter. Silently she stole up behind Steven. To think she'd trusted this man with the good name of Kereru Hills Winery. *Take that!* her brain screamed as she lifted the poker to strike a blow.

She caught her reflection in the window a fraction of a second after Steven did. He twisted, ducking his head behind his arm, releasing the butt of his rifle and striking out at her as the poker fell to the floor.

"Move out of the way, Maggie."

"Max!" Relief turned her knees to putty and tears flooded her eyes again. She didn't have to save herself. Max would.

With Steven fixed in his sights, Max yelled, "Freeze, Dexter!"

Maggie heard Steven's curse as she turned away to where he couldn't reach her, moving like a film run in slow motion. Every action took an age to imprint itself on her mind, yet it was all too clear. Her foot landed on the poker, rolling it back toward the window as she stumbled and went down. One arm stretched out, reaching for the floor, the other twisted sideways as she looked over her shoulder at her brother.

He was coming after her!

She watched as his foot struck the poker, kicking out and up as the rolled steel shot away from him. Weighed down by his rifle, and off balance, he fell backward through the open window in a frenzy of arms and legs.

The ground wasn't that far away, less than one story.

The sound of his rifle firing reached them before the thud of his body hitting the ground.

They met in the center of the room. Max pulled Maggie into his arms as if he'd never let her go. Both hearts pounded, each banging hard against the other through the walls of their chests. "Rowan! Jamie! Have you got him under control?" Max called out. His arms tightened around her as they waited for the answer.

P.C. Bowden replied. "I've got the drop on him, Sergeant," he sang out as if he were in a western. "But he won't be going anywhere soon. He's pretty badly shot up."

Max drew Maggie closer to the window. "Call an ambulance, then."

"Already done, Sergeant. There's one coming for Sergeant McQuaid."

"What the hell?" Max swore and, pulling her along by the hand, said, "C'mon, sweetheart. We have to get to Rowan."

They watched the red taillights of the ambulance till they disappeared. Max's arm circled Maggie's waist and her hand gripped his jacket at the back. She looked worn-out, but the day wasn't over yet.

He lifted her hand and kissed the finger that his ring graced. Apart from the fear in her eyes it was the first thing he'd noticed as she fell toward him. "Let's go pick up my car and get out of here."

"Out of here?" she repeated.

"No way in this world am I leaving you alone again." He'd nearly lost her twice today, and he'd never be so careless again. "I can't stay at the winery. There's still a lot of ends to tie up. Rowan can't do it and Jo looks as if she's in shock."

Maggie slipped her arm under his jacket. Her hand felt cool

through his shirt, but just having her arm around him was enough.

"Is it over, Max?" she asked from somewhere under his chin.

"All over, sweetheart. We've been through enough trouble today to last us a lifetime. I reckon we've done our share, and from now on we're going to have a wonderful life together."

The woman of *his* dreams stretched up on her toes to brush his lips with hers as she whispered, "Absolutely wonderful."

Epilogue

Maggie sat alone in the back of Grant's 1923 Model T Tourer, his pride and joy. Grant, her marketing manager, had decorated it with flowers and ribbons and polished every inch of paintwork till it gleamed like new.

She'd decided to forgo company on this, her last journey as a single woman. Though the distance was short, it was long enough to allow a release of the past. Particularly the happenings in the dead of winter.

Coming to terms with the idea of having been the catalyst that brought about so many tragedies had been tough. And doubts about her suitability to be any man's wife had almost driven her away. But Max had convinced her it wasn't genes that made her uncle and brother the way they were, but life. And his help and belief in her had guided her through the roughest parts.

In some ways she felt sorry for Ed. Fate had thrown its worst at him and he hadn't been able to cope. Maybe confession had brought him some kind of relief. His tell-all statements had proved she hadn't imagined the threat the black car posed. *The stealth bomber.* Oh, she could laugh at it now, but her escape had put Gordon's life on the line. It had been Ed who had taken out Gordon's truck in the Dome Valley as a way of getting close to Maggie.

As for Ivan, he'd died from his wounds. Whether or not he'd gone to a better place depended upon one's beliefs. Yet she couldn't help feeling an ache in her heart for the child he had been, and the potential that had been lost, as proven by the success of his wines at the wine fest less than three weeks ago. She had liked him much better as Steven than as Ivan.

Maggie liked to think that Stella's guilty conscience, about the hand she'd played in Ivan's downfall, had prevented her from contesting Frank Kovacs's will. Even though she wouldn't have gotten very far because of the waiver he had signed when she and Frank had ended their relationship. Maggie would never know the truth. She still hadn't seen her mother—and she had no desire to.

Soon Maggie would have a family of her own. Her hand rested on her stomach. No one but Max and she knew of the secret nestling in her womb. If her own gift had been passed on to the child she carried, it would be well and good. Her experiences had taught her how *not* to deal with such a mixed blessing. Though, from the little family history she knew, the ability was liable to skip a couple of generations.

They were almost there. Almost at the beautiful gardens and sheltered pergolas, whose construction Gordon had supervised from his wheelchair. Max was waiting for her with all their friends as she sent him a message in just one of the wonderful ways they had learned to communicate.

I'm almost there, Max, my darling, my love.

Grant brought the open Tourer to a halt in front of the carpeted walk. Standing up from the back seat, Maggie looked around her. November was such a beautiful month. The vines were covered in soft green leaves and roses bloomed at the ends of the trellised rows. Afterward, when everyone had gone, she and Max would walk there.

The spring breeze tugged at her mauve silk dress, and at the tiny purple violas in her hair—Max's idea—that matched her eyes. He waited for her in front of the priest, with Jo and Carla on one side of him and Rowan, standing with the aid of a cane, and Jamie, who had flown the helicopter to her rescue, on the other.

Max sent her a look of such tender love that her heart turned over in her chest. Her life would never be the same again, and she thanked heaven for such a man as Max Strachan. Grant opened the car door and she took one last moment to look around, her last as Maggie Kovacs. She drew a deep breath, tasting spring, the season of rebirth, then exhaled, letting the breeze carry the past away.

Love met her as she stepped down from the car. Max was waiting. His hand took hers, locking their fingers together. "All gone now?" he whispered for her ears only. "You've let go of the past?"

Maggie nodded, her throat too full of emotion at his gesture of love to speak. Her soul rejoiced. He hadn't wanted her to walk the last of her journey alone.

"I love you," he said, not caring who heard him, and took her lips in a kiss so soft it might have been their first.

Maggie gave herself up to it, and heard nothing past love, past wonder as she sank into his kiss. The chuckles, the asides about jumping the gun, melted away. Only she and Max remained. With love.

As their lips parted she looked at Max, man of her heart, man of her soul. He'd given up so much for her—his career, his world—to train as a vintner. Every day he surprised her with his energy, his enthusiasm as he worked alongside their new wine maker. It was as if he'd been sent to her when she needed him most.

Who knew?

"I love you, too," Maggie answered.

Max's hand shook as he gently ran his fingers down her

cheek and cupped her face. As Maggie looked into his eyes, she knew it hadn't taken a dream to know that Max was the man for her.

* * * * *

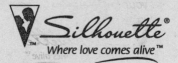

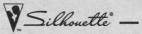

Silhouette®

I N T I M A T E   M O M E N T S™

presents a riveting 12-book continuity series:

A Year of loving dangerously

Where passion rules and nothing is what it seems…

When dishonor threatens a top-secret agency, the brave
men and women of SPEAR are prepared to risk it all as they
put their lives—and their hearts—on the line.

Available February 2001:

SOMEONE TO WATCH OVER HER
by Margaret Watson

When SPEAR agent Marcus Waters discovered Jessica Burke on a
storm-swept beach, bruised, beautiful and in need of his protection,
he never imagined that sharing close quarters with her would lead
to spiraling passion. Or that this young beauty would entrust him
not only with her life—but with her innocence. Now, as they
waited out the danger together, the world-weary agent battled
an even greater enemy to his bachelor heart: love!

*Available only from Silhouette Intimate Moments
at your favorite retail outlet.*

Silhouette®

Where love comes alive™